A POET *of the* INVISIBLE WORLD

ALSO BY MICHAEL GOLDING

Simple Prayers

Benjamin's Gift

A POET *of the* INVISIBLE WORLD

Michael Golding

PICADOR
New York

This is a work of fiction. All of the characters, organizations, and events portrayed in this novel are either products of the author's imagination or are used fictitiously.

For information, address Picador, 175 Fifth Avenue, New York, N.Y. 10010.

www.picadorusa.com
www.twitter.com/picadorusa • www.facebook.com/picadorusa
picadorbookroom.tumblr.com

For book club information, please visit www.facebook.com
/picadorbookclub or e-mail marketing@picadorusa.com.

Designed by Michelle McMillian

The Library of Congress Cataloging-in-Publication Data is available upon request.

ISBN 978-1-250-07128-6 (trade paperback)
ISBN 978-1-250-07130-9 (e-book)

Our books may be purchased in bulk for promotional, educational, or business use. Please contact your local bookseller or the Macmillan Corporate and Premium Sales Department at (800) 221-7945, extension 5442, or by e-mail at MacmillanSpecialMarkets@macmillan.com.

First Edition: October 2015

10 9 8 7 6 5 4 3 2 1

For my beloved friends

Celestial light,
Shine inward . . . that I may see and tell
Of things invisible to mortal sight.

—JOHN MILTON

PART ONE

One

No matter how tired they were from the week's labors, no matter how dull from too much *baghali polo* the night before, no matter how eager to praise God or make tea or milk the cow, there was no one in the tiny village of Al-Kashir who was not stunned by the news that early that morning, in the slant-roofed shed behind the mud-walled house, Maleeh al-Morad had given birth to a bright-faced, screaming boy with two sets of ears. The midwife was so startled when the head popped out that she simply stood there, dumbstruck, as Bina Mardavi, the fourteen-year-old daughter of Maleeh al-Morad's neighbor, stepped in to assist with the birth. A quick-witted girl with dark eyes and large feet, Bina was not afraid when she saw the second set of ears. On the contrary, she was eager for the child to come all the way out so she could see if it was equipped with two of everything. When it finally sprang free, however, the girl was disappointed. For with the exception of the ears—which were placed side by side, like pairs of matched seashells—the flush-faced infant seemed perfectly normal. As she reached for the sewing shears to sever the umbilical cord, she considered giving a quick snip to either side of the head. What use could four ears possibly be to the child? When he was old enough to speak, he would surely thank her. But since she did not possess the knowledge to stop the blood she assumed would gush forth, she decided to leave him as Allah, in His great wisdom, had made him.

As soon as Bina Mardavi returned home and told her father about the ears, the news spread like wildfire. The fat jelly maker left a bowl of sliced apples to turn brown in the sun as he dashed through the fields to tell the ironsmith's wife; the ironsmith's wife left a large pot of lamb stew to scorch on the hearth as she hurried next door to tell the soap and cheese maker; the soap and cheese maker left his goats to go hungry as he raced through the streets to tell the village schoolteacher, who was instructing the children about prime numbers. By the time the children ran home and told their parents, their parents already knew: Maleeh al-Morad—who had lost her husband only three months before—who had eyes so green they caused people to stare—who made the best poppy seed cake anyone in the village had ever tasted—had given birth to a monster. A reptile. A freak.

"Maybe they'll fall off," said Shakiba Benoud. "My sister's first child was born with two sets of eyebrows. But on the third day, the extra set fell off."

"Maybe she can sell him," said Sepantem Verdat. "My cousin

told me that a baby with two heads was born in her village and the Caliph bought him for sixty denars."

"Maybe it's a sign that we should stop talking so much," said Abbas Rashad, "and try to start listening better."

Only Maleeh al-Morad seemed unfazed by the fact of her newborn son's ears. Only she thought the infant a paragon of beauty. A newly crowned prince in her arms. At first she just gazed at him, thrilled by the instant bond between them, lost in the wild love that poured from his eyes. But eventually she reached out her hand and touched the ears. They were perfectly shaped and soft beyond belief. So she began tracing gentle figure eights around their edges—the sign of infinity—delighted at how this made the child coo.

In truth, Maleeh al-Morad had known, long before her child was born, that he would be different from the rest. For on the night before the wheel of her husband's oxcart splintered and he went sailing over the edge of the cliff to his death, Mahsoud al-Morad had awakened from a dream.

"What is it?" asked Maleeh al-Morad, as the large man lay there panting.

"The baby—"

"What about him?"

Mahsoud al-Morad searched the darkness for what he'd seen.

"Tell me!" cried Maleeh al-Morad.

"I can't remember. But I have a feeling we may have to keep him indoors."

At these words, Mahsoud al-Morad rolled over and returned to the last slumber he would ever know. But as the sorrowful weeks passed by, Maleeh al-Morad felt sure that what he'd said was true: the child inside her was somehow marked and she would only know in what manner when it was born. As the moment drew near, she imagined her baby with a pig's snout, a dog's tail, covered in thick fur. So when Bina Mardavi lowered the infant into her arms and she saw the ears, she felt a wave of relief. At least he would hear her when she called.

She realized, as she held him, that she had to give him a name. She considered Farzad, which meant "a splendid birth," but it seemed too boastful. She considered Niyusha, which meant "a good listener," but it seemed too obvious. So instead she chose Nouri, which meant "light," followed by Ahmad, which meant "praiseworthy," and then she threw in Mohammad, figuring how could it hurt. This was followed by the *nasab,* ibn Mahsoud, to denote his father, and the *nisbah,* al-Morad, to denote his tribe. Nouri Ahmad Mohammad ibn Mahsoud al-Morad. Regardless of how many ears the child had, it was a lovely name.

At first, Maleeh al-Morad took the villagers' reactions to her baby in stride. Latifeh Rashad, who was pregnant, had her husband, Azim, scatter garlic across their threshold to prevent her from catching whatever had caused Maleeh al-Morad's baby to be disfigured. Farid ben Ismael fell to the ground and shouted verses from the Qur'an whenever he passed their house. But Maleeh al-Morad simply lay in the grass, threading daisies around her baby's ears and singing songs to delight him:

There once was a child with a gift so rare—
O hear! O hear! O hear! O hear!
That the moon and the stars could not compare—
O hear! O hear! O hear!

It was only when she saw the fear in people's eyes when she ventured out to buy cheese or headed off to the mosque that she began to sense he was in danger. It was only when she was reminded of the village baby who'd been born without a tongue and been set on fire that she began to grow alarmed. And it was only when the double-edged dagger came flying through the kitchen window, piercing the sack of lentils that hung above the hearth, that she knew she would have to remove her child from the tiny village of Al-Kashir before it was too late.

THE CITY OF TAN-ARZHAN WAS LIKE a jewel in the headdress of an Arabian prince. Famed for its great mosque, the Darni Sunim, which had risen to splendor nearly a century before, it had everything a modern city should have: a town square, a public bath, a counting house, a grand bazaar, a public garden (with a running fountain), and three schools, one for each level of education. The layout was square, with four main corridors running from the central axis, and though the northeast quadrant was primarily for the wealthy and the southwest quadrant was primarily for the poor, there was a surprising absence of strife between the classes. Whatever one's lot, life was better in Tan-Arzhan than almost anywhere else. Even the rats felt lucky to roam its colorful streets.

Habbib al-Adib had lived his entire life in Tan-Arzhan. Born in a tiny hovel to an elderly baker and his wife, he'd grown up in the streets, his only education the chores he learned from his father, the prayers he learned from his mother, and the lessons he culled from the twists and turns of the day. He was a happy child, possessed of a sweet, gentle nature. He expected nothing and—with the exception of a leaky roof over his head and three daily meals—nothing was what he got. Like that of most people in the town, his life was set out for him. He would bake with his father until his father was no longer able to bake. Then, if Allah saw fit, he would bake without him.

No one had anticipated the crushing of his hand, which happened on the morning of his twelfth birthday. He'd risen at dawn to help his father with the kneading. Abu al-a-Din—son of Ahmad al-a-Din, one of the richest men in the city—was getting married that day, and Habbib's father had promised to deliver four dozen *naan-e sangak*, six dozen *naan-e barbari*, and as many rosewater-and-pistachio balls as he could fashion between the lighting of the *tanoor* and the chiming of the bells to commence the feast. Habbib's father had never received an order so large. But Mohsen Jawiri, who'd been hired to do the job, had been in bed for six days with a bad stomach flu. So Habbib's father had been asked to step in and he needed Habbib's help.

"Just think of it!" he said, as he roused Habbib in the milky light. "Ahmad al-a-Din has invited everyone to this wedding! If they like what we make, we'll be up to our asses in work!"

Habbib didn't think about the future too much, so his father's words washed over him like the morning mist. And rather than resent having to work so hard on his birthday, he felt that the great outpouring of bread marked the significance of the day. He also knew that his father would set aside a few rosewater-and-pistachio balls for them to have that evening and that if he worked hard he'd be allowed to sleep as late as he wished the next day.

They worked all morning, Habbib kneading the dough and then watching as his father shaped it into rounds and loaves, which he baked to a golden brown in the *tanoor.* Then they loaded up the cart and made their way through the dusty streets until they reached the impressive home of Ahmad al-a-Din. They were led into the kitchen, where a vast team of workers was sweet-braising chicken and pan-frying lamb, then out into the lavish garden that lay at the building's heart. Dotted with cypresses and fragrant lime trees, trimmed with low hedges and graced by a shimmering pool, it would have been enough to take away the young boy's breath. What truly amazed Habbib, however, was the enormous, jewel-encrusted elephant that knelt at the center of it all.

"If I'd known it would be like this," whispered Habbib's father, "I'd have given Mohsen Jawiri a case of the runs years ago!"

As the wedding party had not yet returned from the mosque, there was plenty of time to place the loaves and rounds in an artful manner upon the table, and as they began to do so Habbib's father was suddenly struck with the idea of making a great pyramid out of the rosewater-and-pistachio balls. It took close to an hour for him and Habbib to raise the structure, and they were just placing the last pastry on top when the doors to the garden swung open and the wedding party, flushed with excitement, poured in. Habbib had never seen anything so splendid in his life. The groom, in his white robes, was like a prince from a fable and the bride, in her turquoise veils, was so lovely he had to avert his eyes.

The guests hummed and buzzed as they spread through the garden. Then a great hush descended as Ahmad al-a-Din stepped forward to give the toast.

"We rejoice that our son should be blessed with such a wife! May Allah the Magnificent smile upon you both!"

He raised his cup high and the guests raised theirs.

"May Allah smile!" they cried, giddy with joy. Before they could take a sip, however, the overweight sister of the groom jostled the table—which toppled the pyramid—which sent the fragrant rosewater-and-pistachio balls sailing off in every direction.

Habbib should have just stood there. The pastries, after rolling on the ground, would not have been edible even if he'd been able to retrieve them. But his body was much quicker than his mind and before he knew it he was down on all fours scrambling after the wayward balls. He saw the enormous elephant raise his foot as one of the pastry balls came careening toward him, but he could not stop himself from reaching out for it. And even as the foot came down, he could not foresee how that moment would change his life.

The scream of pain that issued from Habbib was so loud the bride's mother lost her hearing for three days. Yet the cry only made the startled elephant freeze, causing the tremendous weight of his body to bear down on Habbib's hand. When they finally got the creature to raise his foot, the damage was done. With the exception of his thumb—which had managed to remain outside the crushing weight—Habbib's hand had been smashed to pulp and he would never use it again.

When the pain subsided and the bandages were removed and the fact that their son was now a cripple had sunk in, Habbib's parents tried to figure out what to do next. It was clear that the boy could no longer help with the baking, and he would not get far by depending on his wits. So the only thing they could think of was to pay a visit to the small band of dervishes who lived on the outskirts of the city and see if they would take him in. It was not the sort of life that they'd envisioned for their child. But they were old and poor and at least he'd be taken care of when they were gone.

Habbib was still recovering from the shock of the accident when his parents carted him off to the Sufi lodge. Yet the moment he passed through the narrow gate, he knew he was home. It was a simple place with a series of cells for the dervishes, a refectory, a courtyard, a library, and a small chapel mosque. And despite the fact that Habbib did not show the least sign of spiritual yearning, the brothers were happy to take him in.

It soon seemed as if he had always been with them. They gave him the task of sweeping and as he was able to grasp the broom with his good hand and tuck it up tightly beneath the arm of his bad hand, he found that it was a job he could perform. He swept and he swept—his little head bobbing as he labored each morning, his voice murmuring, "Good rest to you" as each day came to an end. He liked the brothers. They were kind and quiet and spent most of their time in either prayer or some form of service to the community. He especially liked Sheikh Bailiri, the leader of the order, whose eyes were like an ocean and whose smile was like the shining beacon of a lamp. And though Habbib always remained slightly apart from them—a worker, not an aspirant—respectful of God, but not inflamed—he was aware that it was a good life, and he was grateful to have it.

Time passed. Childhood gave way to adulthood. And Habbib swept. A few of the dervishes died. A few new ones arrived to join the order. And Habbib swept. His life was as steady as the summer rain. As ordered as a leaf. As predictable as nightfall. So he was unprepared—on that overcast morning, as he made his way out along the river toward the market—when the air shuddered—and the sky opened—and the dearest companion of his life fell into his arms.

IT TOOK MALEEH AL-MORAD ten anxious days to devise the intricate plan that would whisk her baby to safety. The first thing she did was send word to the tiny village of Dursk, where her cousin Hamid lived, to say she was coming. Dursk was a three-day journey away, as far to the east of the city of Tan-Arzhan as Al-Kashir was to the west. She did not explain why she was coming or that she would not be leaving anytime soon. She simply asked Hamid to prepare a small bed and toss a few extra carrots into the soup.

The second thing she did was to arrange for Akbar Zartouf to take her and Nouri to Dursk in his rickety milkwagon. She chose the oily milkman for two reasons. In the first place, he rarely uttered a word, so he was unlikely to tell anyone about her plans to leave the village. In the second place, he was old and coarse and overweight, so he was delighted to accept her body as payment for the trip. So on the morning before the morning on which she wished to depart, she went to his filthy hovel to negotiate the terms.

"I'd prefer no kissing."

"No kissing."

"Or biting."

"No biting. Can we remove our clothes?"

"Yes. But you must close the curtains."

"There are no curtains."

"Then you'll have to find something to cover the windows."

"All right."

"And you'll have to bathe."

He swatted away an insistent fly. "Anything else?"

Maleeh al-Morad thought for a moment. "How long?"

Akbar Zartouf raised his forefinger. "About so." He paused. "Maybe a bit smaller."

"I meant how long will it take?"

"Oh." He paused. "About twenty minutes?"

Maleeh al-Morad shook her head. "Ten."

Akbar Zartouf shrugged and the deal was struck.

It was a vile experience. His hands were calloused, his skin was greasy, and he smelled quite strongly of goat. But as Nouri's safety was at stake, Maleeh al-Morad lay back, fixed her eyes on the gourd-shaped stain on the ceiling, and let the repulsive milkman have his way. He grunted and spat curses and his belly was so large he kept slipping out of her. But she held on tight, until at last—with a cry of *"Bismallah!"*—the fellow was sated.

The rest of the time was spent preparing for the journey. Maleeh al-Morad knew that if her child was to be free of persecution he would have to keep his strange gift hidden from men's eyes. So she drew the large trunk from beneath her bed, removed the dress in which she'd married, and with a pair of shears cut a series of long strips from which she fashioned a covering for his head. It took a number of attempts to get it right. The first made him look like a fledgling pirate, the second like the offspring of some lunatic sheikh. But eventually she managed to create a tiny head garment that succeeded in portraying him as an ordinary, if slightly eccentric, child.

On the morning of the departure, Maleeh al-Morad awoke before dawn, dressed, and headed out through the village carrying a small cloth satchel and little Nouri in his basket. The mist was so thick she could barely see; it swirled in damp clouds about her head as she hurried along. When she reached the home of Akbar

Zartouf, he was strapping a canvas tarp over his milkwagon. Without saying a word, Maleeh al-Morad handed him the satchel and basket, which he proceeded to lower inside. Then she climbed in after them, he closed the tarp, and the journey began.

It was a bumpy ride. For the first hour, Maleeh al-Morad lay curved around the base of a wooden milk drum, her head resting on a small pile of rags, little Nouri sucking contentedly at her breast. Only when she was sure that the wagon had traveled well beyond the limits of Al-Kashir did she unfasten the tarp and peer out. The sky was beginning to lighten and the sight of new trees and new houses filled her with hope. Perhaps life in Dursk would be a new beginning for her and her child.

Toward the end of the first day, they reached a village called Nashtam. After eating some *bureg* and a small sack of figs that Maleeh al-Morad had packed for the journey, Akbar Zartouf tucked the wagon behind the local alehouse, laid a blanket across the seat plank for himself, and left mother and child to sleep between the drums. The following morning, he rose, tossed a few carrots to his horse, and pissed loudly against the alehouse wall. Then he climbed into the wagon, grabbed the reins, and led them back upon their course. The plan was to skirt the city of Tan-Arzhan by crossing the River Tolna, which ran along its northern edge. Then they'd sleep that night in a village called Sourd and—if all went well—they would arrive in Dursk before sundown the following day.

That second morning was cool and clear, the sky freshly painted a perfect blue, the air laced with gillyflowers. As they were now quite a distance from Al-Kashir, Maleeh al-Morad sat in the front with Akbar Zartouf, humming to Nouri, who lay sleeping in her arms. There were no fears to assuage and no problems to solve. There were only the golden fields and the wheeling birds and the steady creaking of the wheels of the wagon as they made their way along.

The sun was at its zenith when they reached the River Tolna. The river was not very wide, but when Maleeh al-Morad saw the flimsy network of struts and ties they were to use to cross it and the silvery water that churned far below, she felt an impulse to throw herself and Nouri from the milkwagon onto the grass. Sadly, the justification for that impulse came a few minutes too late. For they were already on the bridge when Akbar Zartouf placed his hand on Maleeh al-Morad's upper thigh—which caused her to jerk her body away—which caused Akbar Zartouf's mangy horse to lose his footing—and by the time the bridge buckled and the wagon went sailing over the ropes it was too late to jump free.

As she plummeted to her death, Maleeh al-Morad could not help but wonder that her end should so perfectly mirror that of her husband. She felt sure, though, that it was not the end for little Nouri. Even as she squeezed a lifetime of love into the split second of their good-bye, she saw the man strolling along the distant bank, gauged the distance between them, and knew, as she hurled the child in his direction, that he would not only catch him but care for him.

If it had been Pandor the saddlemaker who'd been walking along the river, Nouri's fate would have been to sit strapped in a chair beneath a banner that read "The Wonder of Tan-Arzhan" while people dropped coins into a silver bowl. If it had been Karim the deaf-mute, his fate would have been to remain locked in a toolshed and to be fed *kashk* through a narrow grate. If it had been Fetnem the butcher, his fate would have been to be beheaded in the shit-smeared alley behind the pigsties. But thanks to Allah—the Preserver—the Compassionate—it was Habbib who was strolling along the river that day, and into whose arms the child fell. He'd been thinking about the herb garden he'd planted outside the window of his cell. Salim Rasa, the order's cook, had given him some sage and some basil, but Habbib longed for mint. Just one or two leaves would give zest to his morning tea, and on those special occasions when the brothers prepared lamb, a few handfuls would transform the entire dish. He knew mint was prolific—his mother had planted some when he was a boy and in a few months their backyard was ablaze with it—so as he walked along the river he kept his eyes on the ground, hoping to spy a few sprigs to carry home. Only when he heard the strange whooshing sound and perceived something hurtling toward him did he raise his head. Then Allah smiled and Nouri fell into his arms.

To the end of his days, it would remain the most penetrating moment of his life. And when it was clear that the child was unharmed by his flight—and that no one was going to come rushing out of the woods to claim him—the man with six fingers tucked the baby with four ears into the crook of his arm and they headed off to begin their new lives.

Two

When Habbib reached the lodge, he slipped the infant beneath his cloak. Then he headed for the safety of his cell. As he made his way along, he met Jamal al-Jani, the small, wiry dervish who tended the chapel mosque. When he questioned Habbib about the bulge beneath his garments, Habbib explained that he was sneaking in a sack of potatoes to make a *dolmeh seeb zamini* for Sheikh Bailiri and that he must promise not to say a word. The dervish agreed and Habbib only hoped that he'd remember to go out and get some potatoes, ground meat, and rice to make the dish later in the day.

There were only a few dervishes in the order in Tan-Arzhan, but they were as different as a bedbug from a bee. In addition to Sheikh Bailiri and Jamal al-Jani, there was Salim Rasa, the soft-bodied fellow who cooked most of the brothers' meals; Piran Nazuder, a slender dervish with a grinning mouthful of wayward teeth; Hajid al-Hallal, an elderly dervish with a snow-white beard that flowed past his waist; and Sharoud Ahmirzadah, a dour fellow with a dark cast to his eyes who made Habbib's heart clench. Habbib was convinced that if they knew he'd smuggled an infant into the lodge, both he and the child would be expelled. So he took great care to keep it concealed as he moved through the halls.

When he reached his cell, he drew the baby from his cloak and laid him on his low straw bed. He had large eyes and wisps of black hair and—with the exception of his unusual head garment—he seemed much like any other child. As he lay there gurgling, Habbib suddenly realized that he would have to make him a cradle and bathe him and feed him, as well as a score of other things he could not think of at that moment. Even if his crushed fingers were suddenly restored, he would not be able to do it all himself. He would have to take someone into his confidence, and he knew that that someone was Ali Majid.

Ten years old, brown as a chestnut, and missing most of his teeth, Ali Majid had appeared at the gates of the lodge with a note pinned to his sleeve that read: *"Did he not find thee an orphan and shelter thee?"* The brothers, of course, knew that the words were from the Qur'an. But they also knew that Ali Majid's mother was alive and selling her body nightly in the bazaar quarter, just south of the great mosque. They reasoned, however, that the boy would live a far better life with them than the one that he was living in the streets. So they ushered him in, pronounced him the kitchen boy, and returned to their prayers.

It did not take long to discover that the boy was a bit slow of mind. Hajid al-Hallal was convinced that his ability to stare off into the distance for long periods was a sign of spiritual grace, but the theory was quickly dismissed. He was quiet, though, and he scoured the pots with zeal, so like Habbib he became a part of their lives. Habbib, in particular, had a warm feeling for the boy. He reminded him of the monkey that crouched in the tree that stood beside the *tanoor* where he and his father had baked bread, so he gave him nuts and dried figs, which the boy gratefully gobbled down. It was therefore to Ali Majid that he turned when he realized that he would need help to care for the infant.

It was easy to find him. After years of having to shuffle out of bed during the night when his mother brought a client back to their room, Ali Majid had fallen into the habit of sleeping during the day. Each morning, therefore, after the cups and bowls and plates from the morning meal had been washed and dried and put away, he'd wander into the small garden along the eastern edge of the inner courtyard and slip into a delicious slumber. The brothers rarely disturbed him until it was time to prepare for the evening meal. So when he felt a pair of hands shake him awake, he was rather surprised.

"Habbib asked me to fetch you," said Jamal al-Jani. "He says that he needs your help."

Ali Majid could not imagine why the odd caretaker would need his help. But since there was a good chance he might offer him a handful of pistachios or some chopped dates, he rose to his feet, wiped the sleep from his eyes, and padded off to Habbib's cell.

When he reached it, he rapped loudly on the door. "It's Ali Majid!"

There was a momentary silence. Then Habbib opened the door

and ushered him in. "You must swear you won't say a word to anyone about what I'm about to show you."

Ali Majid swore. So Habbib led him over to the bed, drew back the covers, and revealed the child. Ali Majid was silent a moment. Then he stuck his finger in his ear.

"I like his hat," he said.

Habbib sat him down and explained that the infant had fallen from the sky and that at least for the moment it was best that he remain a secret. Ali Majid did not question the matter. He merely asked Habbib what he wished him to do.

"The first thing is to feed him," said Habbib. "But the brothers will know if we take anything from the larder."

Ali Majid assured Habbib that he could steal almost anything, from the large green melons at the market to the succulent lamb shanks on Karim Rathwalla's grill.

"I don't think he's ready for lamb shanks," said Habbib.

The boy tried to picture what a baby might eat. Rose petals? Dragonflies? Dew?

"What about milk?" said Habbib.

"Goat, sheep, or cow?"

Habbib chose goat and in less than an hour Ali Majid returned with a well-filled bucket. They poured some into a tiny bowl, raised the bowl to the baby's lips, and he drank it down.

Once the issue of nourishment had been solved, they turned to making a cradle for the child. Habbib explained that it had to be large enough to allow room to grow, deep enough to prevent falling out, and soft enough to provide soothing dreams. Ali Majid scampered off to the kitchen and found a small wooden crate, a large sack of rice, and a freshly washed dishcloth. And though

Habbib worried that the crate was too rough, the rice too hard, and the cloth too riddled with holes, when they put them together and placed the baby inside he seemed to like it just fine.

The last thing Habbib asked for was a container in which he could bathe the little fellow. Ali Majid brought him an old soup pot, which he filled with warm water. Then he returned to the kitchen to perform his evening chores.

What with catching the infant and carrying him to the lodge and procuring the milk and the cradle and the pot, it had been a long day for Habbib. So he wished to bathe the child quickly, lay him in his cradle, and go to sleep. He removed the loose gown he wore and laid it on the floor beside the soup pot. Then he slowly began to unwind the slender ribbon of his head cloth. As the first layer came free, a slip of paper floated out and alighted, like a moth, in his lap. Despite the fact that Habbib had shown no spiritual leaning, Sheikh Bailiri had insisted that he learn to read. So he raised the slip of paper to his eyes and mouthed the words that were neatly written upon it:

In the name of Allah, I rain blessings upon you! I am Nouri Ahmad Mohammad ibn Mahsoud al-Morad. If you are reading these words, you have been chosen to protect me!

Habbib lowered the paper and gazed at the child. "Nouri Ahmad Mohammad ibn Mahsoud al-Morad," he repeated. A great smile flashed across his face, and then he bowed his head. "I am Habbib."

As he continued to unwind the ribbon of cloth, he wondered who'd written the note. When he removed the last layer, however, all thoughts disappeared. For that was when Habbib saw the four ears.

He felt no horror. He felt no disgust. He felt no impulse to carry the child back to the river and throw him in. The only thing he felt was a deep sense of wonder. And an overpowering feeling of love.

IF HABBIB HAD FELT THAT Nouri should be kept a secret when he found him, he was certain of it when he discovered his four ears. With the help of Ali Majid, all traces of the child's existence were concealed. And while Sheikh Bailiri noted that Habbib seemed distracted, none of the brothers ever could have guessed that he harbored a magical child in his cell. For one thing, Nouri never cried; whether hungry or sleepy or soiled, he merely gazed out of his curious eyes at the world of Habbib's cell. For another thing, Habbib's simple role in the brothers' lives remained unchanged. He greeted them with the same good cheer in the morning. He swept the smooth tiles outside their cells with the same gentle care. Yet even Habbib should have suspected that Sharoud Ahmirzadah would pose a threat to his scheme.

If one believed the stories that circulated around town, Sharoud had been mean-spirited from the day he was born. According to his mother, when he was first raised to her breast, still sticky and gleaming, he clamped his newborn gums around her nipple so hard he drew blood. She assumed there was no malice in it—he was only three minutes old—but as the days passed, he repeated the action so often she took to squeezing her milk into a jug and spooning it into his mouth rather than letting him anywhere near her naked flesh. When he was old enough to walk, he took to breaking things, yet the damage he did was never random. He went straight for those objects his mother loved most: the earthenware bowl with the four dancing fish, the fluted salt cellar, the vase with the bright blue flowers along the rim. And rather than run off and hide when the deed was done, he would wait beside the wreckage, eyes wide, to observe her reaction when she found it.

His father fared no better. A simple cobbler, whose goods, if a bit rough-hewn, were at least watertight, he received word from his customers, around Sharoud's second birthday, that when they slipped their feet into their newly made shoes they encountered prickly pods, dried beetles, dead lizards, and a sticky mixture of acacia honey and curry powder. When he confronted Sharoud about the pranks, Sharoud just grinned. So the cobbler placed a padlock on the door to his workshop and kept his distance from the child.

Sharoud's parents hoped that when the boy began to speak he would explain what was troubling him. When words finally came, however, he had little to say. In time, they became used to the taut mornings, the hushed mealtimes, the attenuated evenings, and accepted the child as their lot. So they assumed that it was one of his dark jokes, on that late-spring day when Sharoud was ten, when he suddenly announced that he'd had a mystical vision. He stumbled into the house—his face even paler than usual—and claimed that as he was coming home he'd heard a voice say his name, and when he'd looked up, God—who was wearing a blue turban and sitting in a pear tree—had called out to him:

"Be careful, my son! Ill deeds accumulate! There are worlds beyond the one you see!"

Sharoud's mother had a hard time believing that God would appear in a pear tree—or anywhere, for that matter—to a boy like Sharoud. Yet it was quite unlike him to make any sort of reference to his errant behavior. When he further insisted that his future lay with "the sainted ones," his parents didn't argue. They bundled him off to the dervishes and feasted for a week.

When Sharoud arrived at the gates of the lodge, the brothers, as ever, took him in. He was too young to become an initiate, but his conviction that his path lay with God was so fervent it could not be ignored. So they taught him the basic principles of the order, gave him a woolen *khirqa* to wear, and allowed him to participate in *zikr*, the devotional act in which the names of Allah are repeated to infuse the practitioner with the remembrance of God. If he was meant to become a Sufi, the rest would unfold over time.

Sharoud soon found that life in the order—the plain meals, the bare cell, the drab clothes—suited his sober temperament. Yet despite his newfound allegiance to God, his mean-spiritedness did not abate. He poured candle wax on the prayer rug. He carved epithets in the catafalque. He farted, quite loudly, during meals. When these deeds came to the attention of Sheikh Bailiri, the Sufi master responded by giving him a taste of his own tricks. When Sharoud greased the walkway between the cells with *ghee*, Sheikh Bailiri smeared his bed pillow with duck fat. When Sharoud sprinkled the yogurt with black mustard seeds, Sheikh Bailiri laced his soup with bitter cloves. And the farting matches made mealtimes nearly impossible.

Despite the ascetic lifestyle of the brothers, Sheikh Bailiri was quite rounded in his approach to daily life. For one thing, the complex of buildings where the dervishes ate and prayed and slept stood on the grounds of what had once been his family home. Nearly a half century before—after his mother and father had died, one after the other, from a fungal infection and a rancid goat stew—he'd set out upon the Sufi path. A few years later, when his teacher's dwelling had burned to the ground, he'd opened his home to his fellow dervishes to continue their prayers and their studies. In time, the order grew, attracting not only *murids* but wealthy lay members, who paid for their meals and clothes. When it became clear that the brothers were in need of more space, one of the latter offered to raze the simple home and build a mosque, cloister, and cells. Sheikh Bailiri consented, and the lodge was born.

After spending his entire life strolling its gentle grounds and reading beneath its leafy trees, Sheikh Bailiri could only think of the place as home. And since that home had been blessed with an abundance of nature's gifts, he could only encourage his fellow brothers to enjoy those gifts with gusto. The Sufi path was a path of service. Selflessness. Sacrifice. Poverty. But it was also a path of love, so when he assumed the role of *murshid* Sheikh Bailiri could never find fault with his disciples for celebrating life. That was why, when Sharoud arrived, Sheikh Bailiri decided to take the boy's antics in stride. He knew that a strong spirit was needed to follow the path. He knew that even good-hearted play could produce a glimpse of the divine. But Sharoud's pranks were more than just good-hearted play. They showed a lack of respect for Allah. So Sheikh Bailiri knew that he had to do whatever was needed to put a stop to them.

Eventually, Sheikh Bailiri's countertactics succeeded in ridding the lodge of Sharoud's mischief making. Sharoud, however, remained sullen, brooding, an emissary from the dark side of salvation.

His voice quavered when he read verses from the Qur'an, but he was more moved by the sound of his voice quavering than by the meaning of the verses. His heart swelled when he knelt prostrate in the chapel, but he was more thrilled by the thought of how he looked than by any experience of the divine.

Sheikh Bailiri wasn't fooled. But he was convinced that the most frail, most infinitesimal seed of righteousness might someday sprout into a sturdy tree. So he did whatever he could to encourage the youth, and when Sharoud reached the age of eighteen, he allowed him to begin the period of penitential retreat that all true aspirants must undergo. Sharoud survived the trial. So they invested him with the mantle of the order and he became a dervish.

As the years passed, however, Sheikh Bailiri kept his eye on him. For if even the most pious of God's servants had to maintain a vigilant watch over themselves, keeping sentinel over Sharoud would require double duty.

FOR MONTHS, HABBIB TOOK care not to reveal a trace of Nouri's presence at the lodge. Not a word passed between himself and Ali Majid. Not a pattern was interrupted nor a chore left undone. As time passed, however, and the child began to seem a natural part of his life, Habbib began to lower his guard. When Nouri was ready to begin eating solid food, he asked Salim Rasa to make the *aash-e aloo* less spicy. When the weather became too cold to lay the child's clothes on the banks of the river to dry, he began hanging them in the window of his cell. When these things were added to the amount of time he spent in his cell, it became clear to Sharoud that Habbib was hiding something.

What finally gave things away were the elaborate stories Habbib told Nouri before bed. When Habbib was a child, his mother had filled him with tales from the Shahnameh. The story of Sohrab. The seven trials of Rostam. The reign of Ardeshir. She had repeated them, over and over, until each word was etched in his mind. As the years passed, however, the various components of these tales had become confused. Heroes were transformed into villains; young women gave birth to their own grandparents; warriors waged war against kingdoms they'd been sent to protect. Nouri, of course, did not understand a word. But each night, as he lay in Habbib's arms, he would suck on the tips of his withered fingers and coo with glee. What neither Nouri nor Habbib knew was that Sharoud had taken to listening outside the door to Habbib's cell, and heard every word.

At first, Sharoud thought that Habbib was telling the stories to himself. But when he heard the strange sounds of delight, he understood that he was harboring a child. Sharoud could not imagine where it had come from or why, of all people, it had come to Habbib. But it was clear to the dark, brooding dervish that the only thing to do was to flush the creature out. He crouched beneath the window of the cell and beat the *tambla*. He lit sticks of incense and slid them under the door. Yet nothing he did evoked the slightest reaction from either Habbib or the child.

It was only when everything else had failed that Sharoud resorted to using the snake. He was sitting on the low stone bench in the garden when it slithered through the thick grass and darted past his feet. And he instantly knew that it was the means to expose Habbib's secret. Grabbing it by the tail, he carried it to his cell and placed it in an earthenware pot. Then, when the others were asleep, he took the pot to the door of Habbib's cell and let it wriggle beneath. His aim was merely to frighten Habbib, and bring the infant to light. Yet he could not help but thrill at the thought that the creature might squeeze the life out of the child.

The snake, for his part, had no particular agenda. But when he found himself inside the cell, the obvious place to head was the crate that contained the sleeping child. When he reached it, he paused, using his sharpened instincts to discern the best way to slip inside. Before he could do so, however, Habbib bolted up in bed. When he peered through the inky shadows, he saw the snake. But in the split second before he could cry out, the snake recoiled, formed itself into a circle, and began to devour its own tail. That was when the cry issued from Habbib, which quickly led to doors flying open and candles being lit and bodies thundering down the darkened hallway into the cell.

When they saw the infant—not to mention the snake—the dervishes' faces grew wide. But before Habbib could utter a single word, Piran Nazuder suddenly shouted that they must rouse Sheikh Bailiri. Then he scurried off to find him and, a few moments later, returned with the great Sufi master at his side.

"O master!" cried Jamal al-Jani. "We need your help to understand!"

"Surely," cried Hajid al-Hallal, "this is a sign from Allah!"

Sheikh Bailiri stood quietly in the doorway of the cell. He'd seen many things in his seventy-two years. And while he knew that the world the senses could perceive was an illusion, he also knew that a higher world sometimes revealed itself through the senses by using signs. So when he saw the infant with the strange head garment lying in his cradle beside the snake consuming its tail, he knew that he was no ordinary child.

"He's a breeze from God," he declared. "We must treat him with the utmost care."

He paused, half-expecting the child to float up toward the rafters or climb out of the square cradle and dance a *baba karan*. Nouri, however, just lay there and gurgled. So Sheikh Bailiri walked out of Habbib's cell, leaving the room in silence.

Three

Once Sheikh Bailiri gave Nouri his blessing, the brothers embraced him as their own. Indeed, they were so taken by him, Habbib had to petition for his rights as the child's primary caretaker. Eventually it was decided that each of the dervishes would be given a turn to feed the infant, to change his diapers, to hold him in his arms, but only Habbib would be allowed to bathe him and lull him to sleep. When he was asked where he'd found him, he was afraid to reveal that the child had fallen out of the sky. So he replied that an old woman had rushed up to him as he was heading to market, exclaiming that there'd been a fire in the next village and that she'd managed to save the infant in her arms from a house that had just burst into flames. Then she'd handed the baby to Habbib and run off in the other direction. When he was asked why the child wore the strange head garment—for despite the recent decree of the Shah that all men wear turbans, the rule was never applied to infants—Habbib replied that he had a terrible scalp condition and that they must never, never, never remove it. For Sharoud, this was clearly one *never* too many. But after the incident with the snake, he decided to lie low for a while.

So life behind the cool stone walls began to take shape for little Nouri Ahmad Mohammad ibn Mahsoud al-Morad. From the moment he was lifted from his cradle in the morning, he was never alone. Indeed, he was almost never out of the warmth of someone's arms, for when Habbib went to fetch the broom and do the sweeping, Jamal al-Jani or Piran Nazuder or Salim Rasa was always there, eager to hold him. Like a loaf of fresh bread, he was passed from one doting dervish to the next, unaware that he was blessed with the rare privilege of constant touch. Each night before bed, Habbib would rub a mixture of olive oil and crushed rose petals into his ears. Then the boy would listen to one of his fabulous tales and fall into a peaceful sleep.

As time passed, Nouri became a fixture of the community, present at all prayers, all meals, all meditation, his world a haven of order and calm. When he turned one (or thereabouts, as the brothers marked his birth as the day that Habbib had found him), they lit candles around the courtyard, placed Nouri at the center, and chanted the ninety-nine names of Allah. When he turned two, Habbib raised him up onto his shoulders and carried him out through the gates to see the world outside the lodge. When he turned three—after having said little more than "Habbib" and "hello"—Nouri suddenly began speaking in full sentences.

The brothers would listen as he described in precise detail what he'd found in the garden or dreamed the previous night. Words came to Nouri like flight to birds. Each day his vocabulary grew richer, his phrasing more nuanced, his syntax more complex. Until one day he looked around and decided that everything was in need of a new name. *Chair* became "lotan," *book* became "shawd," and the brothers became entrenched in the task of trying to figure out what he was saying. The ritual of renaming, however, did not last long. For Nouri decided that once the objects had been released from the burden of having been called the same thing for so long, they could revert to their former names. The brothers, however, could not shake off the changes so quickly, and for years one might still hear a candle referred to as a "darpash," a plate dubbed a "froost," or a cat called a "kimbaloo."

By the time Nouri turned four, his beauty was undeniable. His eyes, which had wavered between star anise and tamarind, deepened into the richness of black mustard seed. His nose, which might have grown to overcome his face, emerged as noble and straight. His cheekbones were high. His lips were bow-shaped. And beneath his head cloth grew thick waves of hair. Habbib considered that Nouri's bountiful tresses might be enough to hide the two sets of ears. But since he feared that a strong wind would blow in, he left the head cloth in place.

By the time Nouri turned five, it was clear that he was destined to follow the spiritual path. When Piran Nazuder made the call to prayer, Nouri would prostrate himself just like the others. Hajid al-Hallal said that this was merely imitation, that he was too young to know the true meaning of *salah*. When Nouri was late for meals, however, he was usually found sitting in the chapel. And when the poor came to receive the watery soup the brothers doled out twice a week, he was always the first to go among them offering hunks of Salim Rasa's dark, crusty bread. Sheikh Bailiri knew that the boy was too young to begin formal training. But there was a thirst in his eyes that the Sufi master was convinced nothing of the physical world could ever quench. He could feel—just as he'd felt when he'd first seen him—that the child was blessed.

Although the brothers would quite gladly have remained at Nouri's side, they soon found that the child longed to be on his own. If one of them became distracted for even a moment, Nouri would scamper off to some hidden corner to contemplate a leaf or a shattered bowl. When they found him, he'd smile up at them as if he'd never been happier to see anyone in his life. Then, when they turned their backs, he'd hurry off to find something new.

It was with this same curiosity that Nouri considered his extra set of ears. He was aware, from the attention Habbib gave them, that they were special. He'd giggle as Habbib massaged the soothing oil into their tiny lobes and along their gentle curves. He also knew, from the way Habbib added new strips to his head garment as he grew, that they were meant to be kept hidden from sight. He did not actually set eyes upon them, however, until he was six years old. It was a warm, sultry evening toward the end of summer. Habbib was telling the tale of Sam and the *simorgh*, as Nouri sucked happily on a piece of melon at his feet. When Habbib reached the part where the hero heads off into the mountains, there was a sharp knocking at the door.

"It's Ali Majid!" came the familiar voice.

When Habbib went to open the door, he found the gangly youth holding a large oval tray and a pair of candlesticks.

"Hajid al-Hallal told me to polish the silver. But I can't keep my eyes open any longer."

Habbib gazed at the things Ali Majid held in his arms. "Put them there," he said, pointing to the wall.

Ali Majid laid the objects down, knowing that Habbib would bring them to a gleaming shine before morning. Then he thanked the fellow and made his way out of the cell.

Habbib returned to Nouri and the tale. When he finished, however, and sat Nouri on the edge of the bed to massage the oil into his ears, the tray that Ali Majid had placed against the wall caught the child's reflection. And when he unwound the head cloth, Nouri saw his ears for the first time.

He gazed at the image and the image gazed back.

"Why?" he said.

Habbib had been waiting for this moment for years. Yet he was no closer to having an answer to Nouri's question than when he'd first seen the ears himself.

"Perhaps God was bored," he said. "Or perhaps someday we'll all have four ears, and He simply started with you."

Nouri stared at Habbib, unconvinced by either theory. Then he turned his attention back to the face that peered from the tarnished tray. He knew that having two sets of ears made him different. And he had to admit that they were intriguing, like satiny husks from beneath the sea. He knew, however—even at the age of six—that people's thinking was usually not so generous. He'd seen the man who sold eggs at the market mock Habbib's withered hand when his friend wasn't looking. He'd watched the older boys in the village place stones in the path of the blind fishmonger in order to make him trip. And he'd noticed the sullen gaze of Sharoud, and how it was firmly fixed on his head garment.

So Nouri accepted that his ears must remain a secret. And if he underestimated the dark dervish, it was only a matter of time before he learned just how cunning he could be.

ONCE IT SANK IN THAT he had twice the number of ears as everyone else, Nouri began to understand why the subtlest sounds whipped through him like wind through a field of grass. Even with the muffling of the head cloth, Habbib's gentle humming sent shivers down his spine. The clicking of the spoon as Salim Rasa stirred the yogurt made him wince. And if faint sounds were palpable, loud ones were almost more than he could bear. Rain on the roof was a fusillade. A cough was an exploding bomb. The spiraling sounds of the *ney* made him drunk.

As time passed, Nouri found two principal ways to escape from the barrage of sound. The first was to help Piran Nazuder tend the garden. It was as if sound receded while he pruned and watered the plants. The buzzing of the bees no longer jangled his nerves. The song of the morning lark no longer pierced his heart.

The second form of escape grew out of the first. For when he was down on his knees, digging up the rich, dark soil or removing a few withered branches, Nouri's head would fill with words. At first they came single file, like the leaves tumbling down in autumn. *Prayer,* he would think as he cut back the roses, *dragon* or *oxcart* or *brushfire* as he watered the rue. As the days passed, however, they began to cluster into phrases. *The softness of a catkin. A ripple on the pond.* Until at last they began to gather into thoughts:

The pansies that grow along the path have no worries.

The smallest and bitterest seed is sweet to God.

The dinner gong; song of contentment; when will it ring again?

Nouri didn't know that such thoughts were unusual for a child of only six. But when he shared them with Habbib, Habbib felt that they should be written down. Since Habbib had never learned how to write, he asked Jamal al-Jani to become Nouri's scribe. Each night, Jamal al-Jani would come to Habbib's cell with a sheet of paper and record what the child had come up with that day. He'd make no comments as he scribbled the lines down. He'd simply shake his head, or laugh, or wipe away a tear. Then he'd hand the sheet of paper to Habbib and scurry back to his cell.

In time, Nouri's talent for words became a simple fact of the lodge. Salim Rasa would look up from chopping the onions as the boy passed the kitchen and call out, "Say something, Nouri!" Piran Nazuder would follow him around, hoping to witness the birth of a new thought. But it wasn't until Sharoud paid a visit to Sheikh Bailiri that the Sufi master truly contemplated the boy's gift.

From the moment he saw him lying in his cradle beside the self-consuming snake, Sharoud had been watching Nouri. He felt sure that the child had somehow bewitched the creature, and as he followed his development over the years, nothing swayed him from the belief that there was something ungodly about the child. Sometimes he would find him frozen in the courtyard staring at the sky. Other times he would spy him in the branches of a tree, as if it pained him to be too rooted to the earth. Most of all, he was convinced that some mark of the devil was concealed beneath the tightly wound folds of his head garment.

Sharoud knew such thoughts were unworthy of one who had given his life to Allah. So he tried as hard as he could to cast them from his mind. He decided, in fact, that the only way to fight his distrust of the child was to make some gesture toward him. So one morning he decided to pay a visit to Sheikh Bailiri's cell.

The Sufi master was not accustomed to private visits from his *murids,* let alone a visit from Sharoud. So when the dervish rapped on his open door, he was rather curious about his purpose. "How may I assist you, Brother Sharoud?"

"If it's not too much trouble," said Sharoud, "I wish to speak with you about Nouri."

Sheikh Bailiri, who sat cross-legged on the floor, his falcon Kavan perched on his left forearm, gestured to Sharoud to sit. Sharoud complied. Then he launched into lavish praise of Nouri.

"It's not often that a child is so perceptive," he said. "He's a prodigy. A wonder."

Sheikh Bailiri, who by now was as aware as the others of Nouri's gift, nodded. "I agree."

"His seventh birthday is next week. I think we should honor it with a celebration."

The Sufi master shifted his awareness to the geometric patterns in the prayer rug, the weight of the majestic bird upon his arm, the rising and falling of his breath. He did not need Sharoud, or anyone else, to tell him that Nouri was special. Yet he could feel that, despite his dark impulses, Sharoud was making an effort to reach out to the boy.

"It's a fine idea," he said. "Let's make a celebration for Nouri."

As he said this, Kavan turned his head to Sharoud and shouted: *"Kaw! Kaw!"*

And though Sheikh Bailiri did not speak a word of peregrine falcon, he knew that he would have to keep on the alert.

WITHIN DAYS OF SHAROUD'S conversation with Sheikh Bailiri, preparations for Nouri's birthday celebration were under way. The brothers did not have the means to take the festivities too far. But Piran Nazuder erected a tent over the courtyard, Jamal al-Jani got down on his knees and scrubbed the stones, and with the help of Ali Majid—who had sprouted into a loose-limbed lad of seventeen—Salim Rasa spent hours drawing *kashk* out of the yogurt, pounding walnuts and almonds, steaming huge pots of fragrant rice. By the average standards of the people of Tan-Arzhan, it would be a humble meal. But to the brothers, it would be a feast.

On the morning of the celebration, Nouri lay on his bed in Habbib's cell thinking about the dream he'd had the night before. He was wandering through the streets of Tan-Arzhan, yet it was the city and not the city, familiar and yet utterly strange. As he made his way along, he took note of the girl carrying the large clay jug upon her head, the pure white horse drawing the bright green cart, the haggard woman beating the rug. It was a bright day, full of smiles and good cheer. Wherever he looked, there was a sense of purpose. As he approached the town square, however, he felt something dark and sinister dogging his heels. And when he turned he saw a ferocious-looking creature following behind him. He quickened his pace, but he could not seem to lose it. He broke into a run, but the creature did too. Before it could reach him, however, he awoke, heart pounding, in Habbib's cell.

It took a while for Nouri to shake off the dark dream. But eventually he rose and, with the help of Habbib, began to prepare for the celebration. He put on a fresh tunic and trousers and tied a bright blue sash around his waist. Habbib removed his head garment, brushed his hair, and neatly rewound it. Then they went out to the courtyard, where Sheikh Bailiri and the others were waiting.

When Sheikh Bailiri saw Nouri, he led him to a long wooden table laden with food. He gestured to the boy to sit; then he and Habbib took their places on either side. Then the other brothers joined them and the Sufi master raised his cup.

"We celebrate your birth, Nouri! May you live to be ten times seven. And more!"

The brothers raised their cups. "To Nouri!" they cried. Then Salim Rasa leaned forward and shouted, "Say something, Nouri!"

Nouri looked around at the expectant faces. He feared that the brothers endowed his words with a greater wisdom than they possessed. But he closed his eyes and murmured:

"I am the bell on the collar of the cow.
Tinkling. Tinkling.
And I am the breeze that blows the bell."

The brothers were silent. Then Sheikh Bailiri reached for one of the bowls and the feast began.

"You're a poet, Nouri!" said Salim Rasa, as he ladled some of the *mirza ghasemi* onto his plate.

Nouri said nothing. He simply grasped the four withered fingers of Habbib's hand and turned his attention to the meal. No one, in fact, said anything more. Instead, they slipped into a communal trance as the savory tastes danced upon their tongues. Only when the last grain of rice had been devoured did Piran Nazuder suddenly cry out, "We mustn't forget the *sema*!"

The others turned to him, their eyes glazed over.

"Do we have to?" said Jamal al-Jani.

"I'm too stuffed," said Hajid al-Hallal, "to rise up to heaven!"

"One is never too heavy to strive toward God," said Sheikh Bailiri. "And never too humble to perform the *sema*."

Centered on the chanting of litanies and accompanied by the playing of music, the *sema* was deep at the heart of Sufi practice. Some, overcome by the words, would begin to weep. Others, inflamed with joy, would throw their heads back and fall to their knees. But the most sublime response to the chanted words—which had been introduced to the order by Piran Nazuder, who had learned it on a visit to Anatolia—was to spread one's arms on either side and begin to whirl. There were differing theories as to how the practice had begun. Some claimed a Sufi had been so shattered by the loss of his teacher he'd found that only whirling could ease his pain. Some claimed a bowl of oversalted stew had caused a Sufi to start spinning, and when his comrades followed suit they found the movement to be a tonic for the soul. There were rules to observe: one must never move in an affected manner; one must never cry out while one turned. But for those who sought a true union with God, it was an ecstatic form. So the brothers cleared away the cups and the plates and the bowls and removed the table. Then they donned their woolen hats and dark mantles and spread out across the floor. When all were in place, Sheikh Bailiri began reciting verses from the Qur'an, which the others repeated in unison. Then Ali Majid stepped forward with his *ney*.

The brothers would never have thought that Ali Majid would become a musician. He seemed too scattered—too dim—to coax prayer from a simple flute. One morning, however, he saw a *ney* lying in the assembly hall and when he raised it to his lips a perfect note rose into the air. He quickly returned it to where he'd found it, fearful that he'd be punished for touching it. But Hajid al-Hallal heard the clear, sweet sound, received permission from Sheikh Bailiri to give him lessons, and in no time the boy's gift was revealed. He still washed the pots and the pans and sharpened the knives. But his playing became the pulse of the brothers' dance.

Now, as he began to play, Sheikh Bailiri stepped back and the brothers bowed low to the floor. They turned and began to walk in a circle, pausing to bow to one another when they reached the place where the Sufi master stood. When they'd made three rounds, they removed their mantles. Then they folded their arms across their chests and began to whirl. It started slowly, a gentle turning that expressed their longing to be released from their bodies. As the pace quickened, their arms rose up over their heads. Then they spread them wide—their right hands turned upward to receive the grace of heaven, their left dangling down to release their passions to the earth.

Nouri was not permitted to join in the dance like a true dervish, for despite his gifts he was only seven years old. In honor of his birthday, however, Sheikh Bailiri agreed that he could do a bit of turning. So as the music of Ali Majid's *ney* dizzied his ever-sensitive ears, he took his place at the edge of the circle and, in his own simple fashion, began to whirl.

Sharoud whirled too. Inspired by the fever of the festivities, he spun like a giddy top. He was aware of the others as he moved through the space, but he was mostly aware of Nouri. He felt his pulse quicken and his heart pound each time they drew near. And on the tenth revolution—as his taut body floated past the child—he suddenly reached out and grabbed the slender tail of his tightly wrapped head garment.

It was like a spool of white ribbon unfurling. A cocoon being unraveled. A present being unwrapped. But it was only when the music stopped—and the brothers, shaken from their trance, suddenly turned and gaped at him—that Nouri understood that his secret had been revealed.

Four

Nouri sat quietly on the blue-and-gold kilim, his legs crossed under him, his hands in his lap, waiting for Sheikh Bailiri to speak. He'd been sitting in the Sufi master's cell for nearly an hour, but when the dervish entered he seemed to take no notice of him, turning instead to the weathered book on his desk, the goose-quill pen and the crisp sheet of paper, the small bowl of lemongrass tea. He would read for a moment. Then sip the tea. Then write a few lines. And then sip some more. Only after the longest while did he rise from the desk and go to the wooden cage by the window that housed the gray falcon.

He opened the door and placed his arm inside.

The falcon stepped onto it.

Then Sheikh Bailiri drew the bird from the cage and spoke.

"When he dives for prey, he's the fastest creature in the world. But look how calm he is in repose!"

Nouri hesitated, uncertain if he should speak to the Sufi master or simply remain quiet. He'd been aware of the bird from the moment he'd entered the room, however. And Sheikh Bailiri seemed to be waiting for him to respond. So he put aside his fear and cleared his throat.

"What does he eat?" he asked.

"Bats," said Sheikh Bailiri. "And squirrels. And mice."

He moved across the room until the bird was only inches from Nouri, its dark feathers gleaming, its obsidian eyes boring into him.

"I take him out each morning at dawn," said Sheikh Bailiri. "You're welcome to join me if you like."

Nouri nodded. Then Sheikh Bailiri knelt down.

"Would you like to pet him?"

Nouri nodded again. So Sheikh Bailiri extended his arm and the boy reached out and stroked the bird from his head down to his tail.

"His name is Kavan."

Nouri looked at Kavan and Kavan looked at Nouri. Then Sheikh Bailiri carried him back to his cage and placed him inside. He paused a moment, as if he and the elegant bird were exchanging a few words. Then he returned to where Nouri sat and lowered himself beside him.

For seven years, Sheikh Bailiri had been closely watching Nouri. He'd observed his grace, his tenderness, his beauty, aware of the potential for spiritual growth that was lodged in him like a seed beneath the earth. He knew, however, that the first seven years of a boy's life were for his mother and that, without a mother, that role fell to Habbib. So he allowed the simple groundskeeper to care for him, all the while hoping some sign would appear to announce that the next seven years should be his. Now, with perfect timing—indeed, on the child's seventh birthday—that sign had appeared. And Sheikh Bailiri understood what he had to do.

"God's creation is infinite. There are trees. Insects. Mountains. Rivers. Birds of prey like Kavan. There are flowers so fragrant they can make your head spin. There are creatures beneath the sea so strange they would leave you speechless if you saw them."

The Sufi master was silent a moment and Nouri had to work hard not to tumble into his radiant eyes.

"You, my child, are an expression of God's diversity. His abundance. His playfulness. So you must never allow yourself to be ashamed of how he made you."

Sheikh Bailiri paused again. Then a laugh bubbled up.

"Your ears, Nouri! Your ears! If ever there were ears created to hear the Word of God, yours are the ones!"

Nouri's ears, beneath his head cloth, grew hot.

"A seven-year-old is too young to become a dervish. And even after an aspirant has taken his vows, it takes many years to become a true servant of God."

Sheikh Bailiri leaned forward.

"But a Sufi is born a Sufi. It only requires the right teacher to reveal him to himself."

At these words the falcon suddenly cried out, *"Kaw! Kaw!"*

"I'd like to be your teacher, Nouri." He smiled. "Would you like to learn the secrets of the universe?"

Now, there are many things that are hard for a young boy to resist. Riding a camel. Holding a scimitar. Eating *sharbat-e limoo*.

But nothing is more tempting than the chance to learn the secrets of the universe. And Nouri felt sure that if anyone knew them it was Sheikh Bailiri.

"Yes, please," he said.

The Sufi master nodded. And Nouri's education began.

"THERE ARE A GREAT MANY rules to learn. And they must be adhered to with great strictness. But the point—and you must remember this, Nouri—is not to become good at following the rules. The point is to bring discipline to the animal part of your nature. So that your spirit—which is who you truly are—can be free."

It was a crisp winter morning a few months after Nouri had begun his studies with Sheikh Bailiri. They were strolling through the market, past the dried figs and the salted fish and the bowls of ground fennel and sumac and coriander. Sheikh Bailiri found that his mind worked best when he was walking, so each morning, after he'd prayed and broken fast and taken Kavan out to hunt, he would roam with Nouri through the streets of Tan-Arzhan. The boy's head cloth was tied tightly in place—for once he'd seen the stunned reaction of the brothers to his ears, he preferred to keep them safely concealed, even behind the walls of the lodge.

"All is one," said Sheikh Bailiri, as he plucked a large onion from one of the stalls. He held it up to the light as if he was waiting for it to transform into a dove and fly away. Then he handed the man behind the stall a coin, and handed the onion to Nouri. "Things look different. But their inner spirit is the same."

Nouri ran his thumb over the smooth, papery skin and tried to focus on what the Sufi master was saying. He loved his morning walks through the city with Sheikh Bailiri. And for all the curious sights, what truly dazzled him were the sounds that pierced his sensitive ears: the ping of the blacksmith's hammer, the braying of the wine merchant's donkey, the chatter of the spice sellers, the gurgling of the fountain. Yet no matter how alluring these things were, Nouri was always drawn back to Sheikh Bailiri's words.

"God is too great to be perceived directly, which is why He fractured into so many forms. You, Nouri, are one of those forms. When you know yourself, you will know God."

The first thing that Sheikh Bailiri required Nouri to do was to learn the Qur'an. That was the foundation of everything else. The teaching of the Prophet. The Word. Nouri found the book to be both beautiful and direct. But what fascinated him most was the feeling that beneath the words—in the patterns of the syllables and the sounds—was a hidden teaching. After the Qur'an came the Five Pillars of Islam: Faith, Worship, Charity, Fasting, and Pilgrimage to the Holy Land. Only after these things had been explained did Sheikh Bailiri discuss what it meant to be a Sufi.

"Through the Qur'an, the Supreme Being created a holy covenant between Himself and man. A moral guidepost. A set of laws. The Sufis are no less constrained by those laws than any other believers. Their devotion, however, is more inward."

He explained that each Sufi order was led by a sheikh, who had studied with and been confirmed as a teacher by his own sheikh, in an unbroken chain reaching back to the Prophet himself. To be a Sufi was to be a servant of others. And by serving them, to be a servant of Allah. But one could do this only if one remembered that He was present in all things.

"Constant remembrance, Nouri. That is the goal. But I assure you, it is far more difficult than you imagine."

When Nouri had been invited to learn the secrets of the universe, he'd expected to receive discourse on how to alter the pattern of the stars in the sky, turn rocks and pebbles into precious stones, manipulate the workings of time. So all this talk about remembrance and oneness and forms was a bit abstract. But he knew that it was a gift to receive private instruction from someone as wise as Sheikh Bailiri. So he kept his ears open—all four of them—and trusted that understanding would come.

Though what mattered most was the inner meaning of being a Sufi, Sheikh Bailiri also explained the Sufi's manner of dress. A loose frock was worn over the body, made either of a light-colored cotton to express his purity or a patched piece of cloth to express his wish to unite mankind. A battered robe was worn over this to remind him of his vow to poverty. And on his head—sometimes surrounding a domelike hat, which pointed to heaven—he wore a turban.

"The cloth that wraps the head of a Sufi is his funeral shroud," Sheikh Bailiri explained. "So his turban is a constant reminder of death."

To Nouri, death seemed far, far away. Yet he knew that the remembrance Sheikh Bailiri spoke of was somehow connected to it. It was only when they paid a visit to the city's mosque, however—one crisp Sunday in the month of Shawwal—that he caught a true glimpse of what lay beneath the Sufi master's words.

Nouri had gazed at the vast dome and the slender minarets of the Darni Sunim dozens of times, yet he'd never set foot inside. For despite the alluring beauty of the place, the brothers preferred to maintain their worship in the small chapel mosque at the lodge. On this day, however, Sheikh Bailiri slowed his pace as he and Nouri approached the dreamlike structure.

"Allah is as grateful for a simple dwelling as for the most elaborately carved building in the world." He turned to Nouri. "But it's very beautiful. Would you like to see what it looks like inside?"

Nouri nodded. So Sheikh Bailiri escorted him up the six weathered steps, where they removed their shoes and placed them beside the others that were lined up next to the door. Then he took Nouri's hand and they passed through the doorway into the mosque.

As Nouri entered the sacred space, he could feel his breath catch and a shiver run down his spine. The floor was lined with fine woven carpets, the walls were graced with filigreed windows, and the dome—which spread out over their heads—was richly painted with flowers and leaves and suns and moons and stars. But what thrilled Nouri the most was the fact that wherever he looked—on the walls—on the doors—on the frieze that ran in a circle beneath the dome—were the most exquisitely calligraphed words.

"The Prophet came to remind us that we must keep Allah in our hearts at all times." Sheikh Bailiri raised his hand and gestured toward the river of words. "And praise him!"

Nouri gazed at the curving script that sang from every surface of the room.

Words.

In praise of God.

Words.

Words.

Words.

As he stood there in the cool, filtered light, Nouri could feel a peace wash over him. In the corner, a pair of men in white turbans sat on a prayer rug reading the Qur'an. On a nearby ladder, a young man was hanging a brass lamp from a crossbeam. Everything seemed to be floating in space, from the stairs of the *minbar* to the *mihrab* set into the eastern wall. Nouri wondered if the people who knelt before that niche felt the same inner confusion that he did. He wondered if the path he was traveling was affected by his actions or if it was preordained. He wondered why he had to labor to reach God if God was already inside him.

In the rarefied air of that holy space, Nouri's thoughts soared like a dove. So he was utterly unprepared when a voice cried—

"Look out!"

—and the polished lamp that the young man had been hanging came crashing to the ground.

Nouri froze, his hand glued to Sheikh Bailiri's, a strange light dazzling his eyes. He felt as if he could see things as they were. As if he could see himself. The thoughts that crowded his head disappeared. The laws of the physical world seemed to dissolve into the welter of metal and glass at his feet.

"That's it, Nouri!" whispered Sheikh Bailiri. "That's what you're after! That's who you truly are!"

Nouri did not understand what he meant. But he suddenly saw that another world existed. And as its light began to fade, and the contours of his usual world rose over him, he vowed that he would find his way back.

WHEN SHEIKH BAILIRI TOOK NOURI under his wing, Habbib glowed with fatherly pride. He'd spent countless nights gazing at the youth while he slept, wondering what would be his fate. He knew that no one could prepare him for that fate better than Sheikh Bailiri. Yet he could not help but feel a certain sadness at how the new patterns of the boy's life created a distance between them. When Nouri was not out roaming the city with Sheikh Bailiri, he was immersed in a series of small daily tasks: laying the table for the morning meal, lighting the candles in the chapel mosque, filling the water jugs that sat beside the doors of the brothers' cells. Habbib would wait patiently until bedtime, when the child would curl up beside him and listen to one of his tales. On his eighth birthday, however, Sheikh Bailiri announced that he was going to give Nouri his own cell.

"The Sufi must be a part of the community. But like everyone on the spiritual path, he can only find himself in solitude."

So Habbib and Nouri still toiled in the garden and immersed themselves in the stories of the Shahnameh and sat beside each other at meals. But the time they spent together was now a fraction of what it had been.

Even at its most extreme, however, Habbib's reaction to Sheikh Bailiri's devotion to Nouri was mild when compared with that of Sharoud. On the day when he'd unraveled the boy's head garment and exposed his secret, Sharoud had expected Nouri to be cast out into the street. When Sheikh Bailiri instead called Sharoud to his cell and took him to task, the somber dervish could hardly control his fury.

"Surely it must be for the best," he cried, "that such a horror has been brought to light!"

"The Sufi is respectful of others at all times," said Sheikh Bailiri. "You had no right to tamper with the boy's apparel."

"But who knows where he came from?" said Sharoud. "Habbib's story is full of holes!"

"He's a boy with a special gift," said Sheikh Bailiri. "As you yourself pointed out."

Sharoud—not wishing to offend the Sufi master—said no more. But as the weeks passed and Sheikh Bailiri began to mentor the child, he could not hold his tongue.

"How can you honor this creature with your guidance? It's an insult! An outrage!"

"Remember the rules of conduct, Sharoud."

"But he has two sets of ears! It's a sacrilege!"

"No, Sharoud. It's a blessing. A miracle."

But Sharoud was insistent. "He's unfit to be among us!"

Sheikh Bailiri had spent decades on Sharoud: trying to support what was highest in him, helping him to move through his dark, difficult moods. In that moment, however, it was clear that it was he, and not Nouri, who was unfit to be in their midst. So on the following morning Sharoud awoke to find his shoes turned outward at the door to his cell, which meant that he had until sundown to take leave of the lodge. It was a shock to everyone. Sharoud had been a part of their lives for so long it was unfathomable that he should suddenly go. But Sheikh Bailiri was firm, and by the snuffing out of that evening's candles, Sharoud was gone.

As far as the others were concerned, they were not so much dismayed by Nouri's ears as they were amazed.

"No wonder he can invent such splendid verse," said Jamal al-Jani. "He can hear more words than anyone else!"

"With Nouri among us," said Piran Nazuder, "the order is most surely twice blessed!"

So once Nouri's head cloth was retied, he was treated like a rose petal in the washbasin: a flash of color in a world of function, a reminder of the wonder of Allah.

As for Nouri himself, he could not stop thinking about that moment at the mosque when he'd been swept to another world. He wished, more than anything, to go there again. Yet try as he might, he was unable to find his way back. He returned to the Darni Sunim, but its shimmering surfaces remained locked up tight. He held his breath—he pressed his fingers against his eyelids—but nothing came of it at all. He thought that another crash might somehow trigger the experience. So he dropped a ceramic bowl onto the floor. He shattered a vase against the stones of the courtyard. He smashed a plate against the wall. Yet nothing evoked the stunning awareness he'd experienced at the mosque.

Eventually he decided that only a precise reenactment of what had happened could lead him back. So one morning he fetched a ladder from the garden, carried it into the chapel, and placed it beside the small glass lamp that hung from the ceiling. He climbed the ladder, attached a rope to the chain, and climbed back down. Then he positioned himself so that, with one good tug, the lamp would come crashing down at his feet.

He closed his eyes. He tightened his fingers around the rope. But then he heard Sheikh Bailiri's voice.

"Even if it startles you," said the Sufi master, "it won't be the same."

Nouri opened his eyes to find Sheikh Bailiri standing at the entrance to the chapel.

"You can't spend your life pulling down lamps." He crossed the room to where Nouri stood, and he knelt down. "What happened at the Darni Sunim was a gift. To get there again will require effort. And will. Only you can say if you have the strength to remain on the path. Only time will reveal whether you do."

Nouri gazed into Sheikh Bailiri's eyes. He had no idea what awaited him on the path. He suddenly pictured it aswarm with demons. But his destiny beckoned. And there was no way he could turn back now.

Five

So the weeks and the days and the months went by, and Nouri's education continued on.

"You cannot avoid life, Nouri. You have been given it for a reason. You have to move through it—the struggles—the fears—until you can be in it and out of it at the same time."

He explained to Nouri that to be a Sufi was to strive for a direct experience of God.

"Why wait until you die to see Allah," he said, "when you can see Him now?"

As Nouri's ninth birthday approached, Sheikh Bailiri taught him that the world was an illusion.

"There are a thousand veils that cover the Self. You must dissolve them. Anything that separates you from God is a veil."

As Nouri's tenth birthday approached, Sheikh Bailiri taught him about the need to develop the heart.

"You must bypass the intellect. The mind will always obscure the truth. But the heart is a mirror. If you polish away the rust, you can reflect the truth back to itself."

As Nouri's eleventh birthday approached, Sheikh Bailiri taught him about love.

"All service, all prayer, must come from love. The Sufi would give everything he has—even his life—for a friend on the path."

Sheikh Bailiri taught Nouri about the chart of virtues. The science of letters. The magic of numbers. He outlined the Degrees of Ascent and the Seven Stations of the Soul. But most of all, he encouraged the boy to study himself.

"Who are you, Nouri? Are you this creature that eats and sleeps and shits? This vessel of desires? This sack of contradictions? Or are you a particle of God, waiting to reunite with your source?"

As the years passed, Nouri learned how to adapt his head cloth to his spurts in growth. Sometimes he simply needed to add a new strip of cloth to the tail. Other times he had to fashion an entirely new head garment. But he always saw the process of unwinding it—and washing it—and keeping the four ears clean—as a ritual. Whatever the ears meant, they were his, and he vowed to treat them with respect.

Nouri's life might have continued on this way indefinitely had Vishpar not arrived. It was on a sultry morning toward the end of the month of Rajab, just a few weeks before Nouri's twelfth birthday. He was sitting in Sheikh Bailiri's cell, waiting for the day's instruction to begin, when Jamal al-Jani appeared at the door.

"There's a youth at the front gate," said Jamal al-Jani. "He says that he wants to become a dervish."

It had been a long while since anyone had appeared at the front gate wishing to join the order. The process of initiation was rigorous, and Sheikh Bailiri knew that this youth—like most of the young men who had tried—was not likely to make it past the first few days. He was happy to offer him the chance, however. So he told Nouri to rise and they followed Jamal al-Jani to the front gate to meet him.

As they moved down the hall, Nouri pictured the other youths who'd appeared on the doorstep over the years wishing to devote themselves to Allah. Some had been tall and some had been small, but they'd all been pale and enveloped in thick clouds of thought. So when they reached the gate, he was surprised to see the strapping youth who stood before them.

"Praise be to Allah!" said the youth, bowing his head down low as they approached.

Sheikh Bailiri took a step toward him. "What is your name?"

"Vishpar Izad al-Hassan al-Ibrahim."

The Sufi master nodded. "You may raise your head."

The youth raised his eyes to the Sufi master's.

"And what is your purpose?"

"I wish," said the youth, "to know God."

"That is a large aim," said Sheikh Bailiri.

"It is the only real aim that a man can have."

Sheikh Bailiri was silent, and in the space of that silence Nouri studied the youth: his strong body, his hair like spun gold, his face both angelic and fierce. He'd never seen anything like him and he might have kept staring at him forever had Sheikh Bailiri not instructed Jamal al-Jani to lead him away. "Take him to the initiate's pelt," he said, "and explain what he must do."

The youth bowed again. Then he started off into the lodge after Jamal al-Jani.

For the first three days, while Vishpar knelt in silence on the worn pelt that lay beside the door to the refectory, Sheikh Bailiri made a thorough investigation of his past. Everyone he spoke to said the same thing, however: despite his odd coloring—which some said was due to the salt baths his mother had taken while she was carrying him and others said was due to a tryst with a passing infidel—they had never met anyone as loyal or selfless or true as Vishpar Izad al-Hassan al-Ibrahim. On the fourth day, the Sufi master told him that he could still change his mind before embarking upon the penitential retreat. The youth, however, could not be dissuaded from his goal. So Sheikh Bailiri led him to the kitchen and for the next eighteen days he washed lentils, sliced eggplants, and chopped onions while the brothers shouted things like "You numbskull!" and "You're doing it all wrong!" The youth took the barrage of insults in stride. So on the twenty-second day, Sheikh Bailiri handed him the plain muslin shift of the *murid*. Then he set about to complete the long months of service required to become a full-fledged dervish.

The work was hard. Cleaning the tiles on the roof of the chapel. Mending the mortar along the southern wall. Mucking out the sludge and slime from the bottom of the well. But whatever was asked of him, Vishpar responded to it with ardor and good cheer. So when the last of his tasks—scrubbing out the latrines—had been completed, he was ordered to prepare for the ceremony of full confession, which would be followed by his induction into the order.

This was what Vishpar had longed for for years. For from the time he was a child, nothing could dim the fervent gleam of the warrior in his eyes. He was stronger and smarter than the other boys, yet he did not show the least interest in the games they played or the jokes they told or the girls they vied for. Instead, he spent hours roaming the woods beyond the River Tolna on the lookout for thieves. When he was ten, he challenged the other boys to a wrestling match and barely exerted himself as he pinned each one to the ground. When he was twelve, one of the town's wealthy merchants, who bought his saddles from his father, offered to teach him to ride, and Vishpar spent the next several years thundering down the open roads that skirted the city of Tan-Arzhan.

When he was fourteen, something changed. Perhaps it was the perfection of a rose that grew in his mother's garden. Perhaps it was the sight of Sheikh Bailiri moving silently down the street. Whatever it was, Vishpar suddenly knew that not only was he a warrior, he was a warrior of God. He received no visitation from a pear tree like Sharoud had. But his morning walks always wound up at the lodge. And the books he read always paled beside the blazing fire of the Qur'an. So on his sixteenth birthday, he announced his intention to become a Sufi. And the following year, he arrived at the door to the lodge.

On the morning of his induction into the order, the sun rose fat into a pristine sky. Piran Nazuder brought him a *khirqa* and a *sikke*. Then he led him to the courtyard, where Sheikh Bailiri and the others were waiting.

"May your heart flourish," said the Sufi master. "May you draw ever nearer to God."

He placed the *sikke* upon Vishpar's head. Then he escorted him to an empty cell to begin his new life.

Just as he'd knelt for three days outside the refectory, Vishpar knelt in prayer for three more. The door to his cell remained open, however, and the brothers went in and out, bringing him his food and offering gifts of supplication. On the third day, Jamal al-Jani led him to Sheikh Bailiri's cell, where he took an oath of allegiance. Then Sheikh Bailiri invested him with the mantle of the order and pronounced him a dervish.

As was the custom in all orders, the new initiate was to be given a particular area of study to focus upon. And it was here that a competition rose up between the brothers. Piran Nazuder felt that Vishpar should be given to him to train for the *sema*.

"With a body so lithe and graceful," he said, "he was born to whirl!"

Salim Rasa felt that the youth should be given to him to train as a cook.

"With a spirit so forceful, he'll evoke God with a simple stew!"

Hajid al-Hallal felt that he should be given to him to train in languages.

"Imagine the sound of Urdu flowing from his lips!"

Sheikh Bailiri understood the brothers' interest in the boy. His arrival was like an invigorating wind blowing through the lodge. He saw that for all his many gifts, however, Vishpar had the most expressive hands. So he gave him to Jamal al-Jani to train as a calligrapher.

"You won't regret it!" cried Jamal al-Jani. "In no time at all, he'll make the scriptures sing!"

As for Vishpar, he did not really care what he studied or which activities filled his days. All that mattered was that he was now a Sufi. And one step closer to God.

IT WOULD HAVE BEEN NATURAL for Nouri to be jealous of Vishpar. He was so righteous—so radiant—so robust—it was as if he'd stepped out of one of Habbib's bedtime tales. The truth, however, was that Nouri was relieved to have the attention of the brothers drawn away from himself for a little while. So while they hovered like honeybees around the new aspirant, he took long walks along the shaded pathways of the woods and delved more deeply into his studies, grateful for the delicious quiet his solitude brought. He committed the entire Qur'an to memory. Each *sura*. Each verse. And, guided by Sheikh Bailiri, he attempted to grasp the meaning beneath the words. He studied jurisprudence and the Hadith. Astronomy. Arabic grammar. No matter how intently he focused, however—no matter how he tried to remain apart—it soon became clear that he could not stop thinking about Vishpar. If the youth was filling buckets at the well, Nouri would find himself seized by a sudden thirst. If the youth was in the chapel, Nouri would feel the sudden need to pray. He tried not to call attention to himself. He tried not to make eye contact. He tried not to smile. But whenever he found himself near the golden youth his heart swelled.

The truth was, his heart wasn't the only thing that swelled. For Vishpar's arrival coincided with the strange upheaval in Nouri's body called puberty. Dark thoughts tangled his mind. Unsettling urges fevered his blood. And nowhere was the chemistry more maddening than in the constantly distended flesh between his legs. Nouri had always been fond of his penis. It flapped like a catkin when he ran naked through the rain. It bobbed like a glowworm in his bath. But when Vishpar arrived, it sprang up like a lamb sausage toward some voluptuous banquet in the sky, and refused to go down.

He was mesmerized by the youth. Whether Vishpar was toiling in the garden or practicing calligraphy or sitting in *zikr,* Nouri could not take his eyes off him. So he was grateful that the rigors of his life kept him busy. And that his loose cotton shift helped to conceal his tumescent state. And he prayed that the incessant racket his heart made when he was near him could not be perceived by those with only two ears.

ONE MORNING, AROUND THE TIME of Nouri's thirteenth birthday, Sheikh Bailiri received a visit from the *seyhulislam* of the Darni Sunim. A gaunt fellow with a piping voice, he explained to the Sufi master that a wealthy merchant named Abdul Husayn al-Bashir had just died and that his last deed—to secure his place in heaven—had been to donate a new fountain to the gardens of the mosque. The old fountain was about to be removed and the *seyhulislam* had decided to offer it to the dervishes.

"It's beautifully carved," he said, as he raked his fingers through his long white beard. "Though not so ornate that it would offend your simple tastes."

Although the Sufi order was under the jurisdiction of the

mosque, the mosque's leaders felt threatened by its autonomy. In their mysticism and purity of practice, the Sufis were hard to pin down. Sheikh Bailiri therefore knew that the offer of the fountain was a way of reminding him that he and the brothers were still a part of the church. So he thanked the *seyhulislam* and said the brothers would be grateful for the gift.

"It's quite heavy," said the *seyhulislam*. "But a pair of strong lads should be able to manage it fine."

Sheikh Bailiri knew that the obvious candidates for this task were Vishpar and Ali Majid. Yet he could not help but notice Nouri's interest in Vishpar, and he felt that they could only profit from a friendship with each other. So he decided that the fountain was the perfect way to bring them together.

Nouri was elated when Sheikh Bailiri informed him about the task. For despite his intense attraction to the youth—or, indeed, because of it—he and Vishpar had hardly exchanged a word since he'd arrived at the lodge. That night, Nouri barely slept a wink. But when dawn came, he was at the front gate, waiting for Vishpar to appear. When he did, the two youths nodded to each other. Then they started off together down the dusty road.

For a while they were silent, their attention drawn to the cries of the fruit sellers, the smell of baking bread, the light beginning to widen in the sky. Eventually, however, Nouri summoned his courage and spoke.

"It will be nice to have a fountain."

He waited for Vishpar to respond, but the youth said nothing.

"We haven't had a fountain before. It should be refreshing."

Vishpar remained silent, so Nouri said no more. A few moments later, however, he tried again.

"I suppose it will attract birds. Don't you think?"

Vishpar turned now and gazed at the slender boy. He was not really sure what he was doing at the lodge. He was too young to be a member of the order. And though Piran Nazuder had mumbled something about an itchy scalp when Vishpar had asked about the boy's strange head cloth, Vishpar was not entirely convinced by the explanation. He saw, however, how Sheikh Bailiri doted on the youth. So he shrugged his broad shoulders and said, "I suppose."

"And frogs," added Nouri.

"Perhaps."

"And someone will have to clear it of leaves."

Vishpar nodded. "That seems likely."

Nouri could not think of what to say next, so he said no more. But he was delighted to have finally broken the ice.

As Nouri and Vishpar approached the city, the streets began to fill with people. A woman hurled the contents of a slop pot from her window. A wagon came clattering down the road, forcing them to step aside. Eventually, however, Vishpar's curiosity about the boy kicked in.

"You're rather young to be living in a Sufi order."

"The town where I was born was consumed by flames," said Nouri. "Or something like that."

"Do you wish to become a Sufi yourself?"

"Sheikh Bailiri says I already am a Sufi."

"That's impossible! You're what? Eleven? Twelve?"

"I'm thirteen! And besides, Sheikh Bailiri says a Sufi is born, not made. His training only reminds him of what he was already aware of before birth."

Vishpar was silent. He did not wish to contradict Sheikh Bailiri. But this upstart? This stripling? How could he be a Sufi?

"Have you read the Qur'an?"

"Of course!"

"What are the ninety-nine names of Allah?"

"Allah the Compassionate, Allah the Merciful, Allah the King, Allah the Most Holy . . ."

Vishpar cut him off. "What does complete faith consist of?"

"Confirmation by the tongue, belief within the heart, and performance of the basic duties of submission."

"What are the various forms of divine inspiration?"

"Signs, appearances of light, and graces. All of which are ineffable."

Vishpar was silent again. "You know a lot," he said. Then he turned to Nouri. "But what do you *think* about it?"

"What do you mean?"

"There's a great difference between knowledge and understanding. Anyone can memorize rules, laws, articles of behavior. You have to think about them—wrestle them to the ground—if you want to make them your own."

Nouri considered what Vishpar was saying. "Hajid al-Hallal likes to say, 'Allah prefers a strong *murid* to a weak one.' But I think he only says that because he's strong himself. And I don't think the expression is really referring to strength of the body."

Vishpar's eyes widened. "How do you understand the difference between traveling to God and traveling in God?"

"Well, that," said Nouri, "is an important distinction!"

The two youths talked feverishly all the way to the Darni Sunim. And when they got there, and were shown the fountain—a carved basin in the shape of an open lotus with eight petals—they carried it back to the lodge, talking some more. To Vishpar it was like finding the younger brother he'd never had. And to Nouri it was like springtime, a warm bath, and a large bowl of *yakh dar behesht* rolled into one.

It was his first real friendship, outside of Habbib.

And whether he knew it or not, his first love.

Six

Once the new fountain had been installed in the courtyard it became the principal meeting ground for Nouri and Vishpar, the place where they came to discuss the Arc of Ascent or the Conditions of Rapture or the Illusion of the Self. In the morning, after their studies, they would sit by the cool stone basin and discuss the proper conduct of the *murid* toward his sheikh. In the evening, before they retired to their separate cells, they would linger beside it and argue about the state of *hal*. It was a rule of Sufi discipline that a novice should not speak on any question unless he is asked about it. So since Vishpar was a novice, and Nouri not even that, they shared their deepest questions with each other.

"What are the first signs of spiritual intoxication?"

"To what degree does the Shadow of the Absolute reflect His true Being?"

"Why must one pass beyond knowledge, if knowledge leads to truth?"

Such questions were based on the divine possibilities they'd glimpsed more than on anything they'd actually experienced. But they fueled each other's spiritual hunger. And though their natures were different—the poet and the warrior—the rose and the flame—they created a closed circuit between themselves that even Habbib, to his regret, was unable to enter.

At times, Vishpar's spiritual passion threatened to shatter the balance of life at the lodge. For though he always remained respectful toward the brothers, he could not help but notice the gap between what they said and what they actually did. Jamal al-Jani, for example, often spoke about the Sufi's need to divest himself of personal possessions.

"The Angel Gabriel," he liked to say, "strictly warned the Prophet not to accept the treasures of the earth."

When the dervish became ill, however, and Vishpar was sent to his cell with a bowl of *khoresht baadenjaan*, he found a brass candle trimmer and a pearl-studded pouch beside his bed.

Hajid al-Hallal often preached that a true dervish should never reduce himself to begging for alms.

"The Sufi," he liked to say, "must learn to make do with what God provides."

One morning, however, when Vishpar was out walking, he found the old fellow sitting by the side of the road, with his eyes closed, beside a bowl filled with coins.

Salim Rasa would often speak about the Sufi's need for self-sufficiency.

"A dervish must eat only food that he has prepared himself," he liked to say, "or that has been prepared for him by a member of his order."

One day, however, when Vishpar was heading to market, he saw the plump brother munching on a pastry that he'd just purchased from one of the stalls.

When Vishpar attempted to show the members of the order their contradictions, they made feeble justifications or quoted passages from the Qur'an. But this only made the youth more indignant than he already was.

"Sheikh Bailiri is a great man," he said to Nouri. "But the others are so lazy! How can they expect to reach God if they can't harness their own appetites?"

When he went to Sheikh Bailiri to express his concerns, the Sufi master counseled him to be patient.

"Even the strongest spiritual aspirant is filled with contradictions. It takes years to gain mastery over oneself."

Vishpar did his best to do as Sheikh Bailiri advised. He knew that the other brothers were sincere. He wished to become patient. Compassionate. Wise. But his heart remained torn between the need to be submissive to his elders and the need to speak the truth.

For Nouri's part, he had little to say in response to Vishpar's criticism of the brothers. For one thing, he was only thirteen and the impulse to assail the generation above him had not yet fired his blood. For another, he'd grown up at the lodge and the brothers were the only real family he'd ever known. But mostly he remained silent because he could barely contain the feelings that coursed through him when Vishpar was near.

When a friendship took root between himself and the older youth, Nouri felt that he'd found a true *suhba*. Their conversations about remembrance and faith changed his thinking. Their discussions of the Qur'an stirred his heart. Yet all the while—whether they were in the chapel or the garden—whether they were talking by the fountain or sitting together in prayer—Nouri was overwhelmed by a longing for Vishpar that went beyond their intellectual accord. It made his heart pound. It made his head spin. And no matter what he tried—late-night walks around the perimeter of the lodge—plunging into the icy waters of the River Tolna—he could not make that feeling go away.

It never occurred to Nouri that what he felt for Vishpar might be thought of as wrong. But it reminded him, once again, that he was not like anyone else in Tan-Arzhan, and that he never would be. For the first time in a long while, he thought about his ears. Sheikh Bailiri had insisted that they were a benediction. A miracle. Yet Nouri could not forget how Sharoud had looked at him when his head garment had been removed. Like a bird without a beak. Like a puppy with two tails that should have been drowned in the river at birth.

Nouri told himself that he was not his ears. That he was a servant of Allah. That he was Nouri. But there were so many Nouris whirling about inside: the Nouri who studied, the Nouri who prayed, the Nouri who yearned for Vishpar to hold him.

Who am I? he wondered.

Why am I here?

Which of the Nouris is really me?

The only thing that offered Nouri escape from his dizzying feelings was channeling them into words. By now, of course, he had learned how to write. And his thoughts—previously brief and aphoristic—had developed into verse. The brothers had grown accustomed to seeing him frozen in the garden or in the courtyard or on the path, coaxing a few lines into being. He wrote about the sunset and the spiders and the smell of the lamb roasting on the spit and the look on Habbib's face while he was sleeping and the silence during prayer. He learned how to make words skip, crawl, soar, sing. He learned how to make words bow. When he turned his pen to Vishpar, however, he found his friend's virtues too numerous to extol. He would have to focus on something specific. And after he'd been searching for it for months, one hot summer morning, out by the woodshed, it finally appeared.

He'd spent the morning in Sheikh Bailiri's cell, where the Sufi master was explaining that God keeps the hearts of the faithful moving between contraction and expansion.

"When the heart contracts, the aspirant's sensual experiences are extracted from it. Then, when it expands, the veil lifts and he flashes with light."

As Nouri sat on the blue-and-gold kilim, he tried to fathom the Sufi master's words. But with the heat bearing down, and no breeze blowing through the open window, the only thing that he could feel contracting was his throat and the only thing that he could feel expanding was his head and he began to worry that he might pass out. Fortunately, Sheikh Bailiri could see this. So he reached for the clay pitcher on his desk and suggested that Nouri fetch some water from the well.

As Nouri left the cell, his head began to lighten, and as he crossed the courtyard to the well, the tightness in his throat began to release. But when he reached the woodshed, he saw Vishpar chopping wood. He'd removed his tunic, and his torso, covered in sweat, glistened in the blazing sun. Nouri was spellbound by the play of the muscles across his back and the tautness of his skin. When Vishpar raised the ax up into the air, however, the morning light brought his sculpted arms into relief. And as he felt his heart both contract and expand, Nouri knew that he'd found the theme of his poem.

WHILE NOURI COMMENCED WORK on his ode to Vishpar's arms, Habbib began having violent dreams. He'd be walking through the streets of Tan-Arzhan when there'd be an explosion and bodies would start flying through the air. He'd be sitting in his cell when the roof would suddenly cave in. It was strange, for Habbib generally slept like a newborn babe. So when he dreamed that a large bearded man removed Piran Nazuder's head with a gleaming blade, he knew that it was time to pay a visit to Sheikh Bailiri.

In all the time he'd lived at the lodge, Habbib had hardly spoken to Sheikh Bailiri. Except for the warm "hello" he received when he swept his cell and the occasional "good morning," they'd barely exchanged a word. So it was not without a trace of fear that he made his way to his cell on that late-summer morning.

He knocked on the door. There was a brief silence. Then the door opened and the Sufi master stood before him.

"I'm sorry to disturb you," said Habbib. "But I need to speak with you."

Sheikh Bailiri gazed at the small, kind-faced man standing in the doorway, and he realized that it had been years since he'd really noticed him. He always remained in the background, never complaining, never asking for a thing. So Sheikh Bailiri knew that there must be a good reason for him to come knocking at his door.

"Come in," he said.

Habbib entered the simple room he'd swept thousands of times and waited for Sheikh Bailiri to close the door. Sheikh Bailiri gestured to him to sit on one of the pillows that lay strewn across the floor. Then the Sufi master lifted his woolen robe and sat down beside him.

"I've been having dreams."

"What kind of dreams?"

Habbib shuddered. "Terrible dreams." Then he described the shouts and the blasts and the blood that filled his head each night when he relinquished himself to sleep. "Last night all I could see was a pair of eyes peering through the smoke. And the air was filled with groans."

Sheikh Bailiri was silent as he listened to Habbib speak. For the most part, he considered the dream life to be meaningless—a catch pot of random impressions, a tale stitched together from the fragments of the day. Yet he knew that sometimes a dream was a chalice into which a message from a higher world was poured. And he could not help but wonder if the things that Habbib described were a portent of the future.

"I've never had dreams like this before," said Habbib. "So I'd be most grateful if you could tell me what they mean."

Sheikh Bailiri looked deeply into the fellow's watery eyes. He knew that it would only trouble him if he said that his dreams might be an omen. So he did his best to assuage his fears. "It's probably just a confluence of the stars. Or some geological occurrence. I wouldn't worry about it."

Habbib knew that the Sufi master's words could not prevent his awful dreams from coming. But they reassured him. So he thanked him, rose to his feet, and headed back to his cell. Sheikh Bailiri, however, would not forget the gruesome images he'd described. Or shake the feeling that something was on its way.

BY THE TIME THE MONTH of Ramadan arrived and the brothers began their daily fasting, Nouri was well into the writing of his poem. He'd studied the great panegyrics of Asjadi, the epics of Ferdowsi, the quatrains of Rudaki, but after reading the works of Sistani and Salman, he developed a passion for the rhythmic form known as the *qasidah*. He knew that to write one would be a tremendous labor. It would take weeks to map out the *nasib*, in which he would present his subject, the *takhallus*, in which he would describe its effect, and the *madih*, in which he would sing its praise. But it would be worth every effort if he could somehow convey the beauty—the power—the perfection—of Vishpar's arms.

The way his biceps swelled when he was digging in the garden. The way the sun licked the fine golden hairs on his forearms when he sat in the courtyard. The way the network of veins that ran from his elbows to his wrists pulsed as he lay beside the fountain at dusk. Nouri could not say why they brought so much pleasure. He only knew that they stirred something deep inside him, and inspired him to write.

As the summer waned, Nouri worked apace, and he'd soon fashioned the opening lines. The images grew clear in his mind's eye, the metaphors tumbled from his pen, and bit by bit his poem began to take shape. At times, his head became so clogged with words he could no longer think. When this happened, he'd go on long walks along the river, and on one of these walks a strong fatigue came over him. So he climbed into a large, leafy banyan tree to rest for a little while.

It was cool and shady inside the sprawling tree. Nouri found a sturdy branch he could lie down on, with a clear view of the river below. As he stretched out, he thought about the fig tree at the lodge. Each year the figs grew larger and sweeter and hung more abundantly from the boughs. Habbib told Nouri that it was a magic tree—that its leaves granted wishes—that its fruit banished fears—and while Nouri knew this wasn't true, he always looked forward to those fleeting weeks when it offered up its bounty. He'd almost vanished inside the thought of their taste when he heard the sound of footsteps. And when he peered through the leaves, he saw Vishpar making his way toward the water.

Although the rickety bridge where Maleeh al-Morad had fallen to her death spanned the river at a prodigious height, closer to the lodge the water rose to a level where a good swimmer could easily dive in. Vishpar could swim with the best, and Nouri saw that he'd come here now to have one last jaunt before the weather grew cold. He knew that if he revealed his presence, Vishpar would invite him to join him. He also knew that his friend's naked body would arouse him. So he lay very still, and tried not to make a sound.

When he reached the bank, Vishpar paused for a moment. Then he opened his robe and laid it on the grass; he removed his tunic and placed it beside the robe; he undid the drawstring of his trousers and stepped out of them; then, with liquid grace, he dove into the water.

That brief moment when Vishpar soared naked through the air was like a lifetime to Nouri. The curve of his buttocks—the splendor of his phallus floating free from the thick crop of bright golden hair—and those wondrous arms, which formed a tanned parabola over his head. When he reached the water, he disappeared for a moment and Nouri inched forward so he could see him reemerge. But he was so mesmerized by the sight of him slicing through the current that he did not see how far he'd crawled out on the branch. Only when Vishpar climbed out of the water and lay down languidly on the grass did he feel it begin to give way. Then his weight shifted, the branch snapped, and Nouri came tumbling to the ground.

It was not the first time that Nouri had fallen from the sky. And though Vishpar was more surprised than alarmed to find his young friend sprawled like a starfish at his side, it was clear from the look in his eyes that he was not thinking about God.

Seven

In the weeks that followed the incident at the river, there was an unspoken tension between Nouri and Vishpar. Nouri wished that he could explain what he felt in his friend's presence, how it shook him to his roots, but he could not find the words. He realized that neither Sheikh Bailiri nor Habbib had ever spoken about physical love. The closest he'd come to hearing anything on the subject had been when he was at the market with Salim Rasa and a merchant had called out to the dervish:

"What's the use of all your self-denial? For the sake of Allah, don't you desire a wife?"

Salim Rasa had remained silent a moment. Then he'd turned to the merchant and said, "A wife is fit for a man. The stage of man I have not yet reached. Why then should I desire a wife?"

Despite the fact that there were no women at the lodge, Nouri had seen many over the years. The girls who sold eggs and cheese at the market. The women who carried loaves of fresh *naan* and sleeping children in their arms. They fascinated Nouri: their hair thick and glossy, their hands quick and expressive, their eyes, above their tightly clasped veils, flashing with thoughts he could not decipher. Some were fragile, like pale-breasted birds. Some were dark and robust. Yet none made him feel the strange hunger that Vishpar made him feel. And he knew—from the way he'd stared at Vishpar's naked body when Nouri had fallen from the tree—that Vishpar knew how he felt.

The tension between them remained hidden beneath the surface. Yet they spent less time by the fountain talking and they tried to avoid each other's gaze. So Nouri was surprised, one night after the evening meal, when Vishpar leaned in close to him.

"Meet me at the gate after the evening prayer," he whispered. "And be sure to dress warmly."

Nouri could not imagine what his friend had in mind. But when the last movements of the evening prayer had been completed, he went to his cell, threw on his warm woolen cloak, and went to find out.

Vishpar was waiting at the gate when he arrived. He nodded to Nouri. Then, without saying a word, he led him off into the darkness. It was a brisk night and Nouri could see his breath spiral up as they made their way along. At first he thought they were heading to the river, but when they were almost there, Vishpar took a path that Nouri didn't know. It led to a clearing, at the center of which lay the remains of a small structure: a stone floor, scattered with leaves, surrounded by four crumbling walls. A portion of the roof was intact, but for the most part the space lay open to the sky. And Nouri could see that the room—which seemed to hover before them in the moonlight—was a perfect square.

They paused for a moment. Then Vishpar said, "Come!" Then they started across the clearing toward the room.

As Nouri followed after him, his heart began to race. Was something wonderful about to happen? Something terrible? He could hardly bear the suspense.

When they reached the structure, they climbed over the wall. The night wrapped around them. Then Vishpar raised his head to the sky.

"Shooting stars," he said. He lowered himself to the stones and lay back, and Nouri lay down beside him. "They're at their peak. And this is the best place to watch them."

No sooner had Vishpar spoken than Nouri looked up to see a streak of light etch the darkness. He felt as if his body had been turned inside out and his heart was exposed to the night air. He closed his eyes. He felt his breath rise and fall. He felt Vishpar beside him. Then he opened his eyes and gazed at the millions of stars that were scattered across the sky. He waited for another one to go blazing by. He waited for Vishpar to speak. And finally, like a knife piercing the darkness, he did.

"I wouldn't worry about it."

"About what?"

"The feelings you're having." He was silent a moment, and Nouri's supersensitive ears heard the click of each cricket and the rustle of each leaf. "When I see Khaterah? The girl who sells *kefir* at the market? I feel like I'm going to burst through my clothes!" He paused again. Then he turned to Nouri. "There's nothing wrong with it." He shrugged. "It's how we were made."

Nouri took a deep breath. "But I don't feel that way around girls. I feel that way around you."

A star shot across the sky. Then another. Then Vishpar spoke.

"Sheikh Bailiri insists that Allah's manifestations are infinite." He paused as another star streaked the sky. "The Sufi recognizes the earthly for what it is, and tries to maintain his remembrance of God."

"And it doesn't make you uncomfortable? That I feel that way?"

"Not really," said Vishpar. "Besides, in a few years you'll be hiding the tent in your tunic from some dark-eyed girl. It's just a phase. Just a circulation of the blood."

Nouri gazed up at the sky and said no more. Perhaps it was just a phase. Perhaps his longing for Vishpar would sizzle out like the stars, leaving no trace behind. At the moment, however, it burned hot and bright. And he was grateful for the darkness to shield him from the glow of his friend's eyes.

THE SCALES ON THE DRAGON's back and wings were a chalky green, like oxidized copper. But the flesh on his belly was black as the inside of a cave. His claws were like hooks and as he soared through the air, his eyes glinted yellow with fire. He rose in a spiral, growing larger with each turn, the smoke streaming like spittle from his mouth. Then he reared back, spread his enormous jaws, and devoured the sun.

Habbib lay in bed, on his back, panting. It took a moment before he realized that there was no moon that night, that the darkness that enveloped him was the darkness of his cell, and that he'd awakened from another difficult dream. They'd come with such frequency over the last few weeks he was surprised they still shook him. Yet each time a new one appeared, it filled him with terror.

This one was as awful as anything so far. The gleam of evil in the creature's eyes. The whir of its wings. The glee with which it consumed the light. He knew it meant something, but he could not say what. And since he did not wish to bother Sheikh Bailiri again, he rose, threw his cloak over his bedclothes, and headed out into the night.

By the time he'd made his way down the curving road that led into the city, the sky had begun to lighten. He'd not ventured out so early since he'd helped his father deliver the *naan* when he was a boy, and he'd forgotten how fiercely life pulsed in the early-morning streets. Dogs sniffed the alleys looking for scraps, broken-down carts were being hitched to old nags, the smell of frying dough oiled the air. As he moved farther into the heart of the waking city, however, Habbib could feel a tension beneath the surface. On the steps of the Darni Sunim, a trio of men stood whispering. In the public garden, eyes darted left and right. Habbib could not say what it meant, but he knew something was wrong.

Sheikh Bailiri did not need Habbib to warn him that danger was in the air. For the anxious whispers had already reached his ears. According to Atash al-Malik, one of the lay members of the order, the village of Rhuna, about six days north, had been attacked at the height of Ramadan by an army of men. Darwash, to the east, had been sacked, its mosque razed and its inhabitants forced to flee. Sheikh Bailiri knew that if these forces were to reach Tan-Arzhan there would be no stopping them. But he also knew that they might head off in another direction. So he decided that the best way to keep the brothers calm was to turn their attention to a new project.

Sheikh Bailiri had thought of erecting a *chahar taq* over the courtyard for many years. A domed pavilion with four open arches, it would offer the brothers a way to pray in the open air no matter the time of year. With the new fountain at its center, the courtyard would be transformed into a living *mandala*. A place in which to affirm the presence of Allah. So on the very same morning that Habbib awoke from his dream about the dragon, Sheikh Bailiri gathered the brothers in the courtyard to share his vision of the new structure.

"The dome will protect us from the elements," he explained, "but the sides will be open to the air. Think of how lovely it will be to be able to remain outside during a downpour! Or in the summer heat!"

The brothers listened as the Sufi master described the time and the care and the sweat that the project would require. But they were eager to serve. So they agreed, one and all, to undertake it.

Sheikh Bailiri knew that the building of a *chahar taq* would take far more work than any of the brothers imagined. But it would keep their minds off the rumors that were swirling about the town. At least for a while.

OVER THE FOLLOWING WEEKS, the brothers began learning the skills that were required to build the new structure, and raising the funds that were needed to purchase the materials. With the help of a local draftsman, Jamal al-Jani drew up the plans. Then Vishpar journeyed out to the quarry to retrieve the smooth blocks of marble from which it would be made. Piran Nazuder met with a tradesman whose great-grandfather had helped to build the Darni Sunim to learn the methods involved in fashioning a dome. And Salim Rasa designed the pattern for the tiny tiles—which Hajid al-Hallal fetched from a tile maker in Nashtam—that would cover it when it was done.

As the weeks passed and the simple pavilion began to rise, Nouri made a difficult decision. The conversation beneath the shooting stars had only deepened his friendship with Vishpar. And he suddenly felt that it was a betrayal of that friendship not to reveal the strange fact of his four ears. So one morning, while they were working on the southern arch, he leaned over to his friend and said, "There's something I need to show you."

Vishpar wiped a bead of sweat from his brow. "What is it?"

"I can't talk about it here. Come to my cell tonight before bed."

Vishpar agreed and they continued on with their work. But while the older youth hardly gave it another thought, for the rest of the day Nouri could think of little else. What would Vishpar say when he removed his head garment? Would he be repulsed like Sharoud? Would their friendship—which meant the world to Nouri—be cast aside?

That night, after the evening prayer had been performed, Vishpar went to Nouri's cell.

"What did you want to show me?" he asked, as Nouri ushered him inside.

"Is it not written that each man's bird of fate has been fastened upon his neck?"

"It is written."

"Well, mine," said Nouri, "has been fastened a bit higher up."

He paused a moment, his mouth dry, his stomach clenched, his heart pounding. Then he reached up, untucked the ribbon of his head cloth, and began to unwind it.

When the four ears were finally revealed, Vishpar was stunned. But what he felt was neither love like Habbib nor disgust like Sharoud nor the glory of God like Sheikh Bailiri, but rather a deep sense of wonder.

"Amazing."

"I just thought you should know."

Vishpar took a step closer. "Were you born with them?"

Nouri nodded.

"And they function?"

"Extremely well, I'm afraid."

Vishpar shook his head from side to side. "Amazing."

Nouri raised the edge of the head cloth to one of his ears and began binding them again.

"Wait," said Vishpar.

Nouri paused, the ribbon hanging in midair.

"Can I touch them?"

Nouri took another deep breath and nodded. Then he stood very still as Vishpar raised his fingers to his ears. He tapped them. He squeezed them. He moved their tender flaps forward and back. Then—when he was certain that they were real—Nouri covered them again. The following morning they met in the courtyard and continued working. And though Vishpar never mentioned the ears again, Nouri knew that they were closer now.

As work on the *chahar taq* neared completion, the whispers in the city grew louder. It was said that Shadira, a village only three hours away, had been routed. It was said that the invaders had set up camp along the River Tolna and were preparing for a new assault. As a result, many of the merchants in Tan-Arzhan closed their shops. Curfews were imposed, and the wealthier families shuttered their houses and headed south.

Sheikh Bailiri was too wise not to heed the threats. Yet he was convinced that a handful of poor dervishes was unlikely to be the target of an attack. So he instructed Jamal al-Jani to gather the order's few precious belongings—the silver candlesticks, the blown-glass lamp, the leather-bound copy of the Qur'an—and bury them beneath the ash tree that stood by the eastern wall. Then he focused the brothers on the completion of the *chahar taq*.

The morning on which the Sufi master proved to be naive was graced with an unseasonable warmth. So Sheikh Bailiri allowed the brothers to remove their robes and shoes and work in their loose cotton shifts. All that was left to be done was the final sanding of the arches and the placement of the last tiles upon the dome. But by the end of the morning—despite the freedom of their clothes—the brothers were bathed in perspiration.

"It's too hot to go on," said Piran Nazuder.

"What's the point in building a *chahar taq*," said Jamal al-Jani, "if we die of sunstroke before it's done?"

Sheikh Bailiri knew that with a little more effort the structure would be complete. But he could also see that the brothers were exhausted. So he instructed Salim Rasa to fetch a large pitcher of pomegranate juice and some cups and called for a break.

"The last efforts are always the hardest," he said. "But it's important to take things slowly, and get them right."

The brothers sat with their cups of sweet juice. Ali Majid slept. Habbib basked languidly in the sun. Only Nouri, with his two pairs of ears, heard the clamor of the horse hooves in the distance. Only he felt the disturbance in the air and the approaching danger. Before he could issue a warning, however, his ears rang with the music of a single plucked string. Then an arrow went whizzing through the air and struck Piran Nazuder dead.

In a flash, the courtyard was filled with men, their hulking bodies covered in pelts, their beards like black smoke, their eyes glinting with malice. Salim Rasa tried to flee, but he was struck as swiftly as Piran Nazuder. The others dropped down and hugged the ground, hoping that if they cowered they would be spared.

Nouri didn't cower. But neither did he leap up, seize one of the invaders' swords, and start doing battle. That was left to Vishpar. Like a panther protecting his brood, he bounded across the courtyard, toppled one of the attackers, grabbed his weapon, and—in less time than it would have taken to blanch an almond—dispatched a trio of the hot-blooded brutes. At the sight of him in action, Nouri felt a thrill shiver through him. He envisioned his friend single-handedly routing the entire pack. He pictured himself kneeling down before this hero who'd saved his life.

This was the image that flashed in Nouri's mind as someone grabbed him from behind and tethered his wrists. And it would have been the image that stayed with him had he not seen Vishpar rush forward in order to deflect the next blow and be pierced through with a gleaming sword. That was when they slipped the blindfold over Nouri's eyes and the world went black. And though other faces pressed in at the edges of the darkness—Sheikh Bailiri's—Habbib's—Ali Majid's—the look on Vishpar's face as the marauder ran him through was what remained in Nouri's heart as they carried him away.

PART TWO

Eight

Nouri gripped the silver tray with both hands, careful not to jostle it as he moved through the garden, but he was not prepared for the creature that suddenly swooped from the tree and darted across his path. Its body was the most dazzling blue he'd ever seen. And though its head was quite small, its tail was enormous. When it saw Nouri, the creature froze and cocked its head to one side. Then its tail began to spread out until it stood like a painted fan. Nouri remained perfectly still, aware that the pot of tea and the freshly baked *naan* he was delivering would soon grow cold. Yet he could not help feeling that the eyes that were scattered across the tail were staring at him and that if the creature could speak it would say, *"What, in the name of Allah, are you doing here?"*

It was a question that echoed through Nouri's head quite often. For though the conditions of his new life were good—he had a large room and clean clothes and plenty to eat—he generally felt as if he'd taken a wrong turn and stumbled into somebody else's life. Everything around him was strange: the food, the landscape, the faces. When he thought of how things might have turned out, however, he tried to accept the confusion, and focus on the various tasks he was meant to perform each day.

At the moment, he was supposed to deliver the silver tray with the pot of tea, the basket of *naan*, and the bowl of figs to the ornate chamber of The Right Hand. He had no idea why they called the man he'd been ordered to wait upon The Right Hand. When he was first brought to his chamber to meet him, the swarthy fellow had just come from riding and Nouri had half-expected that when he removed his gloves he would find that his right hand was made of wood or covered in scales or scarred by fire. When it was revealed, however, Nouri saw that there was nothing strange about it at all.

The Right Hand was a set of contradictions to Nouri. Gruff, yet deeply attuned to beauty. Powerful, yet easily affected by what others had to say. Nouri heard the danger in his voice when he gave an order. He saw the blood rise to his cheeks when he was displeased. So he did not wish to anger him by bringing him a pot of cold tea, which meant that he had to get past the strange creature on the path.

He stepped to the right. The creature stepped to its left. He reversed his movements and it did so too. But before he could reach for one of the figs and hurl it at its head, the sound of a pair of hands clapping loudly and a voice crying "Shoo!" ricocheted through his head. Then the creature folded its gorgeous tail and flew off to a nearby ledge.

When Nouri turned, he found Leisha, one of the Sultan's serving girls, standing behind him, her thick hair pulled back into a braid, her dark eyes flashing with indignation above her veil. Like Nouri, she was part of the network of servants that flowed through the corridors of the palace. And though he was not sure what her mother tongue was—there was a flatness to her *a*'s and a rough, husky sound to her *h*'s—he'd studied enough Arabic to be able to converse with her easily, as with everyone else at the palace. She was coarse and loud and filled with opinions, which made her seem twice Nouri's age. But she was probably no more than a few years older than he was, if that.

Now, with her hands firmly planted on her hips and her brow deeply furrowed, she seemed ready to knock him to the ground.

"You're supposed to take The Right Hand his tea! Not dance with the accursed birds!"

Nouri wanted to say that he was as eager as she was to see that The Right Hand received his tea. But he knew that more words meant more delay. So he hurried off to deliver the tray.

SO HOW DID Nouri Ahmad Mohammad ibn Mahsoud al-Morad wind up as a tea boy in a sultan's court in a barren country where people wore capes and ate goat and prayed to Moses and Jesus as devoutly as to Allah? What wind blew him westward, and then slightly south? What twist of fate led him from the marauders at the lodge to the bird with the extravagant tail?

For one thing—at least at the start—it was a journey of sound more than sight. For once the blindfold was slipped over his eyes, Nouri's doubled ears took the wheel of his perception and charted his progress forward. The cries of the brothers grew fainter and fainter as the footsteps of his abductor fell upon tile and then stone and then earth. He heard the clatter of horse hooves as they moved through the gates and then a whinny rise up as he was hoisted onto the back of a warm beast and clasped tightly around the waist by a pair of bearlike arms. That was when his sense of smell kicked in: even with a single nose he nearly retched from the terrible stench of the fellow. They sat there until the absence of clinking weapons and the thunder of approaching footsteps announced that the destruction was through. Then orders were shouted and horses were mounted and they set off.

He could not say how long they traveled. Days. Weeks. Time was a mist that tickled his cheeks as they galloped along. His captors would stop every so often to make camp—tossing Nouri a few meager scraps—laying out a hide for him to sleep on—but mostly they just rode. Someone always stayed with him when they descended upon a new village. But while the clash of metal and the gut-wrenching cries grew more familiar with repetition, the memories they evoked of what had happened at the lodge always startled him anew. He tried to press back the images when they came—the blood gathering in shiny pools on the new tiles, the fear in the eyes of the brothers—but over and over they would rise up again and batter his heart.

As they made their way from village to village, Nouri wondered why his blindfold was never removed. And one day, the same thought must have occurred to his captors. They'd stopped by a stream to water their horses and, as the day was warm, they decided to rest. So they lowered Nouri from the horse, tied his wrists with a rope, and bound him to a tree. Then they spread themselves out on the grass and fell into a heavy sleep.

In time, the dissonant clamor of their snoring settled into a steady hum. But before Nouri could give over to the calm, he heard the voice he'd come to recognize as their leader's suddenly bark out a command. In an instant, the others lumbered to their feet. Nouri heard a few of them laugh and a few stop to piss upon the grass. Then they saddled their horses and made ready to depart. As one of them began to untie the rope that bound Nouri to the tree, the leader shouted again. Nouri could feel the attention of the group shift to him. Then the leader shouted a third command and his blindfold was removed.

After weeks of darkness, the sudden exposure to the light was blinding. Gradually, however, rough shapes began to appear: the mountains, the horses, the men whom he'd been with since the attack at the lodge. As his eyes fully adjusted to the light, he saw the savage looks on their faces. Then the leader—a giant of a man, with soulless eyes—shouted again. Then the man who'd removed his blindfold tore off his head garment.

There was a stunned silence as their amusement transformed into horror, and then twisted into fury. One of the men drew his sword and raised it up high over Nouri's head, and Nouri's only consolation was the thought that he would soon be with Vishpar. Before the weapon came slicing down, however, the leader shouted another command, which stayed the fellow's hand.

The air hummed as the leader moved close to Nouri. He raised his choppy fingers to Nouri's ears, but then he recoiled. Then he drew back and—with a look of disgust—he spat in Nouri's face.

He turned. He shouted again. Then the men gathered their things, mounted their horses, and left Nouri bound to the tree.

When the sound of the hooves died away, Nouri could feel the terror inside him begin to release. But as time passed, his mouth became dry and his stomach began to ache and he was faced with the fact that he was tied to a tree by a stream in the middle of Allah-knew-where. He tried to wriggle free of his bonds, but he could not do it. They'd left him, like a helpless beast, to roast in the scorching sun.

The hours crept by. His throat began to constrict and he grew light-headed and dizzy. Then, in the distance, he heard hooves and a pair of men on a pair of ash-colored steeds appeared. When they saw Nouri, they started toward him and he could feel the hope rise in his chest. When they reached him, however, and saw his ears, they spurred their horses and galloped away.

Nouri closed his eyes and tried to fathom his fate. He could not understand why an extra set of ears caused so much revulsion. He could not understand why he'd spent so many years learning so many things if he was meant to die like a sick calf tied to a tree. Was it possible that all he'd been taught was a lie? Could it be that there was no meaning to life after all?

He remained there a long while. But then, once again, he heard the clatter of hooves. And this time, when the riders appeared, they were carrying a large chaise, covered in cloth, that was suspended on a pair of wooden rails. When they reached Nouri, they paused. Then a hand decked with glittering rings parted the cloth and a pair of eyes peered out.

The hand withdrew.

The curtain closed.

Then a parcel of braised meat and a small knife were tossed through the slit. Then a voice shouted a sharp command, and the chaise moved on.

When Nouri saw the meat, he managed to loosen the rope just enough to work his way down the trunk of the tree to the ground. Bending forward, he gripped the hilt of the knife between his teeth and moved it to where he could grasp it with his hands. Then he sliced himself free of his bonds and devoured the meat in a single gulp. It tasted like lamb glazed with honey, but it could have been mule brushed with tar for all he cared. When he was finished, he reached for his head cloth, which lay in the dirt, and re-covered his ears. Then he closed his eyes and lay back against the base of the tree.

Now that the marauders were gone, and he was no longer bound, Nouri was free to seek refuge. The trouble was, he had no idea where to go. He decided to head off in the direction the chaise had taken. But the ground was quite rocky and in no time his flimsy slippers were torn to shreds. A terrible thirst gripped him and it was not long before the sweet parcel of lamb seemed a distant memory. He tried to put one foot in front of the next and not think of how hot the sun was or how tired he felt or how barren the landscape seemed. He would take a few steps, then stop, then take a few more, until he could barely move. Then his head began to fill with fog, and the world went dark.

When he came to, he found himself lying on a thick bed of straw, wrapped in a blanket, in the back of a large wagon. It was night, but enough moonlight streamed down to let him perceive the kindness of the face of the slender man who sat beside him. For the next several weeks, he mostly slept, stirring every so often to find the man holding a damp cloth to his brow or spooning a bitter broth into his mouth. As he slept, he had feverish dreams: Habbib on the back of a large black bull charging toward the edge of a cliff; Sheikh Bailiri guiding a gilded boat down a river; Vishpar holding a bow that he aimed at a dragon growing out of his own body.

When at last he awoke, he found himself in a warm bed in a spacious room at the palace. And though no one ever explained how he'd come to live at the center of this sun-soaked court—with its soaring towers, and its ravishing gardens, and its intricate system that channeled crystalline water from the mountains into its fountains and pools—day by day, he was beginning to accept the place as his home.

Now, as he approached the lavish chamber of The Right Hand, his thoughts were quite far from the path he'd had to travel to get there. He was focused instead on the warmth of the tea, the crispness of the *naan,* and the exacting nature of the man who was about to receive them.

When he reached the chamber, he paused for a moment. He steadied the tray. He adjusted his tunic.

Then he took a deep breath and rapped on the door.

INSIDE THE CHAMBER, PROPPED on a silk pillow on a wicker divan, the man known as The Right Hand was listening to a pair of youths play the most beguiling music. The older one—who was slender and had the faint beginnings of a beard—was playing a haunting melody on the *tar.* The younger one—who was still covered with a layer of baby fat—stood with his eyes closed, his arms floating like tendrils at his side, singing in a seraph's voice:

Away—away—
My beloved has gone—
Far away my beloved has gone.

And I here must stay—
Must stay—must stay—
From dawn until dusk until dawn.

The sounds were like sweet chestnut honey to The Right Hand. They relaxed him and brought thoughts of the pleasures he would partake of on his journey to the nearby city of Amanduena. The Sultan believed it was time to form an alliance between the two courts, and if anyone could grease the diplomatic wheels it was The Right Hand. He had a way of melting resistance. Of making differing points of view somehow converge. But what excited him even more than the political games—or the sumptuous feasts that accompanied them—were the games of seduction. He'd not been to Amanduena for several years, and he felt sure there would be a host of new beauties to choose from. Perhaps he'd find a small laundry girl with a devourable mouth. Or a young kitchen maid with flashing eyes and plenty of flesh to hold on to. He was so immersed in thoughts of the upcoming journey, he did not even notice that his food had not arrived. Only when he heard the rapping on the door did it cross his mind that his breakfast was overdue.

He shouted to the servant boy to enter. Then he studied the boy as he moved toward him with the well-heaped tray. It was clear from the way he spoke that he came from a distant part of the realm. And though the head covering he wore seemed a bit strange—it was not really a turban, and it wrapped right over his ears—he assumed that it was a fashion native to his land. The Right Hand had had many youths attend him over the years. But he could not remember one as tender and sweet-faced as this one.

For Nouri's part—although he'd entered the lavish room dozens of times by now—he never felt completely at ease in the chamber of The Right Hand. For one thing, it was always filled with the cloying smell of incense. For another, it was stuffed with too many glittering objects to allow a trace of Allah to enter in. Mostly, though, he was made nervous by The Right Hand himself: his booming voice, his gruff manner, his heavy-lidded gaze that seemed to peer right into his soul. He was kind to him, though. And he did not say a word about the lateness of his tray. So Nouri carefully laid out the cup and the bowl and the basket and the teapot. Then he poured some tea into the cup, knelt beside The Right Hand's divan, and waited to be dismissed.

By now, the youth who was serenading The Right Hand had moved on to a song about a journey across the sea. As The Right Hand reached for his cup of tea, Nouri listened to the angelic voice pour out into the room. When the song was finished, The Right Hand gestured to the two youths to depart. So they bowed their heads and left the room. Nouri waited for the command to depart, but it did not come. Instead, The Right Hand reached for one of the plump, ripe figs, popped it into his mouth, and—for the first time since Nouri had begun serving him—turned to him and spoke.

"Did you enjoy the music?"

Nouri hesitated. The court was still an elaborate mystery to him, and for all of his attempts to prove otherwise, he had no idea how a tea boy should behave. He knew that he had to say something, however. So he cleared his throat and said, "It was very nice."

The Right Hand reached for a piece of *naan* and tore it apart. "Tell me your name."

"Nouri."

"And you're—let me guess—" The Right Hand peered at him. "Fifteen?"

Nouri nodded.

"And do you play an instrument? The *tombak*? The *tar*?"

"No, sir."

"Do you draw then? Make pottery? Practice calligraphy?"

Nouri shook his head.

"The arts are a strong tonic to the spirit," said The Right Hand. "Here in the court even the servants are encouraged to practice something. That is what it means to be enlightened." He swallowed a hunk of *naan* and washed it down with a gulp of tea. Then he turned to Nouri. "Have you heard the word *enlightened*?"

"Yes, sir."

"Well, then you must find an art to pursue!"

Nouri was silent. He feared that if he said the wrong thing he'd be tossed, like a sack of squeezed lemons, out of the court. But he also feared that if he said nothing he'd find himself studying candle making or puppetry or playing the *oud*. He knew which art to pursue. He'd devoted himself to it for years. So though he worried that he might be speaking out of line, he said, "I like to write verse."

The Right Hand gazed at him for a moment and then laughed. "Verse!" he cried. "Allah the Equitable! To think that a poet has been serving my tea!"

Nouri blushed. But before he could say more, The Right Hand spoke again.

"When you come tomorrow, bring me something you've written." He made a brisk gesture with his hand. "You may go now."

Nouri bowed. Then he rose to his feet and hurried from the room.

He had no idea what he would bring to The Right Hand when he returned with his tea the next day. But he knew that—with the high standards The Right Hand maintained—it would have to be good.

Nine

When Nouri left the chamber of The Right Hand, he headed straight to the kitchen to ask Leisha where he could find paper and a pen. When she asked what it was for and he told her, her mud-colored eyes grew wide.

"A poet!" she said, laughing. "Next you'll tell me you've been appointed to carve marble figures for the Sultan himself!"

When Nouri persisted, she led him to a cramped room at the end of a corridor on the third floor of the palace where a man with watery eyes was copying text from a large leather-bound book. When she told him that Nouri had been instructed to write a poem for The Right Hand, the fellow turned to him and squinted a few times. Then he handed him a few sheets of parchment, a pot of ink, and a matted quill.

"Be sure to use plenty of adjectives," he advised. "The Right Hand will like it if it has plenty of adjectives."

Nouri thanked the fellow. Then he carried the things to his room and returned to his chores.

That night, before bed, Nouri knelt on the floor and came face-to-face with the challenge of the task before him. He'd not written a word since the attack at the lodge, and he feared that if he raised the lid to the place where the poetry came from, the horror would rise up too. So he cracked it only a trace, allowing enough blood to warm the dozen or so lines he laid down about the sleek ginger cat that wandered the court.

When he read it the next day for The Right Hand, he was delighted.

"A poet!" he cried. "A veritable poet!"

He instructed Nouri to bring him a new poem the next day. And the next day. And the next. And soon, like the playing of the *tar* and the singing, Nouri's reading became a part of the morning tea.

As the weeks passed, Nouri grew more and more confident about his poems. Whatever he wrote about—the figs, the fountains, the mountains that ringed the palace, the eunuchs that tended the bathing chamber, the Caliph's horses, the Sultan's robes—The Right Hand would praise him and ask for more. Occasionally, when he raised the lid, a memory would slip out and grip him with terrifying force. But for the most part, the writing brought solace, and a sense of peace. Eventually he decided to find a place where he could write outdoors—with the sun on his cheeks and the open sky overhead—and not lose the solitude of his room. So he set out to explore the hidden corners of the palace and see what he could find.

It did not take long for him to discover that beside each of the stone towers that rose to differing heights throughout the complex lay a courtyard, each with its own name. Beside the Falcon Tower sat the Court of the Finches. Beside the Soldier's Tower sat the Court of the Running Brook. Nouri could not figure out why they were called what they were called—there was nothing sorrowful about the Court of Despair, and the Crimson Tower was a deep ochre—but he felt that he was learning the history of the place by learning the various names. What pleased him even more, though, was his discovery that behind a handful of the courtyards sat smaller courtyards where no one seemed to go. And behind one of these—the Court of Wrens, which sat beside the Tower of Retribution—was the Court of the Speckled Dove. Unlike the larger courtyards, it was clear to Nouri how it had gotten its name: at the center of its broken fountain sat a lovely bird carved of variegated stone. And Nouri knew the moment he found it that it was the perfect place for him to write.

Despite the daily calls to prayer—which were as consistent at the palace as they had been at the lodge—Nouri's spiritual life seemed to have vanished after his abduction by the marauders. The myriad things that Sheikh Bailiri had taught him seemed fragments of another world. His pledge to devote himself to God seemed as distant as a dream. One morning, however, while he was waiting in the kitchen for The Right Hand's tray, he overheard a conversation between the head pastry maker and the Sultan's chief attendant that made it all come rushing to the surface.

"They say that he can make water flow from a rock!"

"Ridiculous!"

"Hossein al-Farid saw him do it! And Ahad Zanzar claims he saw him levitate during *zikr*!"

When they left the kitchen, Nouri asked the pock-faced boy who brewed the Sultan's tea whom they'd been speaking about and the boy explained that a Sufi master named Ibn Arwani had taken a pair of rooms beside the stables on the edge of the city and in a fortnight had attracted a dozen followers. Nouri said nothing. But he felt as if a shaft of light had suddenly pierced the darkness. And though he knew that no teacher could ever match the wisdom of Sheikh Bailiri, that afternoon, when The Right Hand dozed off after a lunch of slow-roasted lamb, fried eggplant, and honeyed dates, he headed off through the winding streets to find him.

As he made his way along, he found it hard to believe that anything remotely holy could rise up from such dirt and din. The streets were scattered with fish bones and rotting fruit, his heels were nipped by chickens and goats, the shouts of food sellers and crying babies tortured his hyperaware ears. When he reached the stables, he found the rooms where the Sufi master had taken up residence. The windows were open, so he approached them and looked in. There were eleven men spread out across the room—their legs crossed, their heads bowed, their eyes shuttered to the world. And while there was no way of discerning the leader of the group by either his clothing or his position in the room, Nouri could instantly tell which one was Ibn Arwani.

He neither floated off the ground nor emitted any strange, heavenly light. But it was clear that he was the master of himself. And while there was no proof that he could teach anyone else to be so, Nouri vowed that he would become his pupil.

Just as these thoughts were taking shape, a horse and cart thundered by carrying the evening's fresh bread. The smell reminded Nouri of the *naan-e taftoon* that would be waiting for him at supper, and the poem he had to compose for The Right Hand for the following day. So he turned from the window and hurried back through the ragged streets to the comfort of the palace.

LEISHA REACHED FOR THE CARVED wooden box, lifted her veil, and held it up to her nose. "I can still smell the cinnamon."

She handed the box back to Nouri, who took a sniff.

"I don't smell anything."

"Cinnamon!" said Leisha. "And a trace of mint!" She picked up the stained cotton cloth and threw it at Nouri's head. "Keep working!"

It was a light-dappled day at the height of summer. Nouri and Leisha were lying on a grassy knoll not far from the palace gates, cleaning the spice boxes. Or—to be more precise—Nouri was cleaning them and Leisha was assessing his work as he went along. While she gazed at the wispy clouds that floated by, Nouri would scour each compartment of the boxes that lay beside him, rubbing away the color and scent with a cotton cloth. Then he'd show the boxes to Leisha, who would invariably tell him to clean them again.

"I don't see why we have to get every last speck," said Nouri. "They're just going to fill them again when we're through."

Leisha let out a world-weary sigh. "That's why you're still just a tea boy. You won't be promoted until you're determined to do a thing as well as it can be done."

Nouri said nothing. He liked being a tea boy and had no ambition to advance to another role. Yet he knew that Leisha's advice was good, so he burrowed the cloth deeper into the compartment and rubbed a bit harder. For the most part, it was easy to detect when the traces of a spice still remained. The saffron left a rust-colored stain, the rose petals a pinkish powder, the parsley, cardamom, and lime various smudges of green. The cinnamon was the color of the wood, however, and he could not always tell when a few specks of it remained. So he depended on Leisha, whose sense of smell was so strong it almost rivaled his acute powers of hearing.

Now, as Nouri pressed the cloth into the corner of one of the compartments, he studied the girl who lay beside him. She was the first girl he'd ever known and from the shape of her body to the thoughts in her head she was an absolute puzzle to him. She generally decided when they'd meet and where and what they would do. And she usually did most of the talking.

"It seems the Sultan's daughter is about to give birth! How anyone could make love to such a cow is an utter mystery to me. If it's a boy, he'll be the sultan himself one day. My friend Kamala is going to be one of his nursemaids. Imagine wiping the crap off the bottom of the future sultan!"

Nouri gave a final swipe to the box he was cleaning and held it out to Leisha, who raised it to her nose.

"It'll do."

Nouri laid the box beside the others he'd finished and reached for the next one. As he did, Leisha raised herself up onto her elbow and gazed at him.

"You've never said a word about your life before you came here."

"There's not much to say."

"Of course there is!" she exclaimed, with a toss of her head. "Was it cold? Hot? Flat? Hilly? Green? Barren? Wretched? Nice?"

Nouri thought back to the lodge in Tan-Arzhan. "It was home."

Leisha rolled her eyes. *"And?"*

"Hot," said Nouri. "Flat. Green." He thrust the worn-out cloth into the box. "Nice."

Leisha lay back. "My friend Kamala says The Right Hand has over a dozen lovers. And that's just within the city gates. He has more in each of the places he visits." She slipped her hands beneath her head. "Isn't that *thrilling*?"

Nouri pictured The Right Hand moving from bedchamber to bedchamber, his eyes growing more glazed with each conquest, thick clouds of incense trailing behind him.

"I'm going to have my own horse someday!" said Leisha. "I'll ride and I'll ride and no one will be able to stop me!"

Nouri spied a smudge of pale yellow in one of the compartments. Was it turmeric? Ginger? Before he could decide, however, Leisha bolted upright, drew aside her veil, and kissed him on the mouth. When she pulled back, she looked deeply into his eyes, her gaze half challenge, half plea. Then she swung her dark braid over her shoulder and lay back on the grass.

"Keep working!" she barked. "They have to be finished by noon!"

Nouri said nothing. Although her lips were soft, the kiss did not evoke the least trace of desire. So he thrust the cloth back into the box and continued on with his work.

LEISHA WAS NOT THE ONLY GIRL in the palace who longed to kiss Nouri. Sarana, the frail girl who pruned the Sultan's roses, had to take care not to chop off their heads when he passed by. Suleini, the plump girl who milked the palace goats, had to make sure not to squeeze their udders too hard when he came to fetch cream for The Right Hand's tray. In the kitchen—at the market—as he wandered through the town—heads swiveled as he approached and eyes lingered as he moved away. For as the seasons passed, Nouri changed from a fair-faced boy to a bewitching youth: his body growing leaner, his cheeks traced with the soft beginnings of a beard, his dark eyes glistening beneath the ever-present head cloth.

"Can't you see how they look at you?" said Little Ahmed, the squashed fellow who helped tend the palace grounds. "I'd drool for a glance like that from the worst of the lot!"

Nouri tried to shrug off Little Ahmed's words, yet he knew they were true: though he'd barely reached the age of sixteen, he could have his choice of any girl in the court. The only thing that compelled him, however—that rattled his brain and kept him up nights—was the daily struggle with words. After The Right Hand had requested that he deliver a new verse each morning, Nouri's afternoons were set aside for him to write. He usually went to the Court of the Speckled Dove, though at times he wandered out along the ramparts or sat beside the star-shaped fountain that flowed beside the Tower of the Sun. Writing was the only thing that made him feel that this Nouri, who wore linen tunics and ate oranges and served tea, was the same Nouri who'd studied and prayed at the lodge in Tan-Arzhan. Each day, to conjure a new poem, he would gaze at the clouds, smell the fragrance of the jasmine, feel the smooth stones beneath his feet. But mostly he would listen—not just to the sound of the water flowing or to the cries of the birds, but to the rhythm of the words as they laid themselves out in his head. Listening was such an integral part of Nouri's writing process, he sometimes wondered if that was why he'd been given two sets of ears.

Day after day, Nouri watched. And listened. And wrote. And listened again. And he might have gone on in this way for a long while had the girl in the white gown not appeared. He was sitting in the Court of the Speckled Dove writing a poem about the morning *naan* when the fountain in the courtyard suddenly rattled and a thin stream of water began to pour from the mouth of the stone bird. This would have been enough to stamp the moment in Nouri's mind forever. But when he turned he saw a girl in a white gown standing at the entrance to the courtyard. She was carrying a large jug upon her head and as he gazed at her he heard the voice of Sheikh Bailiri:

"There are a thousand veils that cover the Self. You must dissolve them. Anything that separates you from God is a veil."

As the words rose up, the girl vanished from sight. And Nouri suddenly saw that, for all the pleasure it brought, his writing was a veil between himself and God. So he carried the pen, ink, and paper to his room. Then he headed out through the winding streets to find Ibn Arwani.

This time when he peered through the open window, the Sufi master, still seated in *zikr,* was alone. Since Nouri did not wish to interrupt him, he waited in silence for him to finish his practice. It therefore came as a surprise when—without bothering to rise or even open his eyes—he suddenly spoke.

"Dogs and other stray animals linger in the street. Men offer their greetings to one another. And make themselves known when they look into a stranger's home."

Nouri was so startled he could barely respond. “Forgive me,” he stammered. “I didn’t wish to disturb your practice.”

“You assume that only words can intrude,” said the Sufi master, as he opened his eyes. “If you wish to enter, the door is on your left.”

Nouri went to the door, pulled it open, and stepped into the room. There was little there: just a low table graced with a pitcher and bowl and, on the floor, just in front of where the Sufi master sat, four burning candles.

“Are you a seeker?”

“Yes.”

“And you know what it entails?”

“Yes,” said Nouri. He paused. “No.” He shrugged. “I’m not really sure.”

“Well, that,” said Ibn Arwani, “is an honest beginning.” He gestured to the floor across from the candles. “Sit.”

Nouri crossed the room and sat on the floor.

“Where do you live?”

“In the palace.”

“Chamber boy? Stable boy?”

“I’m a tea boy.”

Ibn Arwani narrowed his eyes. “And you’re willing to work hard?”

“Yes.”

“And you admit that you know nothing of God?”

Nouri thought for a moment. “Not nothing,” he said. “Not much. But not nothing.”

“Good,” said Ibn Arwani. He leaned forward and blew out the

four candles. "Come back tomorrow at dawn. We'll see what rises in you. And what resists."

Nouri lowered his head to the floor. Then he rose to his feet and departed. He knew that it would not be easy to rekindle his spiritual flame while remaining at the palace. But he was so elated at the thought of resuming his practice, he could not help running all the way home.

Ten

On the following morning, Nouri awoke before the sun was even a glimmer on the horizon and set off to begin his studies with Ibn Arwani. As he made his way through the sleeping hallways of the court, there was hardly a soul in sight. All he saw as he padded by were a pair of the Sultan's serving girls and Little Ahmed and a gaunt-looking fellow practicing *zikr* on a bench in the garden. When he passed by the fellow, a chill ran down his spine.

It was Sharoud.

His childhood foe.

He'd somehow followed him to the court.

As Nouri hurried on through the gates, however, and out into the city, he laughed at this thought. It was clear that some part of himself had conjured up the dark Sufi to trip up his heels as he headed back to the pursuit of God.

As Nouri moved through the streets, he found a seamless shroud lying over the town. Only here and there in the pale pre-dawn light did a cat or chicken dart by to disrupt the stillness. When he reached the rooms of Ibn Arwani, he found a half dozen men already seated in *zikr*. The Sufi master did not acknowledge his arrival. So he quietly took his place among the rest. When the practice was done, Ibn Arwani took him aside and explained what would be expected of him if he joined his teaching. Then the youth made his way back to the palace to prepare The Right Hand's tray.

Thus began Nouri's new double life: part tea boy to the primary adviser to the Sultan, part Sufi-in-training. Early morning was *zikr*; then back to the palace to serve the tea and recite a new verse for The Right Hand; then back to Ibn Arwani for the day's menial tasks; then back to the palace to compose the following day's verse and partake of the evening meal; then back to Ibn Arwani for private instruction; then back to the palace to collapse into bed. Despite his strictness, Ibn Arwani accepted that Nouri divided his time between his spiritual training and his duties at the court. He was still quite stringent in his demands—indeed, he gave him such a string of tasks that Nouri wondered whether he'd entered a Sufi teaching or a work camp—yet he trusted that if the youth's aim was true, he would be able to turn away from the court when the time came to choose.

As for those at the palace, they could only guess what the new tea boy was up to when he crept through the gates before dawn.

"I hear he's become the secret lover of the Widow Alban," said the Sultan's seamstress. "They say you can hear her cries from ten houses away."

"I hear he wanders out through the gates in a trance," said the palace hearth cleaner. "That's how he comes up with the poems that he writes for The Right Hand!"

The Right Hand himself took little notice of Nouri's comings and goings. He registered that the boy seemed a bit tired, but that perception merely grazed his mind for a moment and then disappeared from sight. Only Leisha—for whom Nouri now had no time—was determined to find out what was going on.

"You're like a ghost!" she cried, as she saw him staggering back to the palace one night. "And a frazzled-looking ghost at that!"

Nouri insisted that he was too busy to talk, but Leisha would have none of it.

"I haven't seen you in weeks!" she cried. "You're not going to run off on me now!"

Nouri was too tired to protest. So he followed her out to the gardens that bordered the northern edge of the palace, lay back on a stone bench, and struggled to stay awake.

"You're leading a secret life," said Leisha. "Everyone knows it. You sneak away at dawn—you slip off again in the early afternoon—you vanish in the evening. The only thing that nobody seems to know is what it is you're actually doing!"

Nouri, who ached with exhaustion, tried to respond. But Leisha simply rambled on.

"I think you're a spy! An enemy court planted you here as a tea boy to win our trust. But you're gathering information to help them overthrow the Sultan!"

Nouri shifted his body and felt the cool air swirl about his head.

"It's true," he said. "And what's more, they want me to find an accomplice. Someone who can help me to get top-secret information. And I've decided that you're the perfect candidate for the job!"

Leisha was silent. Then she reached for a clod of earth and hurled it at Nouri. "Very funny! Now tell me what you're *really* doing!"

Nouri hesitated. He did not wish to speak about his spiritual practice, but he knew that Leisha would not let him sleep until she discovered the truth. So he brushed away the crumbs of dirt that sprinkled his chest and said, "I'm striving to become a Sufi."

Leisha furrowed her brow. "A what?"

"A spiritual being. A servant of God." He paused again. "The Sufi tries to free himself from the material world. From the tyranny of thought. His goal is to experience the divine in all things."

Leisha tried to piece together what Nouri was saying. "You mean you're studying with that crazy loon who came to town last month?"

"He's a remarkable teacher. I'm lucky to have the chance to be his *murid*."

"His *what?*"

"His disciple," said Nouri. "His student."

Leisha was silent a moment and Nouri waited for her to begin laughing or to throw something harder than a clod of dirt at him. Instead, she rose and moved through the shadows to where he lay.

"How thrilling!" she cooed. "I've never been with a *murid* before!"

Nouri looked up and saw that her eyes were filled with hunger.

Without saying more, she began to loosen her robes, exposing her soft flesh to the night. Nouri had never seen a girl without clothes and he was curious to know what a pair of breasts actually looked like. When they swung into view, however—ripe as a pair of sun-kissed melons—he felt no impulse to reach up and take them in his hands or lean forward to place his mouth over their nipples. He only lay there, staring at them with a curious disinterest. And Leisha, inflamed as she was, understood.

"You're not normal!" she hissed. Then she gathered her garments and ran off into the night.

Nouri lay back and looked up at the stars. He did not know what it meant to be normal. He only knew what it meant to be Nouri.

Who had four ears.

And was far from home.

And was trying to find his way back to God.

So he rose from the bench and made his way to his room, where he finally gave over to his crushing fatigue.

NOURI RESTED THE SHOVEL against the wall and wiped a trickle of sweat from his brow. He'd been digging for over an hour and his head cloth was soaked with perspiration, yet he knew that he had no choice but to continue on. The ground was rocky and unyielding and it would take a miracle to make a garden take root. But Ibn Arwani had instructed him to do it. So he raised the shovel, ran the back of his wrist across his forehead one last time, and continued digging.

He'd been coming to the simple rooms of the Sufi master each day for almost six months now. And though he was grateful to have found a teacher again, it took time for him to adjust to Ibn Arwani's ways. Where Sheikh Bailiri had been loving, Ibn Arwani was strict. Where Sheikh Bailiri had been patient and reassuring, Ibn Arwani was confrontational. When Nouri said that he wanted to be with God, Ibn Arwani said:

"First you must learn who 'you' are. Then you must learn what it means to 'want.' What it means to 'be.' Then you must learn what 'God' is. Otherwise, it's just a game. A pretense."

When Nouri said that he wanted to know the truth, Ibn Arwani said:

"You must suffer a great deal to know the truth. You must be crushed into powder. People always say they want the truth. But they really want lies. The truth requires sacrifice. The truth requires work."

When Nouri said that he wanted to become a servant, Ibn Arwani said:

"First you must become a warrior. Only with your sword raised high can you become a servant of God."

Nouri listened, and tried to understand. But the image of a raised sword only brought thoughts of the attack at the lodge in Tan-Arzhan. So he focused his energy on the morning *zikr* and the various tasks he was given to perform each afternoon. At times they were pleasant: chopping the walnuts for the *ranginak* or trimming the wicks of the evening tapers. But they were often exhausting, like the labor he was engaged in now. In this case, the grueling task was his own fault. A few days earlier, as he was waiting to be dismissed after washing the tea bowls, Ibn Arwani had said: "What do you think of our gathering place, Nouri?"

Nouri looked around the spare dwelling where he and the

others came to pray. "It's nice," he said. "There's lots of room for remembrance."

"So you don't think it requires any improvement? To be more pleasing to Allah?"

Nouri was silent. He knew that part of being a Sufi was to accept each thing, no matter how simple, for what it was. But he also knew that Ibn Arwani's questions were always a test. And as he looked out through the window at the land that sat behind the two rooms—neglected and overgrown with weeds—he could not help thinking of how a garden would inspire Ibn Arwani's disciples to open their hearts to God.

"I think it would be nice to have some roses," he said. "And maybe a small fig tree."

Ibn Arwani thanked him for his advice. And on the following day he handed him a shovel and told him to begin digging. Nouri found the job rather daunting, but he did his best not to complain. Instead, he tried to picture the fragrant flowers that would bloom when his efforts were through.

Now he was so focused on his labor, he did not even notice the terrible thirst that gripped him. So he was startled when he heard a voice and turned to see Ibn Arwani standing beside him with a pitcher and a cup.

"You look as if you need a bit of rest," said the Sufi master. "Let's sit for a little while."

Nouri rested the shovel against the wall again and then followed Ibn Arwani across the yard to the small patch of shade that the house cast upon the ground. He waited for the Sufi master to sit. Then he seated himself beside him.

"It's a pleasant day," said Ibn Arwani. "Don't you think?"

Nouri hesitated. It was an extremely warm day, especially for digging up rocks. But he knew better than to contradict his teacher. "Quite pleasant."

Ibn Arwani reached for the pitcher and poured a pale liquid into the cup. Then he raised the cup to his mouth and drank.

"A few of the others have offered to help dig." He paused a moment, the soothing beverage perched in the air between himself and Nouri. "But I thought that would rob you of the pleasure of doing it yourself."

He took another sip of the liquid and Nouri felt his throat constrict. He hadn't expected Ibn Arwani to be so severe. He could feel that the Sufi master was quite advanced, yet he could not help but chafe at his methods. Before he could protest, however, Ibn Arwani spoke.

"The part of you that wants to know God is very small. You must strengthen it if you wish to master the part that fears. That desires. That thirsts." He was silent a moment, his eyes boring into Nouri. "The beast or the master. You have to decide which one you wish to be."

At the moment all Nouri wished was a drink of the cool liquid in the pitcher. But he did not say this. Instead, he said, "I should get back to work." Then he rose and went to fetch the shovel that he'd laid against the wall.

He was just about to pick it up when Ibn Arwani called out to him: "By the way—"

Nouri turned.

The Sufi master held out the cup. "Would you care for a drink?"

Nouri felt his tongue rake over his parched lips. Then he nodded.

Ibn Arwani rose, raised the pitcher, and poured more liquid into the cup. Then he crossed the yard and offered the cup to Nouri. It was stronger and more tart than Nouri had expected. But it quenched his thirst. So he handed the cup back to Ibn Arwani, reached for the shovel, and continued digging.

IT WAS EARLY MORNING. Nouri had just returned to the palace from his morning *zikr* with Ibn Arwani when he was stopped in the garden by Little Ahmed.

"The Right Hand is asking for you!"

"But his tray isn't due for nearly an hour."

"Well, if I were you," said Little Ahmed, "I'd go to him now!"

Nouri could not imagine why The Right Hand wished to see him. But he thanked Little Ahmed and headed to his chamber. When he reached it, he found the door slightly ajar. So he pushed it open and stepped inside. The *ney* player was just removing his flute from its silken wrapper and The Right Hand's attendant—a tall boy with long curly hair—was drawing the drapes to let the morning light tumble in. The Right Hand, as always, was seated on the divan, and when he saw Nouri enter, he turned.

"There you are!" he shouted. "Come! Sit beside me!"

The words seemed more a command to Nouri than an invitation. So he crossed the room, lowered himself to the pillow that lay on the floor beside the divan, and—while the *ney* player began an insinuating tune—waited to learn why he'd been summoned.

"The air is so sweet before dawn. So full of possibilities." The Right Hand looked into Nouri's eyes. "Don't you think?"

Nouri nodded.

"Yet there must be something quite special to make you rise so early, and wander away from the court!"

It was clear to Nouri that The Right Hand knew quite well where he was going when he slipped off each morning. And though it was equally clear that he did not approve, Nouri knew there was no point in lying about it.

"I participate in a morning *zikr*," he said. "I hope that doesn't displease you."

The Right Hand smiled. "And how could I be displeased by a morning *zikr*?"

The *ney* player turned to The Right Hand to seek permission to begin playing. The Right Hand nodded. Then the music rose up and The Right Hand closed his heavy-lidded eyes.

"I simply wish to protect you."

"From what?"

The Right Hand opened his eyes and turned to Nouri. "You realize you have a gift, don't you?"

"A gift?"

"You're a poet! It's a talent that's not given to very many."

Nouri said nothing.

"It would trouble me a great deal to see you waste it."

The Right Hand was silent a moment. Then he rose from the divan, went to the large carved cabinet that stood in the corner of the room, opened it, and removed a small book. Then he headed back across the room to where Nouri sat.

"Your gift was given to you by Allah. He wishes you to use it. Not sit in a trance and whisper His name over and over, which anyone can do."

The Right Hand held the book out to Nouri.

"I propose we make a collection of your verses. We'll have the court calligrapher copy them out. We'll have the court illuminator embellish them. Then, when it's finished, we'll present it to the Sultan himself."

Nouri gazed at the slender book. Its cover was made of rich brown leather and its spine was embossed with suns and moons.

"Would you like that?"

"Yes."

"Well, if we're to do this you'll need to devote yourself to your writing. There'll be no time for *zikr.* Or any other activities outside the court." He gazed into Nouri's eyes. "Do you understand?"

Nouri could not imagine turning away from his spiritual practice. But the thought of the Sultan reading his poems was too enticing. Perhaps a short break from his studies would let him digest what he'd learned. He could always return in a few months, when the book was done.

"I'll do my best not to disappoint you."

The Right Hand's eyes flashed with pleasure. "You won't disappoint me," he said. "I'm certain of that."

Nouri wished that he could be as sure as The Right Hand of his success. But the most he could do was wait until he gave him leave to depart, and then race to his room and get to work.

Eleven

When Nouri told Ibn Arwani that he would be taking a hiatus from his practice, the Sufi master shrugged. "There is no break from practice," he said. "One is either with God or one is not."

Nouri wanted to explain that it was only a temporary measure, but he knew there was no point in trying to defend his position. So he thanked Ibn Arwani for his help and headed back to the palace.

As he made his way along, he tried to consider what lay ahead. To compose a few lines of verse for The Right Hand's tea was one thing. To fill an entire book to be read by the Sultan was another. So he searched the streets for the telling image that might inspire a new poem. The man with the sunken eyes carrying the pig to slaughter. The girl lifting her skirt as she stepped through the mud. The light slicing down between the rooftops. The squashed banana. The broken jug. He knew he would need to go further, and deeper, than he'd gone before. Only perfect dedication would allow him to pull it off.

So the veil fell again, and this time with a thud. Nouri was released from his duties as a tea boy. He was supplied with a thick stack of paper and endless pots of black ink. And he was expected to write. From the first strangled cry of the cock to the evening's last guttering candle, he'd conjure up images and weave what he saw into words. He tried to extract meaning from each bud. Each breeze. He tried to experience the simplest object with a sense of wonder.

The Right Hand was pleased by Nouri's devotion to his task. He gave the boy new clothes and had trays of food brought to him while he worked. After weeks of constant writing, however, it was clear that the youth needed a break. So one morning, The Right Hand went to the Court of the Speckled Dove and invited Nouri to go riding with him in the mountains.

"It will do you good! Bring some fresh air into those scholarly lungs!"

Nouri knew better than to refuse The Right Hand. But in truth he quite liked the idea of riding into the mountains. He felt sure that the adventure would yield a poem, or even a few. So he put aside his paper and pen and he and The Right Hand set off.

It was a brisk day, so they hardly broke a sweat as their horses climbed the mountain path. The Right Hand did not say a word, yet Nouri could feel the pleasure he took from the ride. Nouri took pleasure from the silence, which seemed to grow deeper as they went higher, and which soothed his beleaguered ears. Only when they reached a plateau did The Right Hand slow to a halt and speak.

"Magnificent!" he whispered. Then he turned to Nouri. "Don't you think?"

Nouri looked out at the snow-capped peaks that rose in the distance. "Magnificent," he repeated.

"They say that on a perfectly clear day you can see the four corners of the realm."

Nouri knew that this was impossible, but he did not say so. Instead, he tried to press the beauty and grandeur of the landscape into his heart.

"I was thinking that you might enjoy a new room," said The Right Hand. "Something with a more inspiring view."

"I like my room," said Nouri.

"Well, what about a girl, then? Tell me what you like! Large-breasted? Slender? A nice firm ass? I can have whatever you wish sent directly to your room!"

"No, thank you."

The Right Hand threw back his head and laughed. "It's a strange lad who'd refuse such an offer! When I was your age I was on fire! I couldn't wait to find a place to shove my prick!" He was silent a moment. Then he turned to Nouri. "Are you a virgin?"

Nouri said nothing.

"Well, the sooner you let the serpent strike, the better! Otherwise your balls will become inflamed! And you may have trouble pissing!"

Nouri could feel his blood rise at The Right Hand's words. He awoke every morning with "the serpent" stiff and throbbing against his belly. Sometimes it even exploded while he slept, leaving his bed a sticky mess. He knew, however, that he did not wish to lie with a girl. So he thanked The Right Hand for his advice and they said no more.

The weeks sped by and Nouri gave no thought to either his studies or the spiritual labor he'd turned his back on. It was as if an invisible wall had been erected around Ibn Arwani's dwelling, a fog of forgetting more impenetrable than the battlements of the palace. Only now and then did the sound of the *santur* or the setting sun evoke the flashes of grace he'd experienced with the Sufi master. Then a feeling of uneasiness came over him. His room seemed too grand, his clothes too ornate, the cakes too sweet upon his tongue. The feeling only lasted a moment, however. Then he'd reach for the quill and return to the refuge of words.

WHILE NOURI WORKED ON—the verse pouring like clarified honey from his pen—the artisans began to prepare the book for presentation to the Sultan. Each poem, when it was done, was given to the court calligrapher, who painstakingly copied it into the leather-bound book. Then the court illuminator would embellish the words with tiny scallops and arabesques, enclosing the title in a cloud band of shimmering gold. Each step in the process took hours to complete, not to mention the time required to make the title page, which was carefully inked in saffron and moonstone, and the borders, which were lovingly decorated with lapis lazuli, cinnabar, and jet.

For the most part, Nouri was oblivious to these efforts. Yet he found that—when he wasn't writing or riding or sitting on a satin cushion at The Right Hand's feet—he could not stop thinking about how the Sultan would react to his verse. He'd never had any real contact with the man. He'd only seen him sweep by, surrounded by bodyguards, his robes flowing like freshly poured cream from his massive body, his turban gleaming like snow atop his regal head. He envisioned himself being summoned to his chambers and told how deeply his words had touched his soul.

"Such imagery!" the Sultan would say. "Such feeling! You possess a remarkable gift!"

Nouri would blush at this praise, half-forgetting that he'd imagined the entire thing in his head. Yet he could not help feeling that his whole life was about to change.

Despite the sweet tenor of the time, now and then Nouri would dream of the ferocious creature he'd dreamed of on the morning of his seventh birthday. It always appeared out of nowhere—its eyes gleaming—its teeth bared—and followed hot on his heels. Nouri always awoke in an icy sweat before it managed to reach him. But he was aware that with each successive dream it was getting closer.

One morning, as Nouri sat writing in his room, The Right Hand paid him a visit.

"I've asked the court painter to paint your portrait," he said. "On the final page of the book!"

Nouri worried that he was going too far, yet he could not find the strength to refuse. "It will be an honor."

"I've arranged for him to meet you this afternoon in the Court of the Speckled Dove. He'll be waiting for you after the midday meal."

So that afternoon Nouri put on his new clothes, wrapped his

head garment around his head with extra care, and went out to his favorite spot to have his image laid down.

When he reached the courtyard, he found the court painter—a large fellow with a bulbous nose and a wild black beard—preparing his easel. A small boy was seated behind him, his head on his knees, fast asleep.

"Welcome!" cried the man, as Nouri approached. "It's time to commit you to eternity!"

Nouri crossed the courtyard to the wooden stool that had been placed beside the fountain and sat. Then he drew himself up very tall and nodded to the painter to begin. The fellow worked intently, with great zeal, and every so often he would call out to Nouri:

"Imagine you're on a boat on the open sea!"

"Imagine you're in a sunlit meadow!"

"Imagine you're on an elephant storming through the jungle!"

Nouri didn't see how he could be on a boat, in a meadow, and on an elephant all at the same time. But he tried his best to relax and let the court painter paint. For the first hour or so, it was easy to sit still. Nouri placed his attention on his breathing and took pleasure in the court painter's focus and concentration. Eventually, however, the sun caused beads of sweat to trickle down his neck. Then an insistent mosquito appeared, which made it difficult not to squirm. So he was grateful when at last the court painter lowered his brush and announced that the portrait was done.

Nouri was eager to see the finished work. But before he could go to it, the court painter clapped his hands and the small boy sprang up and scurried to the easel. He waited as the court painter removed the clips that held the book in place. Then he lowered the book into the boy's hands and he carried it to Nouri.

When he reached him, the boy held the portrait up like a mirror before Nouri's eyes. And Nouri was startled by what was reflected back to him.

His chin was lifted in pride. His mouth beamed with self-satisfaction. And his eyes, though dark and glistening, seemed covered by a veil.

"A perfect likeness!" cried the court painter. "Don't you agree?"

As Nouri gazed at the portrait, he was suddenly reminded of Ibn Arwani and the spiritual struggle from which he'd turned away. But no sooner did the thought rise up than it vanished again. So he turned his eyes from the portrait and nodded.

"Perfect," he said.

The boy lowered the book and carried it back to the easel. Then Nouri headed to his room to finish the poems.

NOURI LAY ON HIS BACK, on the floor, his knees raised, his head on a pillow, waiting for the final image to take shape. He was describing the faint swirls of fog that nestled in the mountains before dawn, and he knew that when the image was perfectly clear he would know how to express it. He closed his eyes. He listened. Then, when the words finally came, he sat forward, reached for the pen, and scribbled them down. When he wrote the last word, a strange quiet came over him. Then he took the poem to the court calligrapher to be inscribed in the book and went to tell The Right Hand that his work was done.

When he reached the familiar door, he knocked.

"It's Nouri!"

There was a long silence. Then The Right Hand called out: "You may enter!"

When Nouri pushed open the door and stepped into the room, he found that it was unusually still. There were no servants to be found, nor any sign of a musician. Only The Right Hand, stretched out on the divan, his eyes balanced between thought and sleep.

"What brings you?" he said, as Nouri approached.

"It's done."

"What do you mean?"

"The book."

"The book?"

"It's finished. I've just taken the last poem to be inscribed."

The Right Hand was silent. Then Nouri's words penetrated the fog. "The book!"

Nouri nodded. "It's done!"

The Right Hand combed his fingers through his luxurious beard. Then he clapped. "We must celebrate!"

He gathered his loose robes, slipped his feet into his slippers, and rose from the divan. Then he crossed the room to the large cabinet from which he'd fetched the leather book and removed a glass bottle and a pair of silver cups. He placed the cups on the desk that stood beside the open window that looked out over the city. Then he removed the curved stopper from the bottle, poured a dark amber liquid into the cups, and offered one to Nouri.

"To your achievement!"

Nouri gazed across the room at The Right Hand. He'd been in his chamber many times, yet he had never seen him like this. His eyes glittered and a heat rose from his body. Nouri wondered what he would say when he introduced him to the Sultan. Perhaps he would be made a member of his circle and be asked to recite for him each day, as he had done for The Right Hand. At the moment, however, The Right Hand's arm was outstretched. So Nouri pressed all thoughts from his mind, crossed the room, and took the cup from his hand.

The Right Hand reached for the other cup, raised it to Nouri's, and drank down the liquid in a single gulp. Nouri drew the cup to his lips and did the same. Then The Right Hand turned to the open window.

"Look at the city, Nouri! Perhaps someday everyone out there will know who you are!"

Inflamed by both the liquor and the praise, Nouri lowered his cup to the desk, moved to the window, and looked out past the weathered ramparts and the rain-washed towers at the tumult of the streets beyond. He felt a deep urge to describe what he saw. To compose a true hymn to the city. But before he could even frame the opening words, he felt The Right Hand move close behind him.

"It's exciting, isn't it?"

Nouri felt his heart begin to pound. Then The Right Hand parted the curls that hung down from his head cloth and pressed his lips to his neck.

"Have you taken care of that problem we spoke about?"

At these words, The Right Hand reached around Nouri's body and grasped the serpent. Nouri recoiled. But the serpent, stirred by the contact, began to stiffen, which only emboldened The Right Hand.

"There are many ways to deal with these things," he whispered.

He kissed Nouri's shoulder. And then his back. Then he pressed him down against the frame of the window and tore open his trousers.

"All things," he whispered, "come at a price!"

It wasn't the first time Nouri had experienced staggering pain. When he was six, he had found a wasps' nest in the grass and when he carried it through the garden to show Habbib, he was stung, sixteen times, on his arms and face. When he was ten, while he was helping Salim Rasa prepare some *khoresht annar-aveej,* he had sliced off the tip of his left thumb. But what was happening now so stunned him he could not actually believe it was occurring. His mind dissolved. His body became a field of flame.

Somewhere, from deep within the pain, he felt The Right Hand reach beneath him and grasp the serpent again. He resented the delicious tremor that shot through him. It brought pleasure into the bargain, which only confused him more. As he lay there, pinned between the heated body and the cool marble ledge, he saw Leisha walking by on the path below. He wanted to cry out to her, but he could not make a sound. So he watched as she moved on, unaware of the outrage that was happening a short distance over her head.

The Right Hand drove on. Nouri felt as if the breath had been expelled from his body and his blood had turned into dust. He could not imagine it lasting much longer, but as The Right Hand's passion approached its peak, he began thrusting harder. Nouri was too consumed with pain to see that, in his fever, his assailant had wound his fingers into his head garment and, in a moment of fury, had torn it off. Only when The Right Hand's groans rose into a furious wail did he realize that his ears had been revealed.

"Demon!" cried The Right Hand, as he reared back. "Spawn of Satan!" He reached out and squeezed Nouri's ears to be sure that he was not seeing double. "I'm fucking a goddamn monster!"

Nouri gripped the ledge, grateful for the sudden interruption of his abuse. He knew that what was likely to come next was his demise, but to his surprise, The Right Hand reached neither for an inkpot to crush his skull nor a dagger to pierce his heart, but instead began pounding him even harder. Nouri wondered if this was how he intended to kill him. But then, like a lightning-struck ox, he suddenly spasmed, and collapsed on top of Nouri's battered frame.

Nouri waited for The Right Hand to regain his senses, certain that when he did he would call for the guards to come fetch him and take him to some dark corner of the palace, where they would chop off his head. But the body, having lapsed into a sated swoon, only grew slack. So Nouri slipped out from under the leaden weight, gathered his torn clothes, and hurried off.

PART THREE

Twelve

The snow covered the woodshed and the granary and the pasture and spread like a gentle sleep over the hills. It had fallen, in a great silent downpour, during the night. So when Nouri awoke and looked out through the little window over the place where he slept, there was neither a footprint nor the tracks of either a cart or a plow to mar the perfect white. Nouri had never seen snow in his life. So he could only think that some *djinn* had cast a spell over the landscape to make it disappear.

He knew, however, that, *djinn* or no *djinn*, he had to climb down the ladder and throw off his caftan and put on his warm clothes and head out into the icy air to tend the sheep. There were twelve of them: four rams, six ewes, and a pair of newborn lambs. It was his job to lead them out into the pasture to feed, to remove the twigs and dirt that matted their coats, and to make sure that they did not wander off. And while the snow was likely to complicate these tasks, he knew there was no choice but to carry them out.

Had someone asked him, Nouri would have been unable to say how long he had lived in the dusty barn on the simple farm on the side of the stony mountain. He assumed that his seventeenth birthday had come and gone, but he could not say when. One day blurred into the next, the heel of bread he consumed each morning varying only in the degree to which its crust was burned, the watery soup he ate for lunch never wavering, the bowl of grain he was given for supper being augmented with a scrawny carrot or a small scrap of meat only now and then. He rose. He worked. He slept. Each breath was an act of forgetting. Each action was a denial of all that had come before.

When Nouri had fled the wounding embrace of The Right Hand, he felt light-headed and dizzy. It was the hour of siesta, so no one saw him as he staggered over the colored tiles and back to his room. He removed his clothes, rolled them into a bundle, and changed into something unsoiled. Then he hurried through the palace, out the gates, and over the sleeping streets until the city was far behind him.

He had no destination. He just ran and ran—down the dusty roads, through the choppy fields, along the dried-up riverbanks—until he spied an abandoned farmhouse where he could spend the night. He was cold and hungry and there was little comfort to be found in its forgotten rooms. But he curled himself up into a ball beside the lifeless hearth and relinquished himself to sleep.

In the morning, he rose and went out to the parched garden, where he found a well. He drew enough water to fill the tub that sat on the broken porch. Then he removed his clothes and sank in. He did not think about what had happened the day before. He did not think about anything. But when he stepped from the water, it was as if his life at the court had never occurred.

Over the following days, he continued north, stealing food from the fields and gardens he passed, stopping only when his tired body could move no more. At times he found a barn or an old windmill where he could spend the night, but for the most part to keep himself warm he had to huddle in the clefts of the dry earth that were scattered along the way. He followed the roads, but took cover when he heard the sound of horse hooves. Even the simple gaze of a pair of eyes was too much for him to bear.

As he traveled on—his only motive to get farther from the court—he began to perceive that he was moving higher. The ground was less beaten, the air more fragrant and less tinged with salt. As he pressed on, the path grew narrow and snaked upward through great crags of rock. This meant that Nouri had to climb, and that there was less food to be found.

One morning—after tucking himself into a tiny cave he'd found on the side of a great bluff—he awoke to find that he was not alone. Surrounding him, in a fleecy ring, were ten sheep, their eyes closed in a communal sleep, their bodies filling the space with warmth. When he sat up, they stirred, but they showed no signs of fear. They simply blinked their elliptical eyes and bleated a few times.

Nouri felt safe at the center of the flock. But having drunk his fill from a meandering stream he'd passed the night before, he felt the need to piss. So he climbed over the circle and stepped out of the cave into the morning light. As he released a steady stream upon the ground, the sheep turned their heads to listen and watch the steam rise up. Then, when he'd brushed the dirt from his clothes and headed back to the path, they rose and started after him.

At first, Nouri was confused to find the wooly creatures dogging his steps.

"Be gone!" he shouted.

He waved his arms and tried to shoo them away. But their dark, vacant eyes just stared at him, and he soon realized that after being alone for longer than he'd ever been alone in his life he was grateful to have them near. So he turned back to the winding road and let them follow behind.

They remained at his heels the entire day. When he paused at a stream to drink, they drank too. When he came upon a patch of grass, he waited while they grazed. And when dusk came, he found a crevasse in the side of a mountain where the entire flock could spend the night. It was not as spacious as the cave where they'd sheltered the night before, but it was dry and protected from the wind, and both Nouri and the sheep seemed happy at the thought of settling in.

He removed a few stones scattered on the floor of the enclosure. Then he led the sheep in and they hunkered down. Before he could lay his own weary body beside them, however, he felt a shiver run through him, and when he turned he saw an old man hovering in the darkness. He was carrying a small torch, which cast shadows across his haggard face. But his eyes, set deep within his skull, blazed brighter than its flame. Nouri feared more for the sheep than for himself. But then the man suddenly shouted:

"Ven!"

The cry made Nouri's tender ears throb. But as the sheep rose to their feet and started toward the old man, Nouri knew that the flock was his. When they were gathered around him, the man turned and started off, and the sheep—just as they'd done with Nouri—followed behind. After a few paces, however, the man turned back. He glared at Nouri through the fading light and Nouri feared that he might draw a knife from the heel of his boot and slice open his throat. Instead he shouted:

"*Venga!*"

Then he jerked his head to indicate that Nouri should follow him too, and so he did.

By the time they reached the old man's farm, it was dark. Nouri watched as he led the sheep into an enclosure. Then he followed the old man into a small stone house, where he gave Nouri a hunk of bread and some tasteless soup. After the spare meal, he led Nouri out to the barn, showed him the ladder that led up to the narrow loft, and left him to sleep. When Nouri awoke the following morning, the old man handed him a wooden staff. And Nouri understood that his new job was to tend the sheep.

In the time since then, the weather had grown cold and Nouri had settled into life on the farm. In exchange for looking after the sheep, he was given food and shelter. The rest of the old man's world—the cultivation of the scraggly vegetable patch, the tending of the orchard, and whatever went on in the little house outside the times when Nouri was welcomed for meals—was none of his affair. Nouri performed his chores and followed his tasks. Each day was like the day that had come before.

Now, however, he'd awakened to find that the world had gone white. So he shook off the last traces of sleep and scrambled down the ladder to see what the strange substance was like. For with the past erased, and no guarantee of any future, what could match his state of mind more completely than a landscape that was hushed and numb?

AS TIME PASSED, A SIMPLE fondness grew up between Nouri and the old man. With no common language, they had to depend on looks and gestures to communicate. If the old man raked his fingers across the sky it meant that more snow was coming. If Nouri mimed turning a key in a lock it meant that the sheep were in for the night. Nouri kept waiting for the old man to make some sort of reference to his head cloth, but he never did. So he assumed that it just seemed like another expression of his strangeness to the old man.

There was a flurry of activity when the two lambs were born. The first came quite easily, on a clear afternoon, and Nouri did little more than hold the bucket of warm water and watch as the sticky creature entered the world. The second, however, came at night, and was breech, so Nouri had to assist while the old man pushed it back, grasped one of its legs and pulled it into the birth canal, did the same with the other, and then guided the lamb out to safety. With no words to use, the old man was unable to tell Nouri what was needed, yet it was as if some deep-seated intelligence moved in and explained what to do. When it was clear that both the lamb and the mother would survive, the old man clapped Nouri on the back. It was a moment of connection. Otherwise, they simply nodded to each other as they performed their chores and, from time to time, stood together beside the barn to watch the sun slip behind the hills.

It wasn't until several months had passed that Nouri learned the old man's name. Nouri was sitting beneath the yew tree where the sheep liked to graze when he looked up to see the old man striding toward him. He assumed that he'd done something wrong, but when the old man reached him he peered into his eyes and thumped loudly upon his chest.

"Enrico!" he shouted.

Nouri was silent. Then he suddenly remembered that he also had a name. "Nouri," he said, as he thumped his chest in return.

The old man nodded. Then he turned and marched back to the house and that was that.

Considering the amount of time he spent with them each day, Nouri was surprised he did not feel a deeper kinship with the sheep. He fed and watered them; he brushed their coats and took them on long rambles along the steep mountain paths; he even named them: the four rams were Abtin, Omid, Siamak, and Javeed, the six ewes were Ashtag, Chalipa, Yasaman, Ghamzeh, Malakeh, and Rasa, and the two lambs were Poupak and Kamal. But all that had occurred over the previous year kept his heart locked up tight, and the lambs could not enter in.

Sometimes, when the dullness of not feeling was almost as painful as the pain had been, Nouri would kneel down and pray. But without any access to his heart, the simple words that formed were just words. So he rose each morning and tended the sheep and slipped back into bed at night.

Wanting nothing.

Expecting nothing.

Content to let each excoriating day trickle into the next.

WHEN HE FIRST HEARD the singing—augmented by his ears into the sounds of a choir—Nouri looked up, for he was certain that music so sweet could only come from above. He was carrying the hay out to feed the sheep, but the singing stopped him in his tracks. And when its source finally appeared—climbing the winding path that led up the mountain—he was surprised to find that it was merely a girl, about the same age as he was, carrying a large basket covered with a cloth. As soon as she saw Nouri, the girl stopped singing. But she kept her eyes on him as she approached, and when she reached the place where he stood she spoke.

"He traído el jamón para Enrico."

Nouri, who could make little sense of the odd language, said nothing. He was unused to seeing a girl without a veil, so he could only stare at her dark, lovely face.

"Es especialmente bueno este año." She gestured toward the basket. *"Estoy seguro que le va a gustar."*

The girl waited for Nouri to respond, but he just stood there. So she smiled a faint smile and then headed toward the house. As she left, Nouri watched her: her dark hair swinging behind her, her feet making a slender trail in the snow. She reminded him of someone, but he could not say whom. He only knew that he was happy to see her.

When she reached the house, she rapped on the door. Then it opened and Enrico ushered her in. So Nouri shook the encounter from his mind and continued on toward the sheep. As he approached them, they bleated a few times and Nouri noted how they blended into the snowy landscape like chunks of *panir* in a bowl of unseasoned rice. With great care, he laid out the straw for them to eat. Then he made his way back to the barn, climbed the ladder to the loft, and peered through the window, hoping to catch a glimpse of the girl. She did not appear, however. So he assumed that she must have departed while he was tending the sheep.

Two days passed. Then six. Then eight. Then, when he'd nearly forgotten all about her, the girl returned. He'd just finished brushing down the sheep and was sitting on the bench in the orchard when the sounds once again pierced the air. When she saw him seated beneath the empty plum tree, she went to join him. She smiled and sat down beside him on the bench. Then she began speaking again in that strange fluted tongue. And though Nouri did not understand a word, he was comforted just to hear the sound of her voice.

As the weeks passed, the girl came again and again. And each time she went to Nouri, and began speaking, and gradually the mysterious language began to unfold.

"*Casa,*" she would say as she pointed to the house.

"*Cielo,*" she would murmur as she gestured toward the sky.

Nouri would listen carefully to each word and then try to repeat what she'd said. And eventually, he began to join in the game. He'd point to the well and the girl would say: "*Pozo.*"

He'd gesture toward the sheep and the girl would say: "*Ovejas.*"

Sometimes she'd nod as he pronounced the sounds. Other times she'd laugh, and correct him, and he'd try again. There were times when it seemed hopeless, a mass of dark phrases that he would never penetrate. But he persisted, and in time he began to understand the new tongue.

Once he could make sense of the words, he learned that the

girl lived on a farm on the north side of the mountain, that she had a younger sister and an older brother, that she came to Enrico's to exchange the salt pork that her father cured for the milk from Enrico's sheep, and that she had a name.

"Soledad," she said, when he finally asked.

Nouri did not know what it meant. But he knew that when she said it, it made him feel safe.

Even with the language uncorked, Nouri found that the words failed to flow with Enrico. He was now able to say "thank you" and "good morning" and "good night." He was now able to ask if he needed help chopping the wood or if there were a few extra spoonfuls of soup. Enrico would say *sí* or *no* and an occasional *allá* or *más tarde*. Otherwise they continued on in silence as before.

There were moments, as he and Soledad sat talking, when Nouri sensed a movement inside him and he thought that he might actually feel something again. But despite the vague stirring, his heart refused to quicken. So he sat on the bench and tried to be grateful that, in this cold, empty time, a friend had appeared.

Thirteen

It snowed and it snowed. Great fat flakes poured from a creamery sky, endless white shrouding the house, the hills, the trees. Sometimes Nouri and Soledad would sit in the barn, watching the torrent fall outside the open door, obliterating everything except the cold, dry space where they sat. Other times, when the sky would clear, they'd climb high into the mountains, where broad vistas would appear and great birds would swoop over their heads.

Once Nouri understood the girl's language, they spoke less and less, as if words had been needed to forge a connection that, once made, needed no words. They could spend hours without a sound passing between them, aware that it was pointless to give shape and color to things that could not be expressed. At times, however, something would rise up to remind them of the distance between them. And then the questions would appear.

"Why do you wear that?" asked Nouri, as he pointed to the wooden cross that hung from Soledad's neck. So she told him about the child of Bethlehem and how he'd offered his life to redeem the sins of mankind. Nouri listened carefully to the tale, and saw how the light gleamed in her eyes as she spoke. But he was too far away from his own god to make sense of anyone else's.

"Why do you wear that?" asked Soledad, as she pointed to the tattered head cloth Nouri never removed. Nouri, feeling compelled not to lie, merely said that his ears were sensitive—omitting the fact that he had four instead of two.

One morning, when Nouri peered out through the window above his bed, he found Soledad waiting outside the barn. So he hurried down the ladder, threw on his clothes, and went out to meet her. When she saw him, she cried, "Come!" Then she started over the field toward the path that led down the side of the mountain. Nouri wanted to ask where they were going, but before he could say a word she was halfway across the field. So he tightened his scarf about his throat and doubled his pace to catch up. As they hurried along, he could feel Soledad's excitement. But only when the path suddenly branched and they took the route that led to a house and a well and a pen of stout pigs did he realize that she was taking him to her home. As they approached the pen, he saw a girl a few years younger than Soledad laying out scraps for the pigs. When she saw them, a great smile spread across her face and she ran into Soledad's arms. Soledad held her. Then she turned to Nouri.

"This is my sister, Concepción."

Nouri nodded.

"And this," she said, turning back to the girl, "is Nouri."

The young girl's smile flashed again, and Nouri's heart cracked—ever so slightly—and a trace of her sweetness trickled in.

They moved toward the house, the pigs loudly grunting their disapproval as they started away. As they approached the door, a man with a head of thick black hair opened it wide. He beamed at the sight of the two girls, and Nouri knew that he must be their father.

"My angels," he whispered, as he kissed the tops of their heads.

"This is Nouri, Papa," said Soledad. "The boy who lives at Enrico's."

The man turned to Nouri and his black eyes bored into him.

"Welcome," he said.

Before Nouri could answer, the man turned and went into the house, and Soledad gestured to Nouri to enter as well. So he crossed the threshold and the two girls followed behind.

It was a simple place, with a large, open hearth and a few pieces of rough wooden furniture, yet it exuded a warmth that Nouri had not felt in a long time. A small, broad-faced woman crouched beside the hearth, turning a loaf of bread over the flames. Nouri guessed that this was Soledad's mother, and when Soledad's introduction confirmed this, they exchanged a smile.

The woman pulled the bread from the fire and placed it in a woven basket. Then she carried it to a table by the wall, which was laden with salt pork and fresh cheese and a bowl filled with oil. Soledad led Nouri to the table, and when the others had joined them, they clasped their hands and lowered their heads. Then Soledad's father closed his eyes and murmured a brief prayer.

"Thank you for the food. And for our health. We are grateful."

They whispered, "Amen." Then Soledad's mother drew the bread from the basket, tore it apart, and began handing the pieces around the table. Nouri watched as the others dipped the bread into the oil, and placed the pork and cheese on top. So he pushed aside the feeling of being an outsider, and did the same.

No one spoke as they ate the simple meal. Nouri found the bread a bit dry and the pork a bit salty, but he was grateful to be welcomed to the table. Just as he was beginning to relax, however, a voice called out: "Save some for me!"

Concepción's face flashed with joy and everyone turned toward the door.

"There's always food for you, Fortes," said Soledad's father. "Put down the shovel and come join us."

Nouri turned to look at the young man standing in the doorway. Broad-shouldered, with long black hair and the imperious air of an avenging prince from one of Habbib's bedtime tales, he was clearly the older brother that Soledad had told him about.

"Who's this?" said Fortes, leaning his shovel against the frame of the door and entering the house.

"Nouri," said Soledad. "My new friend."

The young man looked into Nouri's eyes and Nouri felt a wave ripple through him. It reminded him of the yearning he'd felt for Vishpar. And the pain he'd endured in the chamber of The Right Hand. And since the feelings that these memories evoked—sorrow—anger—shame—threatened to seep through the crack in his heart, he nodded brusquely to the fellow and averted his gaze. Then he returned to the table. And the food. And to feeling nothing at all.

THE STREAKS OF RED STOOD out from a great distance against the sweep of white. At first, Nouri thought that some rogue had stumbled into the drifts and upended the contents of his wine pouch or that some strange current had bubbled up through a fissure beneath the snow. As he moved closer, however, he understood that the streaks were blood, and when he reached them he saw the ram lying half-hidden in the snow. Its eyes were closed, and the blood, which had come from a gash in its side, was caked in its curling wool. Yet there were no footprints leading to it or from it, for the wind had scattered the snow during the night to conceal the source of crime.

As Nouri stared at the lifeless form, it seemed to bear no relation to the creature that he had brushed and watered and grazed. But he knew that he had to tell Enrico about it. So he trudged through the snow to the house, where he was tending the hearth. When he described what he'd found, the old man showed no emotion.

"No tracks?"

"No tracks."

"And they just left it there?"

Nouri nodded. "So it seems."

The old man said no more. Then he threw on his coat and they went out into the snow to retrieve the dead body. When they reached it, they hoisted it up and then carried it to the shed behind the house. Nouri assumed they would dig a small grave, say a prayer, and then bury it. But instead, Enrico fetched a pair of sharp knives and began to butcher the creature. First he cut the skin back from the legs and broke them just beneath the knees. Then he tied a stick between the legs and hung the carcass from a strong elm. Then, as if he were peeling a shiny apple, he began stripping away the skin. When the creature was bare, he broke open the sternum to remove what was inside. And though occasionally he would ask Nouri's help—to carry away the intestines—to feed the heart and stomach to the dogs—for the most part Nouri simply watched, in a state of wonder, as a life devolved into a series of random parcels before his eyes.

Over the following days, Enrico prepared roast mutton, braised mutton, mutton broth, mutton stew. But though the smells of the various dishes were enticing, Nouri could not eat a bite.

THE WINTER WANED, and the snow began to give way to fresh patches of grass and tiny wildflowers and longer days. Nouri took the sheep out to graze and helped Enrico with the pruning and the planting. He also spent more time at Soledad's, helping her father with the salting, helping her sister with the pigs, and joining the family for the odd meal. He could tell that Soledad's father was somewhat wary of his presence; Soledad was young, and Nouri was a boy from a distant land. But he knew that he could never explain that it wasn't his daughter he desired.

Soledad understood this without being told. She'd been to the village and had seen how the men stared at her—as if she were a piece of pastry—as if she were walking down the street without any clothes on. Nouri's eyes were always chaste when they fell upon her. She felt safe when she was with him. There were times, though, when she saw him gaze at Fortes like the men in the village gazed at her. And one evening she decided to speak to him about it.

They were sitting on the small wooden porch behind her house. Nouri had just come from feeding the sheep and was content to watch the sun descend while Soledad mended her father's trousers. After a few moments, however, Fortes arrived to fix the broken wheel of the grain cart that languished beside the shed, and Nouri's attention was drawn to the handsome youth. The arc of his body as he labored over the cart. How the muscles tightened beneath his shirt. He was different from Vishpar—more solid—less tinged with light—yet he stirred in Nouri the same longing. Nouri tried not to show it: he shifted his body away from the shed and only darted occasional glances in his direction. But Soledad could tell what Nouri was feeling.

"He's beautiful, isn't he?"

Nouri said nothing.

"I've always thought so. Even when we were small."

"He reminds me of someone I once knew."

"Someone you cared for?"

Nouri nodded. "Someone I loved."

Soledad drew the needle through the cloth and tightened the stitch. "I know how you feel," she said. "Love is a powerful thing."

They said no more. But Nouri could feel that the bond between them had deepened.

As the days grew warmer, Nouri began to find his sleep interrupted by violent dreams. They usually involved The Right Hand, who would appear like a dark *djinn* out of nowhere and pursue him through forests, down rivers, across vast, sun-dried plains. When he reached him, a struggle would ensue, which always ended with Nouri taking The Right Hand's life. When he awoke, however, there was no feeling of triumph. Only a harsh, metallic taste on his tongue and the effort to press the memory from his mind.

Nouri worked hard to fill his days with activity. He offered to help Enrico enlarge the vegetable patch, which meant digging up the rocky soil that lay along its southern border, putting down fresh, fertilized loam, and helping him decide what to grow. When it rained, he made sure that the hay stayed dry. When the sun beat down, he filled buckets from the pump to keep the sheep well watered. And in the evenings, despite the feelings that it evoked—or perhaps because of them—he climbed down the mountain to visit Soledad's farm.

One morning, as Nouri was washing himself at the pump, Enrico came to him.

"It happened again," he said. "Come."

He turned and headed off toward the enclosure and Nouri knew that another ram had been killed. So he dried himself off, put on his clothes, and followed the old fellow to where the body lay sprawled. This time, there was no snow, so the blood had seeped into the ground. And Nouri could only wonder what strange flowers would grow from such sullied soil.

A few weeks later, a third ram was killed. Enrico made no attempt this time to conceal his despair. He hacked up the creature as before, but he could not eat it. A shadow descended over the farm. There were still enough ewes to give milk, but with only one ram—and the fear that it too would be attacked—the future seemed grim. So Enrico began sleeping with the flock, his gutting knife sharpened and ready in his hand.

For Nouri, it was a time of confusion. Why would someone kill three healthy rams, yet leave their bodies behind? Why only the rams and not the ewes? Was it some sort of warning? Did someone have an ancient grudge against Enrico?

Nouri couldn't say. But the killings only increased the bleakness of his life on the little farm.

Fourteen

One night, as Nouri was returning to Enrico's from Soledad's, the answer came. He'd been invited to join Soledad's family for supper; the eldest sow had given birth to a litter of six, and there was a feeling of celebration in the air. Soledad's mother made fritters, which she served with a bitter lemon compote, while Soledad's father roasted loin chops and brought out a jar of trotters he'd smoked the previous fall. When the eating was done, Concepción sang a song and, with the help of the others, persuaded Soledad to join in. Then Soledad's father and Fortes became engaged in a discussion about the best methods for harvesting grain. They seemed, point by point, to disagree with each other, yet their exchange was playful. And though they left Nouri out of the conversation—which was wise, since he knew nothing about harvesting—the evening made him feel as if he was a part of something again.

As he climbed the mountain path, he was free of thought, the air cool and dry, the small copper lantern flashing its light as he moved along. When he reached the farm, he paused for a moment and looked up at the endless pinpricks of light that punctured the darkened bowl over his head. Then he made his way toward the barn past the small enclosure where Enrico slept with the sheep. As he approached it, a wave of gladness washed over him, followed by the need to piss. So he placed the lantern down, lowered his trousers, and released a warm stream upon the ground. He felt strangely content. Relaxed. At peace. As he raised his trousers, however, he noticed something glinting near his feet.

He knelt down and brushed away the dirt. A blade appeared. He tried to wriggle it free and managed to loosen a small knife from the soil. It was heavily crusted with something dark and dried. But it was only when he grasped the handle and felt the weight of it in his hand that the memories came rushing back.

The anger.

The fury.

The struggle.

The bloodshed.

The pain.

The pain.

The pain.

The pain.

The violence of Nouri's dreams had been real. But rather than vent his rage on The Right Hand, he'd killed the rams. And the only thing more shocking than this realization was the fact that he'd managed to bury it so far down in the dark corners of his mind, he hadn't even known that he had done it.

WHEN NOURI RETURNED TO THE BARN, he fetched a bucket, filled it with water, found an old rag beside the pump, and in a hidden corner beneath the loft began to scrub away the dirt and dried blood that befouled the knife. He rubbed and rubbed until the slender blade gleamed. Then he carried it up the ladder, slipped it beneath the thin straw mattress, and lay down to sleep.

It soon became clear, however, that sleep would not come. His heart was too anguished at what he'd done, and he was concerned that if another dream came he might do it again. He knew that he would have to go to Enrico in the morning and confess his crime. But he feared that when the old man found out, he would reach for his knife and kill him on the spot. If he didn't, he would be sure to ask why he'd done it, and Nouri would not be able to answer without explaining what had happened with The Right Hand, which he knew that he couldn't do. So he lay there—counting the knots in the beams—listening to the buzzing of the insects—as the hours crept by.

The following day, he avoided Enrico, fearful that the exchange of even a glance would betray his guilt. And the following night he lay awake, on the theory that if he could keep from sleeping, he could keep from enacting the violence of his dreams. After three tortured nights, he could no longer resist. He slipped beneath the waves and remained submerged until Enrico came to rouse him several hours after the sun had risen. What he found, however, when he shook off his slumber, was that the simple awareness of what he'd done had changed the structure of his sleep. It was as if a sentry now stood guard in his head, monitoring his thoughts in the night. So he let himself drift off the following night, and the next night, secure that he would neither wander from his bed nor do any harm.

One morning, about a week after he found the knife, Nouri awoke to a terrible itching. It started in his legs, a crawling sensation, as if a band of ants had burrowed beneath his skin. Then it spread up his body to his belly, his arms, and finally his ears. He knew that if he removed his head cloth and began to scratch, he would never stop. So he gave up trying to figure out what had caused it—a bug bite?—something he'd brushed against?—something he'd eaten?—and tried to find something to take it away. He soaked his body in both warm water and cold. He rubbed it with acacia honey. He covered it lightly with salt. But none of these things seemed to bring the least bit of relief. So since he was still somewhat chary of Enrico, he took the problem down the mountain to Soledad.

When he reached the farm, she was kneeling beside a small basin of water, washing a stack of clothes.

"I need your help."

Soledad looked up.

"I have a terrible itch. And I can't seem to get rid of it."

"Where is it?"

Nouri took a deep breath. "*Everywhere.*"

Although Soledad did not profess to have any medical knowledge, she asked Nouri if she might examine his body. Nouri agreed. So she took him inside the house, led him into the small room that she shared with Concepción, and told him to remove his clothes. As she studied his legs and his chest and the warm hollows beneath his arms, they were both keenly aware that this moment was creating a new intimacy between them. But when she asked him to remove his head garment, he declined, for the memory of The Right Hand's reaction when he'd discovered his ears still filled him with terror.

When Soledad was finished with her examination, she told Nouri to slip back into his clothes. Then she asked him to remain where he was and she left the house. About an hour later, she returned with an old woman with milky eyes, whom she introduced as Señora Inez. The woman spread a large cloth over Soledad's bed and told Nouri to remove his clothes again and lie down. Then she proceeded to sponge his body with a solution of vinegar and antimony. She followed this by massaging oil of violets into his skin. Then she covered him with a red chalky substance, wrapped him in muslin, and left him to rest.

At first, Nouri thought that the odd treatment had worked. The vinegar was cooling, the violet oil was numbing, and the chalky substance seemed to draw the itching away. His body relaxed and he fell into the first sleep he'd known in days. A few hours later, however, he awoke to find the muslin torn from his body and his fingers clawing his flesh.

It was only then that Soledad's father stepped in. Nouri was sitting in a chair by the window, wrapped in a thin blanket. He was lost in thought and had not even noticed that the taciturn man had entered the room. Only when he heard the low voice did he turn and see him standing in the shadows.

"I hear you've got an itch."

Nouri nodded.

"An itch is bad."

Nouri nodded again and there was a long silence. Then Soledad's father folded his arms.

"I know a fellow who can help you," he said. "But you'll have to travel far to see him."

"If it would stop the itching," said Nouri, "I'd go to the moon."

Soledad's father did not respond. So Nouri spoke again.

"How do I get there?"

The gaunt man was silent. Then he shrugged. "I guess I'll have to take you."

The offer came as a surprise to Nouri. "Thank you," he said.

"We'll leave in three days."

Soledad's father stared at Nouri a moment. Then he left the room.

Nouri could not imagine going off on a journey in such a condition. But the thought of remaining where he was, with no relief from the itching, was far worse. So he closed his eyes and prayed that he could keep from removing his skin before it was time to depart.

THE FOLLOWING DAYS WERE filled with preparations for the journey. Soledad sewed a small tablecloth into a sack and her mother spent hours baking bread and wrapping olives and sausages and cheese into small bundles to fill it up. Concepción gathered handfuls of dried grass and wove a pair of broad-brimmed hats to protect the two travelers from the sun, while Fortes fashioned a pair of sharp knives to slice the sausages and the cheese—not to mention the throats of any strangers on the road who might try to harm them.

The most difficult thing for Nouri was to tell Enrico about the trip. He'd avoided him for weeks and still found it hard to look him in the eye. He finally managed to mumble it to him one morning as he stood drawing water from the well, and though the old fellow barely said a word Nouri knew that the news had struck him hard. The most Nouri could do was reassure Enrico that he would come back soon, and that the sheep would be safe while he was gone.

The morning of the departure was overcast and gray. Soledad helped Nouri and her father gather their things together and load them into a pair of satchels. Concepción gathered handfuls of wildflowers to hand them and Soledad's mother gave Nouri an ointment of beeswax and juniper berries to ease the itching until they reached their destination. They said their good-byes: Soledad giving her father a tender embrace and Nouri a heartfelt look, Concepción running into the house, Fortes hanging back on the porch. Then they hoisted their bags and set off down the mountain.

They walked in silence, the sky clearing to a searing blue as they made their way down the winding path. When the land leveled off, they came to a small farm, where an elderly man gave them a pair of brown steeds. Soledad's father drew a rasher of pork from one of the bags and gave it to the man. Then they loaded their things into the satchels and headed out over the dusty terrain.

They rode all day, not exchanging a single word. When night fell, they tied the horses to a tree and laid a pair of blankets on the ground. Then they ate a bit of the pork and cheese and, with the intricate beadwork of the stars overhead—not to mention the aid of Soledad's mother's ointment—they managed to get some sleep.

On the second day, they set out at dawn, the dust clouding their eyes, the heat parching their throats, the sun blazing down like an evil *djinn*. Nouri knew that the journey would be less oppressive if he and Soledad's father conversed. But the heat dulled his brain, and Soledad's father said nothing. So they rode on together in silence. On the third day, they came to a tiny village where they bartered their salted pork for fresh hay for their horses. Nouri wanted to linger awhile to gaze at the new faces. But Soledad's father said they still had a long way to go, so they mounted their horses and continued on.

They traveled until Nouri lost track of time. Days of riding, the heat a dull weight pressing down on his body, the itching a steady presence beneath the skin that threatened to break loose at any time. When hunger came, they stopped to eat. When night fell, they laid out their blankets and slept. But mostly they just rode and rode and rode.

One afternoon, they reached the crest of a large hill that they'd been climbing most of the day, and Nouri looked out to find an expanse of sea so blue, so light-dappled, so seemingly endless, he could hardly believe his eyes.

"We're close now," said Soledad's father. "The boat will be waiting for us at the water."

Nouri did not point out that there'd been no talk of a boat or any passage across the water, especially not a sea as vast as the one they faced now. Instead, he merely followed as Soledad's father gave a sharp kick to his horse and continued on toward the coast.

When they reached the sands that bordered the sea, they reined in their horses and dismounted. Then Soledad's father told Nouri to wait with the tired steeds while he went to search for a man named Alfonso. About an hour later, he returned with a ruddy-faced fellow with piercing eyes who told them to entrust their horses to a boy who tied them to a tree. The fellow led them to a small wooden boat, helped them aboard, and proceeded to pull up anchor. Then, with a gentle breeze at their backs, they set off.

It was the first time in Nouri's eighteen years that he'd ventured out upon the water. So it took him a little while to get used to the buoyancy and the salty flavor of the air. As they moved away from the coast, he saw the water change from dark green to turquoise to a silvery blue. But even more alluring than the water was the light: it seemed to pour in from every direction, sending a warmth through his body that licked at the ice that surrounded his heart.

They slept that night on the boat, Alfonso laying blankets over the seat planks and making *ceviche* for them to eat from the carp that he caught. Nouri, however, spent most of the night wide awake, thinking of the relief from the terrible itching that would finally come when they reached their destination. In the morning the sun rose golden and sleek, and when Nouri looked out he found that land was within sight. As Alfonso guided them in, he saw boats hugging the shore and people scattered across the beach. And as the smells wafted in from the food being cooked on a series of open fires, it was clear they were entering another world.

When they reached the shore, Alfonso dropped anchor. Then Soledad's father stepped from the boat and gestured to Nouri to do the same. They waded through the low water until they reached the sand. Then Soledad's father paused.

"How do we find him?" Nouri asked. "The man who can help with my itching?"

Soledad's father raised his eyes to the clay-colored towers that loomed at the far edge of the beach. "There is no man."

Nouri stared at him, not comprehending.

"I know you killed the rams," he said. "I don't know why you did it. But I know." He was silent a moment, his eyes still locked on the distance. "On top of this, I see how you look at Fortes. This is not natural." He was silent again. Then he turned to Nouri. "So I've brought you to a place where this god of yours abides. Let him deal with you." He stood there to make sure that his words drove home. Then he waded back to Alfonso's boat.

Nouri closed his eyes and tried to press back the feeling of dread that rose from his gut. But he could not avoid the fact that he was stranded in a foreign land with no friends—no money—and an itch like a madman roiling beneath his skin.

PART FOUR

Fifteen

Despite the number of twists and turns he had to take, the sleeping dogs sprawled across narrow alleys, the rancid smells rising from sun-soaked courtyards, Nouri knew when he saw the slender man draped in the tiger skin and seated beside the pipes that he'd reached the place he'd been sent to find. The pipes—which were strewn across the steps that led to the curtained door—were of all shapes and sizes: long wooden tubes topped with circular bowls, elegant hookahs of knobbed silver, carved ivory wands that curled up to flirt with the smoke that issued from their mouths. Exposed to the harsh glare of the midday sun, they seemed tame and ornamental. But Nouri could tell, from the faraway look in the man's eyes, that they were conveyors of real magic.

After living in the windswept town for nearly a week with no relief from his itching, Nouri needed whatever magic he could find. When Soledad's father had abandoned him on the beach, he'd just stood there, staring at the sea. When he finally turned back to the land, he was overwhelmed by the activity: the fishermen untangling their brightly colored nets, the women carrying large woven baskets on their heads, the men grilling fish in open pits that smoked like the portals of hell. So he crossed the beach to a narrow shelf that was sheltered by a string of palms, lowered himself to the cool white sand, and sat staring at the horizon, where the world he knew lay smashed like a broken toy.

He sat there the whole day. And the next day. And the next. And he might have sat there until the life drained from his tormented body had a man with a thick beard and dressed in a dazzling blue robe not approached and held out a ripe, gleaming pear.

"Unless you're just a figment of my imagination—in which case I should be home in bed and not selling fruit in a moth-eaten tent on the beach—you must be as hungry as a fucking mule after sitting here, staring at the whore-loving sea, for the last three days."

Nouri was so stunned by the man's florid speech—not to mention the fact that the entire thing was in Arabic—he could not say a word.

"Take it," said the man, as he offered the pear. "Or I'll slice your head off and sell it as an exotic melon."

Nouri reached for the pear, took a bite, and a stream of sweet juice trickled down his chin. Then, in a single gulp, he devoured the rest.

"As I see it," said the man, "you have three choices. Either you get up and go back to where you came from—which I assume, from the way you look, is a journey you're in no condition to make—or you come with me. Which will at least prevent the mosquitoes from eating you alive."

Nouri waited for the man to go on, but he said no more.

"That's only two choices."

The man gazed at Nouri and shrugged. "Or I'll slice your head off and sell it as an exotic melon."

Nouri tried to consider the options. But he knew that returning to where he'd come from was not a choice. And despite the relentless nagging of his thoughts, he still valued his head. So he rose and shook the sand from his clothes.

"Lead the way."

The man nodded. Then he started across the beach and Nouri, still light-headed and confused, did his best to follow behind. As they made their way through the crowded streets, he learned that the fellow's name was Sayid, that he'd spent his whole life in the bustling city, that he'd tried selling spices and leather before he'd settled on fruit, that he'd been with over three dozen women, that he could spit farther than any man he'd ever met, and that Nouri was welcome to stay with him until he figured out what to do next. Nouri had never heard anyone talk so much. One sentence flowed into the next until he was swept away on a torrent of sound. But he was tired, and hungry, so he let the fellow jabber away as he led him on.

When they reached Sayid's room—which was stuffed with books and jars and rugs and hides—there did not seem to be enough room for Sayid, let alone for Sayid and himself.

"There's a pump in the alley for water," said Sayid. "And a place to shit. As for food, you can help yourself to whatever I have. Which isn't much. But then life can be lived on quite little, if you know what you like."

Nouri was too dazed to respond, so Sayid took a broom, thumped the thin straw mattress that lay on the floor a few times, and told him to lie down.

"Sleep!" he cried. "The elixir of Allah!"

Nouri removed his shoes and added them to the clutter. Then he crawled onto the lumpy bed and fell into a deep sleep. When he awoke, Sayid presented him with a mouthwatering *tagine*—laden with lamb, dotted with prunes, drenched in a sweet cinnamon sauce—which Nouri wolfed down. Then he took him out on a tour of the humming city. It was filled, he explained, with a hodgepodge of contradictions. Christians and Muslims. Tradesmen and clerics. Crusaders and pirates. Its bright face was as shining as its dark, hidden underbelly was grim.

"There's nothing you can't find here," said Sayid. "And if you do think of something you can't find, there's always someone who'll venture off to where you can and bring it back."

Nouri was amazed by the place: even the great city of Tan-Arzhan seemed lifeless by comparison. So when Sayid returned to the beach to sell his melons and pears and tangerines, Nouri continued on along the footpaths and through the alleys and the courtyards, intrigued by the fair-haired Berbers, the scholars dressed in their crisp black gowns, the long-masted galleys that towered like gray-haired wolves above the wharves. But though everything he saw filled him with wonder, he still felt as if a battle were occurring beneath his skin. So since Sayid had insisted that one could find anything in the clamorous city, he went down to the beach to inquire where he could find something to remove his itching.

When he reached the tent where Sayid hawked his fruit, the loquacious fellow was filling a small basket with kumquats. When Nouri told him about his itch, he just stood there a moment, stroking his black beard.

"There's a woman across the way who sells salves. And there's a man who lives near the countinghouse who can put people into a trance." He waved his hand over a basket of ripe figs to scatter the flies. "But if you want my opinion, neither of these things amounts to a pile of cat puke."

"Well, there has to be something."

Sayid narrowed his eyes. "I guess it depends on how badly you want to escape your pain."

"Badly," said Nouri. "Very badly."

Sayid was silent. Then he reached for an apple, threw it up high into the air, drew his sword, and as it tumbled back down toward the ground, sliced it in two, catching both halves with his other hand. Then he slipped the sword back into his belt and offered one of the halves to Nouri.

"Then I've got just the thing for you."

That was when he told Nouri about Abdallah, who with a few draws from one of his pipes would make Nouri's itching go up in smoke. So Nouri followed the path that Sayid had described through the maze of streets until he arrived at the place where he stood now.

"Sayid sent me," said Nouri. "He said to tell you that you should give me a 'first-class passage.' "

The man draped in the tiger skin looked up. Then he rose to his feet and began to climb the crumbling steps, and Nouri followed behind. When they reached the top, the man drew the curtain aside and they entered a dark room. Nouri saw that he was in a narrow cell with no windows, the only light the flickering flames from a series of oil lamps that were scattered across the floor. Beside each lamp lay a man sprawled on a worn-out rug, sucking at the end of a slender pipe topped with a bowl that he held, inverted, over the flame. The tiger man—who by now Nouri assumed must be Abdallah—gestured to Nouri to take his place on one of the empty rugs. So he lay down beside a vacant lamp and waited to be shown what to do.

The man shuffled off to the far side of the room. Then he returned to Nouri with one of the long, lovely pipes. He opened the lid and placed a small pealike bundle in the bowl; then he replaced the lid, turned it over, and lowered it over the flame. Nouri watched as the heat rose in wavering plumes from the small glass chimney and warmed the contents of the bowl. Then the man handed the pipe to Nouri and nodded.

"Breathe!"

Nouri slithered close to the lamp, slipped the pipe between his lips, and drew in not smoke but a warm stream of vapor. Its taste was so acrid he wanted to pull the pipe from his mouth. But he decided that if the others could bear it, its reward must be great. So he persisted. Until at last his body relaxed, and his head grew light, and a sweet euphoria swept over him and carried him away.

THE BARGE WAS VAST, and tipped with gold, and floated, cloudlike, over the vermilion water. Nouri lay back on one of the cushions that were strewn across the deck and gazed out at the men washing their camels along the shore, the glittering domes of the mosques, the round ships and cogs and *feluccas* taking their turns in the afternoon light. He felt weightless. Blissful. Without a care in the world. So he was unprepared when the deck suddenly lurched and he bolted forward as something—a schooner?—a whale?—struck the side of the barge.

"You can't just lie there all day, my indulgent friend! For the sake of Allah, it's time to wake up!"

Nouri opened his eyes and gazed at the smoke-stained ceiling. He was not on a satin cushion on a golden barge on a silver sea. He was in Sayid's room and it was neither a whale nor a schooner that had disturbed his calm but a sharp kick from Sayid's foot.

"No one understands the lure of Abdallah's pipes better than me. But you have to crawl out of the fog now and then. You have to eat. You have to piss." He gave Nouri another kick. "And you have to work! Do you think such delicious visions come free?"

It had been two weeks since Nouri had first gone to the windowless room and inhaled the transporting vapors. And the pleasure he felt was so sublime—no itching—no sorrow—and a palpable muting of the sounds that assaulted his ears—that he returned each day until the narcotic fog enveloped him wherever he went. At night, he lay in Sayid's room, dreaming delicious dreams of the past: talking with Vishpar, laughing with Habbib, walking through the streets of Tan-Arzhan with Sheikh Bailiri. When he awoke, he stumbled off to Abdallah's and lay down with the pipe, never thinking about who was paying for his sweet escape. So despite the fact that Sayid's words came as something of a shock, he could only stare up from the sweaty mattress, not knowing what to say.

"Get up!" cried Sayid. He paused a moment and then gave Nouri a final whack. *"Now!"*

Nouri attempted to raise himself from the bed, but he faltered. So Sayid went to the washbasin, lowered a cloth into the water, wrung it out, and brought it back to the bed. Nouri pressed it against his face and it dissolved a few outer layers of the fog. Then he went to the table, where Sayid fed him some dates and a bit of cheese.

"The woman who runs the local laundry," said Sayid, "is in need of help. It's a stinking place. I can promise you that. But as far as I can tell, you're in no position to be choosy."

Nouri couldn't argue. So Sayid rose from the table. "Come," he said. "Before you float back into the clouds."

Sayid led Nouri into the street. Then they moved through a series of shadowed passageways until they came to an open doorway that belched great billows of steam. When they entered, Nouri found himself in an airless room hung with caftans and bedsheets and turbans, all dripping in the filmy air. Sayid looked around the room and, when he found no one there, cupped his hand around his mouth and shouted:

"Shoh-reh! My speckled quail egg! It's Sayid!"

There was a momentary silence. Then a large woman, dressed in a tentlike shift, her face damp with sweat, strode into the room. "I've no time for fucking, Sayid! I've got too much work!"

"I'm not here to fuck. I'm here to introduce you to a friend."

The woman looked at Nouri, a bead of moisture dangling from one of her chins. "For him, I suppose I can find the time."

Sayid shook his head. "He's not here to fuck either. He's here because he needs a job."

The light in the woman's dun-colored eyes went out. "I need help with the stirring," she said. "And the wringing. And the hanging." She drew a rag from one of the folds of her voluminous shift and wiped it across her brow. "You can start now." Then she turned and vanished into the sea of clothes.

Nouri stood there frozen. So Sayid gave him a shove. "Get going!" he cried. "There are worse ways to pay for a journey to the stars!"

Nouri closed his eyes. The room was dank, and foul smelling, but then he remembered the bliss that awaited him at Abdallah's. So he took a deep breath and headed off into the haze.

WORKING AT SHOHREH'S LAUNDRY was much harder than Nouri had expected. From the moment he arrived each day, just as the sun was coming up, until he staggered out, as it was setting, there was an endless list of things to be done. Once Shohreh had taught him the various tasks, she left him to tend to them on his own. As soon as he finished one stack of fetid clothes, however, the next would appear. By the end of the first week, his skin was raw, his hands were blistered, his back was knotted and sore. But the coins that Shohreh gave him at the end of the day felt smooth and cool in his pocket. And when he handed them to Abdallah and he handed Nouri the pipe, all thoughts of the grueling labor drifted away.

Day after day, Nouri shuttled between the laundry and the smoke-filled den: in the former, enveloped in clouds of steam; in the latter, in clouds of forgetting. The streets became a tunnel he floated through, the people he passed vague phantoms, Sayid a blur at the edges of sleep. At times, the fog in his head was so thick he could not find his way back home. At other times, his mind was so clear it was as if the rest of his life had been immersed in fog. He still slept at night, but as the weeks passed, his dreams began to sour. Instead of sweet memories of his days in Tan-Arzhan, he saw Habbib, tied to a wagon, being dragged through the streets, Soledad tending a flock of bloody sheep, Vishpar and Fortes making love. So despite the fact that the sweet vapors of Abdallah's pipes were able to relieve his itching, they could not take away his pain.

One night, as Nouri staggered out of Abdallah's den, he passed an alley from which an alluring scent beckoned. He rarely wandered off the familiar path that led from Sayid's to the laundry to Abdallah's and back to Sayid's. The streets that jutted off from his accustomed route were merely deviations from his daily pattern of work, intoxication, and sleep. The fragrance was beguiling, however—a heady mixture of rosewater and lime—so he decided to head down the alley and find out where it came from.

It was a moonless night, so the only thing he had to light his way were the twitching candles in the darkened windows over his head. As he moved along, he could feel eyes peering from those windows, but he was unable to trace them to their sources. The smell that had lured him upon his course was soon smothered by other smells: frying onions and sandalwood and the stench of rotten fruit. His ears, ever alert—even beneath his head cloth and the haze of Abdallah's pipe—could hear snatches of conversation, tree branches scraping against clay-tiled roofs, cats scurrying by. Whirled by the sharp euphoria of Abdallah's magic, the night rattled and roared.

At the end of the alley, he saw a figure in a doorway: head lowered, arms folded across his chest, one leg drawn up against the door. As Nouri moved closer, the man raised his head and peered at him through the darkness. Nouri could feel his heart begin to pound and a flash of heat pass through him. He wanted to stop. To turn. To say something to him. But all he could do was continue on.

As he started down an alley that ran perpendicular to the one he'd just traversed, he could feel the man walking behind him. It was as if the fellow was leading the way from behind: under the low stone arches, over the cobbled courtyards, until they reached the narrow street that spat out onto the wharves. As they entered it, the man quickened his pace, and Nouri could feel the fear course through him. Before he could think what to do, however, he felt a hand on his shoulder. So he stopped. And he turned. Then the man took a step closer, lowered his hand, and grasped the serpent.

Nouri stiffened. But so did the serpent. And though the fear now gripped him, he could only gasp as the man raised his tunic, and opened his trousers, and fell to his knees.

For the first time in as long as he could remember, he thought of God. Then a wave of such pleasure passed through him, even God was gone.

Sixteen

On the morning after his encounter at the wharves, Nouri awoke in a state of arousal, the covers tented around the insistent hardness of the serpent. As he slipped from the bed and splashed water on his face, he could not stop thinking of what had happened the night before. He kept hearing the man's footsteps—seeing his coal-black eyes—feeling the heat of his desire. As he followed the path from Sayid's to the laundry, he felt sure each person he passed knew what he'd done. He felt sure Shohreh knew too: she kept pressing her body against him and could not stop speaking about the soiled bedsheets. Yet even Nouri's discomfort at her closeness did not cause the serpent to relax. It jutted against the steam press and thudded against the vats and remained a general nuisance throughout the day.

When he was done with the day's labor, he continued on to Abdallah's. But the moment the luscious vapors took their effect, he hurried off in search of the man. When he reached the place where he'd found him the night before, there was no one there. But a bit farther on he found another man—this time leaning against a rusted gate—he could relinquish himself to.

A new daily pattern emerged: rising in the morning, trudging to Shohreh's, hurrying to Abdallah's, and then heading out to find the next man. Sometimes he wandered for hours without success. Other times he'd barely stepped into the dark alley before he found the next warm body. Each night was an adventure, each man different from the one before. Some were strong and thickly muscled. Some were wraithlike. Some were small. Some were covered with bristling hair. Some were smooth like stones washed by the sea. Some were charcoal. Some were fair. Some cried out when they came. Some whimpered. Some moaned.

All were on fire.

Few spoke a word.

And despite their vast number, he never encountered the same man twice.

As Nouri moved deeper into the world of the flesh, his body continued its passage from boy to man. His shoulders broadened. His face grew lean. His voice—which had been a piping *shawm* when he'd left the lodge—settled into the warmth of a resonant *oud*. More significant than these physical changes, however, were the changes in how he related to the world. He no longer felt the need to be looked after. To be approved of. To be told what to do. And after months of sating the needs of the serpent, he no longer felt ashamed at watching it rise and fall.

The months slipped by. The Sharqi blew in from the east and the sultry days grew shorter. And night after night, Nouri gave himself over to the pleasures of the body. Not even the delirium of the pipe could make the world so completely disappear. Each night, however, before he could carry his spent body back to Sayid's, the persistent itching would return. And all he could do was tumble into a restless sleep, and begin a new cycle the next day.

IF SHEIKH BAILIRI HAD BEEN a part of Nouri's new world, the Sufi master would have explained quite clearly that nothing remains the same for very long, that the senses dull, that pleasure fades, that left to their own devices all things, no matter how sweet, will inevitably decline. He was not there, however, and his voice—which had once echoed in Nouri's ears—was now buried beneath layers of thick gauze. So Nouri could barely register the fact that it took longer to accomplish less at the laundry, that it took more draws from Abdallah's pipe to produce the desired effect, and that the men he caressed in the hidden pockets of the night were becoming not only interchangeable but unappealing. He only knew that when he awoke in the morning he felt drained, that the smell of Shohreh's soap made him queasy, and that he often had to search all night before he found someone to whom he was willing to offer himself.

Sayid—who rarely saw him anymore—found him a perfect

model of dissipation. "I've watched many people pass through here. It's a stewpot. A magnet for every vice. But I've never seen anyone fall so hard for the city's lures. You're impressive, my friend!"

Shohreh, on the other hand—who saw him every day—found him a perfect wreck. "I wouldn't fuck him now," she exclaimed to Sayid, "if he was the last prick in town!"

More important, she was no longer sure that she wished him to work at the laundry. His stirring was listless, his hanging erratic, and he seemed in need of a good pressing himself. So one morning, after a particularly impassioned night, she announced that he needed to either shape up or find a strong camel to ride out of town.

"If I'd wanted to look after a child, I'd have had one! Get the clouds out of your head! Or get out!"

To be honest, Nouri was grateful for the ultimatum. For he knew that his life was a mess and could not go on much longer as it was. But if he lost his job at the laundry, he could not pay Abdallah for the pipe; if he could not use the pipe, his itching would increase; if his itching was not tempered, he could not bear the touch of even the gentlest stranger; and if he did not lose himself in his nightly trysts, he could not bear the sorrow in his heart. So he swallowed his pride and begged Shohreh to give him another chance.

As a test of his pledge to work harder, the gruff laundress gave him a particularly difficult task. Rashid al-Halil, one of her most steadfast customers, had just lost his wife. Consumed by grief, he'd ventured off to receive succor from a band of religious fanatics who lived in the mountains a few hours south. He'd remained there a month, and was so touched by the kindness they'd shown him, he wished to offer them a kindness in return. So he sent a pair of his servants to gather each towel, bedsheet, window curtain, tablecloth, and stitch of clothing the brothers possessed and take it to Shohreh's to be cleaned.

"White!" Shohreh shouted, as she led Nouri to the absurdly large basket that the great heap of goods was piled up in. "Everything is fucking white! And I've been told to make certain it's all even whiter when it goes back!"

Each item, she explained, had to be soaked in a solution of hot water mixed with vinegar and soap, then wrung out by hand, then rinsed with cool water, then wrung out again, then hung in the courtyard, then rinsed again, then wrung out again, then hung out again, then pressed in the steam press, then folded, and then carefully stacked in the enormous basket. Rashid al-Halil's servants would return for the basket a few hours before sundown. So it all had to be done as swiftly as it could.

"They say the stupid fools barely eat!" Shohreh exclaimed. "So at least you won't have to deal with shit stains in their drawers!"

Nouri found this scant consolation for the long day of labor that lay before him. But he rolled up his sleeves and set out to do the best that he could do. First he made a fire to heat the water for the vats. Then he added the vinegar and the soap. Then he gathered the sheets and towels and tunics from the basket and lowered them in. Once they were submerged beneath the scalding water, he reached for the long birch stick and began to stir. By now his arms were quite used to the exertion—indeed, after working at the laundry for almost half a year, they'd grown nearly as strong as Vishpar's—but the steam that rose from the boiling vats stung his eyes, and the sound of the churning water deafened his ears, and his thoughts, spurred by Shohreh's ultimatum, began to turn in his head.

Maybe I can stop roaming the streets at night.

Maybe I can stop smoking the infernal pipe.

Maybe I can dive into one of the steaming vats and be cleansed like the laundry.

He worked all day—stirring, wringing, rinsing, hanging, pressing, folding, and stacking. By the end, he was so tired he could barely lift the most gossamer sash from the plate of the press. Yet he knew that once he'd laid the final item in the basket he would head for Abdallah's. So he balanced the last stack of things on the basket's edge, raised his eyes to the steam-wrecked ceiling, and prayed for help.

It had been so long since he'd turned to Allah, he did not really know what to say. But then he saw a white robe hanging from a wooden dowel, and he thought of Soledad. He realized that he'd been waiting for her to appear—leading a herd of goats over the hill—walking barefoot across the blazing sand—to help him sort out the mess he'd gotten into. So he closed his eyes and sent up a tender plea—not to God, who he felt quite sure had given up on him, but to his absent friend.

"Help me," he whispered. "I'm lost. And I can't seem to find my way back."

Nouri could not have said what he hoped would occur. A sudden dispersal of the steam? A flash of insight? A flash of light? Or perhaps merely the simple strengthening of his will? He never could have guessed that the dowel that held the robe would suddenly snap, causing the garment to float into the air like an angel. Or that the splintered halves of the rod would come crashing down to knock him hard on the head and hurl him into the cavernous basket at his side. Or that the stack of clothes he'd placed on the basket's edge would topple down and cover him. Or that he'd be so gone to the world he would not feel a thing as the men who'd been sent to deliver the finished laundry hoisted the basket and carried him away.

IT WAS A PERFECT MORNING: bathed in sunlight, laced with birdsong, soothed by a fragrant breeze. A few pale clouds were reflected in the tiny pool that sat at the center of the garden, and the argan tree that stood near the southern wall cast its shade on the grass. For the man in the thin white shift seated cross-legged on the ground, however, a veil covered the day. So he pressed his bare legs into the grass and tried to push through it.

Despite the loss of his parents to a virulent plague that had swept through his village when he was six, the destruction by a savage dust storm of the farm he'd been taken to live on when he was twelve, and the trampling to death of his best friend by a runaway steed when he was twenty-one, Sheikh Abu al-Husain al-Ibrahim al-Khammas always insisted that his life had been exceedingly good. He'd always had food to eat, a roof over his head, and, most important of all, he'd found the purpose of his life at an early age. There was never any doubt that his path was toward God. The moment he heard the first words of the Qur'an, he knew there was nothing else worth pursuing. When he asked his elders how to take his devotion to a deeper level, they saw the mystic in his soul. So when he reached the age of sixteen, they sent him off to become a Sufi. He studied with a teacher named Sheikh al-Faraj al-Farid for nearly thirty years, until he was chosen to travel into the mountains to head the order in the clouds. He'd led that order now for even longer than he had studied and practiced at the first. And though its heyday had come and gone, and its ranks had dwindled, it still offered him what he needed to progress on his inner path.

After six decades of practice, Sheikh al-Khammas found that nothing was left but his desire to be with God. The laws of a higher world had been revealed and they rendered mute the laws of common existence. He was no longer fooled by ambition or greed. He no longer felt the need to control anyone else. Such freedom, however, was accompanied by an inner wildness, which he tried to hide from his fellow Sufis. For with the loosening of the doctrines of his faith, he was left to govern himself.

He knew, however, that as long as he had skin, blood, and bones he would have to labor to reach God. As he splashed the cold water on his face in the morning. As he roamed the hushed corridors at night. So now, as he sat on the grass, in the garden, by the pool, he attempted to pierce the veil that kept them apart.

He tried to see the shadows of the branches that fell upon the gravel path. He tried to hear the rustle of the leaves. Then he raised his head, leaned back, and gazed up at the sky. A great scalloped cloud floated by like a galleon, at the center of which was a small square of blue. So he focused upon it, until he felt himself pass through into the void beyond.

He could not say how long he remained on the other side. Time split its confining husk and ceased to exist. But eventually the light began to recede, and the damp grass began to penetrate his shift, and the thoughts—from which he'd been so blissfully free—came rushing back.

How could he have let Rashid al-Halil take his clothes? The bedsheets? The tablecloths? The towels?

Was Allah trying to say that he was meant to do without?

After so many years, did he still need reminding of such things?

Before he could spiral off any further into thought, he saw Abbas al-Kumar and Omar al-Hamid moving toward him.

"Forgive us for interrupting you—"

"Either now—"

"Or at any time—"

"But we thought you should know—"

"That the basket of laundry—"

"Has returned!"

Sheikh al-Khammas gazed up at the two men. They were as different as goat's milk and ink: Omar al-Hamid was thin and frail and myopic, Abbas al-Kumar was large and utterly rooted to the earth. After working and eating and praying together for so long, however, they were like the flip sides of a coin, and Sheikh al-Khammas had grown accustomed to hearing their words overlap as they finished each other's thoughts.

"They must have brought it back in the night—"

"While we were sleeping—"

"And then crept away—"

"Into the darkness—"

"Like a panther—"

"Or a thief—"

"But now it's just sitting there—"

"Like a battleship—"

"Or an offering—"

"Outside the gate!"

Sheikh al-Khammas pressed his hands against the ground and rose. "Allah takes away. And Allah gives back." He brushed the dirt from his hands and removed a twig from the hem of his shift. Then he started toward the entrance of the lodge and the two dervishes followed.

When they reached the enormous basket piled high with laundry, Sheikh al-Khammas raised the lid, and the contents, now flawlessly white, gleamed in the sun. He instructed Abbas al-Kumar and Omar al-Hamid to carry it inside. But when they tried to lift it, they found that it was absurdly heavy.

"Perhaps," said Omar al-Hamid, "the weight of cleanliness is greater than the weight of grime!"

"Perhaps," said Abbas al-Kumar, "it's been filled with rocks!"

Even when Sheikh al-Khammas lent a hand, the basket was too weighty to budge. So he decided that the only thing to do was to remove a few things at a time and carry them into the lodge. He reached in and pulled out an armful of towels. Omar al-Hamid scooped up an armful of nightshirts. When Abbas al-Kumar took his turn, however, he froze. Then he cried out:

"Fart of a choleric dog!"

It had been thirty-four years since he'd last uttered this epithet, so he was as surprised as Sheikh al-Khammas and Omar al-Hamid to hear the words fly from his mouth. When they ran to the basket to see what had caused the outcry, however, all thoughts disappeared. For there—beneath the gleaming curtains—below the sparkling robes—lay a beautiful youth in a strange head garment, who seemed utterly dead to the world.

Seventeen

The stupor that Nouri fell into after he'd been abandoned by the marauders had lasted for several days, just like the one he had fallen into after he'd been deserted on the beach by Soledad's father. This time, however—his body exhausted by his days at the laundry—his bloodstream corroded by the fumes of Abdallah's pipe—he tumbled down to the bottom of a dark chasm, where he remained for nearly a month. Upon finding him in the basket, Sheikh al-Khammas instructed Abbas al-Kumar and Omar al-Hamid to carry him into the lodge, remove his clothes, dress him in one of the freshly laundered tunics, and place him in one of the beds in one of the empty rooms. He advised them, however, not to disturb the strange head cloth he wore, as he was unsure of its spiritual implications.

They left him to sleep for several days, checking in on him every so often to be sure that he was still breathing. When he refused to rouse after nearly a week, the Sufi master brewed a strong tea of black horehound and bayberry leaves and carried it to his room. Then he slapped him quite hard on both cheeks and when Nouri opened his eyes he placed the steaming liquid against his lips, and Nouri drank. That was when the struggle began: the fierce blood battle as Nouri's polluted body tried to break free of the grip of Abdallah's pipe. He thrashed in his sleep. He sweated through his bedclothes. He cried out unintelligible phrases. And day after day Sheikh al-Khammas poured the cleansing elixir into his mouth. Eventually, the thrashing and sweating gave way to nausea and trembling. Sheikh al-Khammas added ginger to the brew and had Omar al-Hamid massage Nouri's feet. And at last the hallucinatory flowers worked their way out of his system.

When Nouri finally opened his eyes after his tormented sleep, he was confused to find himself in the bright, airy room. The weeks since he'd been struck on the head at Shohreh's laundry had seemed a feverish dream. And though he'd registered the presence of the man with the white beard—especially when he slapped his face and forced him to drink the foul tea—he was surprised, when the fog finally lifted, to find him sitting beside him.

"You've come back."

Nouri looked into the old man's eyes, which were tinged with fire. "Yes."

"It may take a while for your strength to return. But there's no rush. You're safe here."

Nouri closed his eyes for a moment. Sheikh al-Khammas drew himself to his feet.

"Rest," he said. Then he left the room and Nouri went back to sleep.

When he awoke again, Nouri found himself alone, and for a long while he just lay there, trying to figure out how he'd reached such a sheltering port. Eventually, however, he rose and went to explore his surroundings. He surmised that he was in a lodge like the one in Tan-Arzhan. But unlike that place—whose walls seemed to protect it from the world—his present surroundings seemed to hover above the yearning of everyday life. As he moved past the windows that opened, in every direction, to the sky, it was as if the world had disappeared.

When Nouri reached the doors that led to the garden, he stepped outside. Then he crossed the trimmed lawn to where the man with the white beard was tending the roses.

"They're a bit temperamental this year," said the Sufi master as Nouri approached. "You don't happen to know anything about roses, do you?"

"A bit," said Nouri. "I used to help in the garden when I was a child."

"Well, perhaps you can coax the life back into these."

Nouri nodded. "I can try."

Sheikh al-Khammas pulled a few brown-edged leaves from a stem. Then he turned. "What's your name?"

"Nouri."

"I am Sheikh al-Khammas." He turned his attention back to the roses and snapped off a withered bud. "You must be hungry. Let's go and find you something to eat."

He led Nouri into the lodge, down the hallway, and into a small kitchen that held a table, a pair of benches, and a bookcase lined with bowls and ceramic jars. He told Nouri to sit at the table. Then he drew a series of jars from the shelves and removed their lids. He reached for one of the bowls and filled it with a lumpy mixture. Then he added some seeds and a few cubes of cheese and sprinkled some oil on top. When he offered it to Nouri, it was not very appealing. But Nouri was hungry, so he reached for the heel of bread that Sheikh al-Khammas placed beside the bowl and gobbled it down.

When he'd finished eating, he looked up. "How long have I been here?"

"About a month."

"And how did I get here?"

Sheikh al-Khammas smiled. "You seem to have taken flight in a basket of laundry."

Nouri thought back to that moment when the dowel had snapped and could only praise Allah for having devised such a means to deliver him from a life of fever and fumes.

"Do you know where you are?"

"In a Sufi order."

"And you know what that means?"

Nouri thought back to the lodge in Tan-Arzhan. "I was raised in one. But I seem to have lost my way."

"A true Sufi loses and finds his way many times. Often in a single day." Sheikh al-Khammas paused. "You're welcome to stay here. We're a small order. But our aim is true."

"Thank you," said Nouri. "I would like that."

Sheikh al-Khammas gazed at him a moment longer. Then he left the room and headed back to his cell.

It had been years since anyone had joined the order. And

though he did not wish to burden the arrival of this newcomer with any expectations, Sheikh al-Khammas could not help but feel that the youth would be with them for a while.

OVER THE FOLLOWING DAYS, Sheikh al-Khammas told Nouri the history of the order. Nearly eighty years before, a band of Sufis had made a trek into the mountains and had been so struck by the splendor of the views that they'd decided to create a new order in the clouds. It took twelve years to build the stone complex, and a few years more to cut the path that led up the side of the mountain to its doors. As soon as word of the place got out, however, it attracted devotees from near and far. At one point, nearly sixty dervishes lived beneath its roof, and Sufis came from the farthest corners of the realm to use it as a retreat.

One day, however, the leader of a nearby order proclaimed that it was prideful to perch so high above the heads of the common man. He condemned the order, insisting that moving closer to the heavens could not bring one closer to Allah. A crisis ensued, and the order began to dwindle. That was when Sheikh al-Khammas was brought in. He turned the lodge into a hospice for the ill, trusting that the fresh mountain air would help to heal the infirm and that the task of caring for them would be a spiritual boon to the brothers. But it soon became clear that the times were changing. The young men who chose to embrace the Sufi life no longer wished to live in the clouds. The elder members of the order died. Eventually the lodge became a relic, its heyday described by wandering Sufis on long journeys across the desert or in the middle of the night when it was too hot to sleep.

Now, in addition to Sheikh al-Khammas, there were only four dervishes left: Abbas al-Kumar, Omar al-Hamid, a frail fellow named Yusuf al-Wali, and a dervish known to the rest as "Brother Shadow," who was off on the *hajj* to the Holy City. They swept away the sand that blew up from the desert. They tended the gardens. They cooked one another meals. And they cared for the sick and the needy when they appeared at the door.

"We no longer seek alms," said Sheikh al-Khammas. "With so few of us, we can live on what our lay brothers provide. Which allows us more time to care for the ill. And to commune with God."

For Nouri, the new surroundings were a relief. There was light, and space, and his supersensitive ears were not bombarded by sounds. On top of this, the terrible itching had disappeared. For the first time in as long as he could remember, the world was calm. He stood at the window of his room for hours watching the eagles wheel in the sky. He took long walks in the mountains and sat in the garden beside the pool. When he closed his eyes, however, either to sleep or to pray, he was greeted by painful memories. And though he tried to resist them, he could not seem to shake them away.

One morning, as he was sitting on the curving terrace that had been carved into the western face of the mountain, Sheikh al-Khammas approached.

"May I join you?"

Nouri nodded. "Of course."

The Sufi master lowered himself to the stone bench.

"I'm curious about the head garment you're wearing. I've never seen one that completely covers the ears."

"I'm quite sensitive to sound," said Nouri.

Sheikh al-Khammas nodded. "Sensitivity," he said, "is a great gift to a Sufi."

There was a brief pause. Then the Sufi master spoke again.

"Whatever you've been through, it was designed to make you stronger."

"I know that," said Nouri. "But I can't stop the difficult thoughts from coming."

"Let them come," said Sheikh al-Khammas. "And then let them go."

"When I let them come, I feel like I'm on fire."

"Fire purifies. If you don't resist, it will burn off the poisons in your heart."

Nouri wasn't sure that he could bear the heat. But he tried his best to follow Sheikh al-Khammas's advice. When thoughts of the attack on the lodge in Tan-Arzhan rose up, he tried not to will them away. When memories of The Right Hand pressed in, he allowed himself to burn. He found that if he didn't resist, the fire burned hotter, and then gradually faded. He found that if he focused on the smooth stones beneath his feet or the vast sky over his head, the dark thoughts began to fade.

So once more Nouri became a part of the new world to which fate had carried him. He rose each morning and ate breakfast with the brothers. Then he helped Sheikh al-Khammas tend the roses and keep the reflecting pool free of debris. He enjoyed the work. It brought memories of his childhood. It made his new surroundings feel almost like home.

To Sheikh al-Khammas, Nouri was a conundrum. Having been raised in a dervish order, the youth adapted swiftly to life at the mountain lodge, and his manner suggested the humility and depth of a true Sufi. Yet the fact remained that he had never been inducted into an order. After his month in bed, however—not to mention the trials that seemed to have preceded it—Sheikh al-Khammas felt the rigors of the penitential retreat would be too strenuous for him. So he assigned him the task of washing and feeding the sickly lodgers, and gave him a large stack of books to read. Many of the volumes were familiar to Nouri. The poems of Attar. The writings of al-Ghazali. The holy pages of the Qur'an. But many—like the Hindu Vedanta and the Gnostic Gospels and the Vinaya Pitaka—were new.

"The Sufi finds truth wherever it lies," said Sheikh al-Khammas. "In the pattern of the stars. In the temple of the Jews. It is no insult to the glory of our own Holy Book to examine the wisdom of the others."

So Nouri read. And read. And read.

When he was finished with one stack of books, Sheikh al-Khammas gave him another. The teachings of Zoroaster. The philosophy of Plato. The instructions of the Egyptian papyri. It was like returning to his studies with Sheikh Bailiri when he was a child. But in the range and depth of what he gave him, Sheikh al-Khammas pushed him further. He toppled the boundaries between the faiths, and expanded the limits of Nouri's mind.

One morning, after a few months had passed, Sheikh al-Khammas instructed Abbas al-Kumar to bring Nouri to the garden, where he asked him a single question:

"What is it that keeps you from God?"

Nouri was silent. Then he raised his eyes to Sheikh al-Khammas's. "Nothing can keep me from God if I truly desire to be with him."

The following day, Sheikh al-Khammas sent Omar al-Hamid to Nouri's room with a *khirqa* and a *sikke*. Then he escorted him to the meeting hall and the Sufi master invested him with the mantle of the order.

That was when the real teaching began, as day after day Sheikh al-Khammas brushed the cobwebs from what Nouri had learned when he was a child. Many of the concepts were the same: the need for constant remembrance, the need to place the mind within the heart. Yet it often seemed to Nouri as if he was hearing them for the very first time.

"If knowledge puts you to sleep," said Sheikh al-Khammas, "throw it away. It's pointless to merely repeat what you've been told. You must learn how to think. You must learn how to choose. You must learn how to observe the mind—all its certainty—all its doubt—and root your sense of yourself in what observes, and not in what you observe."

So Nouri tried to observe the contradictions inside him. He practiced remembrance. He struggled with the veil. And as he persisted—day after day after day—the pain of all he'd been through since the attack on the lodge in Tan-Arzhan began to loosen its grip on his heart.

ONE EVENING, A FEW WEEKS after his twenty-first birthday, as Nouri and the others were sharing a bowl of mashed lentils, Sheikh al-Khammas announced that Brother Shadow was about to return.

"A letter arrived this morning from Tlemcen," he said. "He should arrive in a few days."

When Nouri asked why he was called "Brother Shadow," the others smiled.

"It's a reminder—" said Abbas al-Kumar.

"That we each have a dark side to our nature—" said Omar al-Hamid.

"And of the fact—"

"Which we must try to remember—"

"That it can be mastered."

"It's a term of affection," said Sheikh al-Khammas. "For in spite of his manner, Brother Shadow is a man of great spiritual depth."

Yusuf al-Wali twisted his beard. "A true Sufi!"

When Nouri asked how long he'd been away, Sheikh al-Khammas explained that while it was customary to make the journey to the Holy City in the month of Dhu al-Hijja, Brother Shadow preferred to go when it was less besieged. He also preferred to travel alone—following the inland route rather than making his way along the coast—so that he could ride for long periods with only the occasional nomad or a wandering camel herder to disrupt his solitude. He generally remained for an entire season, convinced that the Holy City lent strength to his daily practice. He'd therefore been away for several months, and the news of his return brought the brothers joy.

It was during the evening meal, on the third day after Sheikh al-Khammas's announcement, that the absent Sufi finally appeared. The brothers were eating a stew of preserved lemons and goat when Yusuf al-Wali felt compelled to share a vision he'd had that morning.

"We were seated together in the prayer hall, each with a bowl of fresh milk placed before him. And there was a sixth bowl, which I took to be Brother Shadow's. We reached for our bowls and drank them down, but when we lowered them to the floor we saw that the sixth bowl was now empty as well. Then slowly it began to rise, until it hovered between the ceiling and the floor. It remained there, suspended. Then it shattered into pieces. Then the vision was gone."

The room was still. Then Abbas al-Kumar broke the silence.

"Perhaps Brother Shadow has come to harm—"

"Or perhaps—" said Omar al-Hamid, "it's an omen—"

"About his spiritual condition!"

"Maybe it's a good omen," said Nouri. "When the milk has been drunk, there's no need for the bowl."

There was another silence. Then a soft voice spoke.

"The truth is that our souls hang in the balance until our final moment. We fluctuate between grace and sin and only Allah can say what will happen when the bowl finally shatters."

At the sound of the voice, Nouri turned to see a slender man standing in the doorway.

"Brother Shadow!" cried Abbas al-Kumar.

The man took a step into the room.

"Welcome home," said Sheikh al-Khammas. "I trust that your journey was profitable?"

"How could a visit to the Holy City," said Brother Shadow, "be anything less?"

Sheikh al-Khammas turned. "I'd like to introduce you to the new member of our order. This is Nouri."

Brother Shadow bowed his head. “It’s always a pleasure to meet a fellow traveler on the path.”

Nouri bowed his head in return. But when he raised it, and looked into the dervish’s eyes, he felt an icy hand grip his heart. For though the years had aged him—and the gaunt face was now hidden behind a salt-and-pepper beard—it was perfectly clear that the piercing eyes peering into his were none other than the eyes of his childhood nemesis, Sharoud.

Eighteen

Over the following days, Nouri kept waiting for the moment when Sharoud would suddenly announce to the others that Nouri was a freak—a slip of the hand of Allah—and once again he'd be forced to leave what he'd just begun to call home. For though he knew that Sheikh al-Khammas was as loving as Sheikh Bailiri, who'd taken Nouri's ears as a sign of grace, he could not take the risk that if the *murshid* found out what was hidden beneath his head cloth, Sheikh al-Khammas would deem him unworthy to be a Sufi. Sharoud, however, did not say a word, and Nouri could only assume that he did not connect the young man he now was with the boy he'd been when they'd last parted ways. There were countless fellows named Nouri in the world. And the mountain retreat was a great distance from the simple Sufi lodge in Tan-Arzhan. So Nouri had hope that, against all odds, his secret was still safe.

The weeks passed and Nouri's studies with Sheikh al-Khammas continued. They took long walks into the mountains, and though the Sufi master was nearly four times Nouri's age, he seemed to have twice his stamina. At times he was playful. At times he was aloof. At times he brimmed with the kindness of Sheikh Bailiri and then suddenly cut deep with the directness of Ibn Arwani. The only thing that Nouri could be sure of was that whenever he thought he knew what Sheikh al-Khammas was about to say, he would say something else.

One morning, Sheikh al-Khammas asked Nouri to place new bulbs in the pots that bordered the entrance. So he fetched a spade and a small pail from the garden shed, went out to the entrance of the lodge, and began to work. It was a warm day, and as the sun beat down the sweat began to gather on his neck and brow. When he reached up to wipe away the drops with the back of his hand, he heard a voice.

"Would you like some water?"

Nouri paused. Then he turned around to find Sharoud standing behind him.

"No, thank you."

He turned back to the pots and the bulbs and the dirt, but then Sharoud spoke again.

"Of course, you'd be a good deal cooler if you removed your head garment."

Nouri froze. Then he lowered the spade to the ground and turned back to Sharoud. "How long have you known?"

"From the moment I first saw you."

"But you haven't said a word."

Sharoud's eyes glinted. "What's there to say? Our paths are obviously destined to converge."

Nouri stared at Sharoud. "Are you going to tell them?"

"I don't see the point. If you're some sort of demon, Allah will take care of you." He shrugged. "I have my own demons to fight."

Sharoud paused for a moment, his eyes fixed on Nouri's. Then he turned and walked back into the lodge and Nouri returned to his planting.

It was clear that Sharoud had softened over the years. That his pride had diminished. That his righteousness had dimmed. Yet Nouri was not convinced he'd developed the strength not to reveal his secret. And no matter how much the dark dervish had changed, Nouri knew that it would be a long while before Brother Shadow would win his trust.

WHAT, THEN, IN THE DOZEN or so years since he'd been banished from the order in Tan-Arzhan, had Sharoud been through? What path had he traveled from the time his shoes were turned out at the lodge in Tan-Arzhan to the time when he was a respected member of the mountain order? To be sure, the journey had not been easy. And while it might have been less painful than Nouri's, it was no less marked by twists and turns.

On that first morning, when he'd moved through the braided gates for the last time, Sharoud had been so filled with rage he'd kept walking until the city was far behind him. He slept by the side of the road, his mind teeming with schemes for revenge. All he could think of was how he'd been wronged. All he could see were those monstrous ears.

One day, he stopped at a small village to find water. When he reached the town square, he saw a fountain, but as he approached it he came face-to-face with a young woman whose child had climbed up to take a drink. When their eyes met, he saw fear in the woman's face. Then she scooped up her child and hurried away. And in that moment Sharoud saw how far he had strayed from Allah.

His only choice was to head south into the desert, where he found an oasis that he proceeded to make his home. He remained there for nearly a year, trying to dissolve his rage. His skin darkened to the color of a sweet gum tree, and his body became as thin as a blade of grass. Only when he awoke one morning from a dream in which he was circling an enormous cube did he understand that the only way to cast the anger from his heart was to make his way to the Holy City.

He knew that it would not be an easy path, for Sharoud had no money for either a mount or provisions, and the journey would take many months. So he walked until he came to a city called Shariwaz, which, despite its heat and distance from the other cities of the region, was packed with the pious, and where there was a large Sufi order to take him in. He stayed there for several months, so impressing the head of the order with his zeal that he was given a camel and a small parcel of food so that he might join the *hajj* caravan when it was ready to depart.

The trek across the blazing terrain was grueling. Many turned back and many did not survive the trip. But the rapture that filled Sharoud's heart when he finally entered the Holy City made the effort required to get there seem small. The streets were scattered with pilgrims from each corner of the realm and in the intensity of their fervor Sharoud could feel a collective shout thunder up to God.

On his first evening, Sharoud found lodging at a hospice and began to settle into his new life. He chose to remain in the white *ihram* he'd been given at one of the stations outside the city and—in accordance with the rules of the garment—to refrain from cutting his nails and hair. As a result, he became one of the city's odd progeny, moving through the streets like a streak of white chalk or peering, like a holy specter, from the window of his room. He found that when the pilgrimage month had passed, the harshness of the climate grew worse. His decision to stay therefore symbolized his wish to place his worship above the comforts of his body.

As the months passed, however, Sharoud could not avoid the fact that his heart remained filled with pride. And one morning, as he passed a wizened Sufi leading his disciples through the streets, he saw that his anger at Sheikh Bailiri had kept him from finding another master, and that he could not progress any further without one. So he fastened his *ihram* a bit tighter around his ever-thinning body and set out to find his next teacher.

There were dozens of options scattered along the streets: stout sheikhs who beamed with the confidence of the righteous, gaunt sheikhs who burned with the flames of self-denial, sheiks so ancient they seemed as if they'd crossed over to the other side while still keeping residence in their crumbling bodies. They all appeared wise, and were surrounded by followers. Yet none inspired Sharoud to kneel down and abandon his will to theirs. One evening, however, as he ventured toward the well where the archangel Gabriel was said to have brought water to Abraham's wife, he saw a man seated half-naked upon a wall, bathed in an aura of such peaceful transcendence he could not help but approach him and ask: "Do you know the way to the truth?"

The man gazed serenely into Sharoud's dark eyes.

"I know nothing," he said.

It was not what Sharoud was expecting to hear, but it so pleased him he begged the man to allow him to be his disciple. The man merely shrugged. So Sharoud stripped half-naked, and for the next several years they traveled together across desert and mountain—begging for alms, sleeping beneath the stars, emptying their hearts of all feeling and their minds of all thought. At times, Sharoud found the journey unbearable. But eventually he felt the anger inside him lift and a wonderful lightness take its place.

He might have continued on this way forever. But one day the half-naked saint suddenly spoke. "You've made progress," he said. "Your spirit is stronger than it was. But now you need to be tested."

He then explained that he would take Sharoud to Cairo, where he would be placed into service as a camel attendant in the court of the Sultan. The challenge would be to remain as empty in that teeming city as he was now, on the barren road, beneath the open sky. If he could achieve this, then Allah's dominion over his heart would be secure.

Sharoud had no choice but to follow his master's will. So in less than a fortnight he found himself in the sprawling metropolis along the Nile. To his purified senses, the city was a shock: like riding on the back of a wild stallion or drinking twelve cups of black koshary tea. He found, however, that he enjoyed the simple task of tending the camels. And nothing—from the bustle of the Bayn al-Qasrayn to the frenzied cries that rose up from the *khans*—seemed to threaten the inner quiet he'd attained.

He was therefore unfazed when it was announced one day that the Sultan would be traveling to a foreign court and that, as he would ride no camel but his own—a proud Bactrian the color of skimmed goat's milk that he called the Pearl of Giza—Sharoud would be required to go along. So he prepared the noble beast for the journey and they set out through the gates of the palace and over the dusty roads to an elegant barge that took them downriver to the sea, where they boarded an enormous five-masted vessel that carried them safely across the water. When they reached the far shore, they disembarked. Then they traveled on until they arrived at the foreign palace, where the two potentates sat down to tea and tried to convince one another that each was wiser and wealthier and more filled with an inviolable love for Allah than the other.

The great men conferred for three days, during which time Sharoud was able to explore the grimy city that clung, like a canker, to the palace gates. He found a mosque where he could pray, and spent most of his time either there or in the small windowless room he'd been given to share with the other attendants, who were far too distracted by the city's charms to pay heed to their unsociable companion. On the third morning, however, he decided to venture out to the palace gardens to practice *zikr*. His heart was light and as he settled himself on a marble bench he could feel Allah beckon from the fountains and the stones. Before he could dissolve in remembrance, however, he heard the sound of footsteps, and when he turned he saw a boy about the age of sixteen scurrying down the path. Sharoud would not have given him another thought had he not perceived, in a blinding flash, that it was none other than Nouri Ahmad Mohammad ibn Mahsoud al-Morad. For on that morning when Nouri had crept through the palace at dawn and had imagined he'd seen Sharoud, he hadn't imagined it at all. And though the youth shook the thought from his mind the moment he moved through the palace gates, Sharoud was consumed by the thought of Nouri from that moment on.

In the mosque—on the street—as he moved through the glittering halls of the palace—all he could think of were the ears that lurked beneath the youth's head cloth and the injustice of having been made to leave the order in Tan-Arzhan for bringing them to light. The thorn he'd tried for eight years to remove from his side was still deeply embedded. The poison he'd struggled to purge from his quarrelsome heart still flowed in his veins. And this was no more evident than when the three men with whom he shared the tiny room stumbled in, after an evening of carousing, and he sprang up in his bed and cried:

"For the sake of Allah, shut your polluted mouths and be still!"

A hush fell over the room as the revelers gaped at their seething bedfellow.

"He speaks!"

"It's a miracle!"

"He's actually human!"

Sharoud said nothing. But human was precisely what he did not wish to be. So when they returned to Cairo, he went to the *seyhulislam* of the palace mosque and asked for help.

"My heart is unclean. I need to remove myself from the world." He paused for a moment. "Again."

The *seyhulislam* was not a Sufi, yet he knew from the burnished glint in Sharoud's eye what he needed. So he sent him to join the order in the clouds, where Sharoud began his life as Brother Shadow.

It had been five years now since the mountain retreat had become his home. And little by little the clean air and the daily prayer and the simple coexistence with the brothers restored the peace to his heart. He knew, though, that that peace would be tested. So when he returned that evening to find Nouri sitting at the table in the kitchen, he felt neither anger nor surprise. Only the keen understanding that—no matter where he traveled—no matter how deeply he prayed—this boy was a challenge that he could not avoid.

FOR NOURI, THE MAIN CHALLENGE was to prevent Sharoud's reappearance from creating a veil between himself and God. For from the moment Sharoud revealed that he knew who he was, Nouri's peace of mind was completely shattered. Resentment rose up. Insecurity. Fear. He tried to remove them with prayer, but the more that he looked within, the more flaws he observed. Obstinacy. Naïveté. Self-pity. Self-doubt. How could such a tainted vessel draw near to God?

He went to Sheikh al-Khammas to seek advice. But the Sufi master's words only confused him.

"The Sufi Way is the way of self-knowledge. God knows himself. When you know yourself, you will know God."

For the first time, Nouri began to contemplate making the long and arduous journey to the Holy City. Sharoud seemed to have been deeply affected by his trips and, despite it being one of the basic pillars of the faith to make the pilgrimage at least once, Nouri had never been. He'd observed that Sheikh al-Khammas never spoke about the *hajj* or gave any indication that he should go. When he told him of his wish to make the journey, however, the Sufi master's response was immediate.

"The caravan leaves from Cairo in six weeks. Omar al-Hamid will accompany you until you reach the posting station. Then you'll continue on with the others."

The following day, Sheikh al-Khammas found a lay brother named Faraz al-Aziz who was willing to provide Nouri with a camel. So Nouri set about to gather his provisions—and his strength—for the journey.

On the morning of his departure, Nouri bid farewell to the other brothers. Then he and Omar al-Hamid started down the mountain path. They continued through the village, across the desert, for days and nights, until they reached the place, just east of the throbbing city, from which the caravan would depart. Nouri was amazed at how many pilgrims there were: thousands of men, women, and children, each determined to place his or her feet on the soil where the Prophet had been spoken to by God. When the last of them had gathered, they headed out in an orderly procession behind the Sultan's *mahmal*, traveling eastward until they reached the oasis of Kuman. From there, they headed south, through the mountains, until they reached the city of Nadiz. They paused in Nadiz for several days to water their camels and rest. Then they continued on through the wretched terrain that stretched between there and Medina, the last stop before they reached the hallowed city of Mecca.

The journey from the posting station to Medina took forty-six days. Some pilgrims died of exposure along the way. Others of thirst. Some forgot the reason they'd made the trip. Others forgot their names. But when they reached Medina, their spirits rallied. They visited the Prophet's tomb and the Prophet's mosque and intoned their collective thanks to Allah. Then they loaded their camels with fresh provisions, rode to a station outside the city—where the men removed their clothes, bathed, and put on their *ihrams*—and set off on the final leg of the dusty journey.

It was a crisp autumn morning when Nouri finally entered the Holy City. He was struck by the power of the place, but whether that power was due to the fact that the Prophet had been born there, the fact that it was where he had received the Holy Book, or the sheer number of bodies that overflowed its narrow streets, he couldn't say. He only knew that he was swept along on a sea of prayer to the center of the Haram, where he joined in the impassioned circling of the great stone cube.

Nouri spent fifteen days in the Holy City. The constant eruptions of sound—the donkeys, the bells, the booming calls to prayer—were overwhelming to his ever-sensitive ears. But he stuffed them with some wax he purchased from a candlemaker and soldiered on. He found lodging at a Sufi hospice not far from the Grand Mosque, which allowed him to go there whenever he liked. He also performed the other rites of the *hajj*: the prayers at the Maqam Ibrahim, the "Running" between the hills of al-Safa and al-Marwa, the "Standing" beneath the Mount of Mercy on the plain of Arafat. At the end of the visit, he joined the Feast of the Sacrifice. Then he removed his *ihram* and headed home.

The journey back was even longer than the journey there. When they reached Nadiz, an illness swept through their weary ranks and the caravan had to remain there for nearly a month before they could travel on. A windstorm impeded their progress to Cairo, and by the time Nouri reached the gates of the mountain lodge he was gaunt and sun-dazed and aching with fatigue. The brothers were eager to hear of his adventures and Nouri did not hold back. But only Sheikh al-Khammas knew the truth, which he conveyed in a single glance.

The journey was thrilling.

Inspiring.

Exalting.

And, in the end, it did not change a thing.

"You would never have believed me if I'd told you," said Sheikh al-Khammas. "You had to learn the truth for yourself: the real Holy City is within."

Nouri wasn't sorry he'd made the trip. It had stirred his heart and strengthened his will. But he knew that Sheikh al-Khammas was right. So he focused his efforts on finding the Mecca within. He poured himself into the world of nature. He sat in the chapel mosque, trying to merge with a higher world. At times, the sharp line around things would melt and he would unite with a bird or a cloud or a tree. But the moment would always pass, and the feeling of separateness would return.

Perhaps he hadn't suffered enough.

Or paid enough.

Or prayed enough.

"Who are you, Nouri?" Sheikh al-Khammas would say. "You must keep asking yourself. Over and over."

So the members of the tiny order in the clouds fell to the ground and lowered their heads and extended their arms and tried to observe who they were and who they were not.

I am not this withered body, thought Sheikh al-Khammas.

I am not this resentment or this disdain, thought Sharoud.

I am not these yearnings or these fears, thought Nouri. *Or these ears.*

And the days passed. And Nouri's connection with God flickered on and off, like a torch in a storm. And he prayed that he could find the strength to keep it from going out.

PART FIVE

Nineteen

So time began to change shape at the little Sufi lodge in the mountains. The days came and the days went and Nouri and Sheikh al-Khammas and Sharoud and Abbas al-Kumar and Omar al-Hamid and Yusuf al-Wali tried to empty themselves and love God. And they moved closer to the mark and they drew further away. And they struggled. And they plummeted. And they soared. And the final layer of softness was whittled from Nouri's cheeks. And Sharoud's hair turned from black sprinkled with white to white sprinkled with black. And Abbas al-Kumar grew fatter. And Omar al-Hamid grew thinner. And Yusuf al-Wali grew frailer. And Sheikh al-Khammas's skin became so gauze-like it revealed the fine tracery of the capillaries that feathered beneath it. And two years, and five years, and eight years passed.

And Sheikh al-Khammas continued to mold Nouri. To temper him. To confound his logical mind and shatter the constructs within him that kept him from God.

"You must be vigilant," said the Sufi master. "The house is on fire. And you just sit there, staring at the flames."

When ten years had passed, Sheikh al-Khammas sent Nouri to an order in a nearby village to teach. Nouri didn't feel he was ready, but Sheikh al-Khammas knew the only way he could progress further on the path was to share his understanding with others. Nouri spent an entire year there, trying to impart what he'd learned from Sheikh al-Khammas. And though he could not say, when the year had passed, if he'd deepened the understanding of any of the brothers he'd taught, there was no doubt in his mind that he'd strengthened his own.

Another year passed. Another two. Another four. Nouri was now thirty-eight—nearly twice the age he'd been when he'd first arrived at the lodge. Yusuf al-Wali had died that spring, reducing the brothers' number from six to five. And while they'd grown used to one another's habits and quirks over the passing years, Sheikh al-Khammas was always aware of the unspoken tension—subtle as the fragrance of a peach blossom—between Nouri and Sharoud. Despite the countless meals they'd shared and the countless times they'd knelt beside one another in *zikr,* they always seemed to avoid each other's gaze. So one day—just as Sheikh Bailiri had found a way to bring Nouri and Vishpar together so many years before—Sheikh al-Khammas devised a plan to dissolve the distance between Nouri and Sharoud.

On that sunlit morning, the Sufi master and Nouri were sitting in the garden, as they had sat, almost daily, for so many years.

Nouri—whose beard had grown thick and whose gaze was now firm and sure—was splitting open the large seedpods the carob tree had scattered upon the grass and was launching them, like tiny *feluccas,* onto the surface of the pool. They rarely spoke as they sat together. Nouri had asked all the questions worth asking and Sheikh al-Khammas had imparted what wisdom he could. But today there was a plan to hatch, so the Sufi master broke the silence.

"It's been years since anyone came to receive succor. It's not good for us. We're cut off from the pulse of life."

"We need a good sickness to strike the village!" said Nouri.

"Don't say such a thing!" said Sheikh al-Khammas, laughing. "Allah hears!"

He reached for one of the pods that lay near his feet and gave it to Nouri, who cracked it open and added it to the fleet.

"Besides, there is a sickness in the village. A kind of blood fever. I've been told that the hospice is nearly full."

"We should go and help them."

"I agree. But I'm too old to travel down the mountain. And Abbas al-Kumar and Omar al-Hamid are useless with the infirm." He paused. "I think you and Brother Shadow should go."

Nouri was silent a moment. Then he nodded. "We'll head out this morning."

An hour later, Nouri and Sharoud met at the front gate and began the long walk down the mountain to the village below. They'd circled each other for years now, each one insisting that time and the grace of Allah had melted the hardness between them, yet each fully aware that it wasn't so. So they walked in silence—Nouri trying to keep Sharoud's piety at the forefront of his mind,

Sharoud trying to suppress the ever-disturbing thought of Nouri's ears.

When they reached the hospice—a flat-roofed building with a dormitory, a kitchen, and a small room for the gravely ill—they were welcomed in. Nouri was given a cloth, a bowl of water, and a bottle of vinegar to cool the patients' brows. Sharoud was given a pail of soapy water and a mop to keep the place clean. They worked all day at their separate tasks. Then they made their way back through the village and up the mountain to the lodge.

Over the following weeks, they met each morning and accompanied each other to the hospice. But whether they walked together in the wide morning light or the gathering shadows of dusk, they did not utter a single word. One day, however, about three weeks after they'd begun their labors, as they were heading down the mountain, Sharoud spoke.

"I need to stop for a drink of water," he said. "There's a dwelling at the foot of the mountain. I've been there before."

Nouri was so accustomed to the silence that always shrouded them on their walks that he was unable to respond. So he followed Sharoud to the foot of the mountain and then on to a small building that stood a few hundred paces from the path. When they reached it, Sharoud knocked loudly upon the door. There was a moment's pause. Then it opened, and a spindly man whose arms and hands and face were covered with dark smudges peered out.

"I've come for water," Sharoud shouted at the man.

The man—whom Nouri assumed must be deaf—said nothing. Instead, he turned and began to make his way across the room. As he did, Nouri looked inside and saw that it was a workshop, the floors strewn with pieces of charred wood, the table scattered with hammers and ratchets and bowls filled with an assortment of colored powders. There was a strong smell of sulfur in the air, and the walls and ceiling were covered with dark smudges, just like the man. When the man reached the far wall, he fetched a pair of cups from a shelf. Then he hobbled back to where Nouri and Sharoud waited, gave them the cups, and closed the door.

Sharoud—who seemed to think nothing of the fellow's strange behavior—turned. "Follow me," he said.

He led Nouri around the building to a well, where he drew fresh water to fill the cups. They drank. He refilled the cups and they drank again. Then he turned back to Nouri.

"We should return these to the fellow before we go."

Nouri nodded, and reached out his hand. "I'll take them."

Sharoud handed his cup to Nouri. Then they started back to the door.

As Nouri made his way over the dusty ground, he thought of the rheumy-eyed patients who awaited him at the hospice. There was one in particular who brought a smile to his lips: an old fellow with a kind, lumpy face who reminded him of Habbib. When Nouri sat pressing the moist towel against the fellow's forehead, he could see his old friend walking along the river, kneeling in the garden, telling him stories before bed. He was so lost, in fact, in this double layer of imagination—imagining himself at the hospice, where he would imagine himself at the lodge in Tan-Arzhan—he almost believed that he'd imagined it as well when a sound louder than anything he'd ever heard suddenly ripped through his ears and hurled him to the ground.

When Nouri came to, he felt the ground hard beneath him and the crumbling dirt stinging his eyes. But as he lay there, watching smoke pour through the open window, he felt a strange sense of calm. The feeling was undisturbed when the door flew open and the man stumbled out, gasping for air. But it was only when Nouri saw Sharoud running toward him—mouth open—seeming to cry out—that he realized he could not hear a thing.

FOR SOMEONE ACCUSTOMED to a lifetime of intensified shouts, screams, sobs, wails, growls, yowls, yammers, whimpers, grunts, snarls, barks, bleats, bangs, clangs, squawks, tweets, thumps, thuds, yawps, yips, honks, snorts, hoots, whispers, buzzes, howls, hollers, hisses, cackles, screeches, moans, groans, clicks, clacks, whines, cheers, moos, coos, clinks, squeaks, jingles, jangles, booms, shrieks, yelps, yaps, whoops, bellows, woofs, quacks, trills, caws, clucks, whinnies, yells, and roars, the sudden absence of sound made it seem as if Nouri had been transported to another world. He watched as the spindly man staggered toward him. He watched as Sharoud knelt down and rolled him over onto his back. But without the crunch of the dirt beneath their feet or the sound of their voices, it all seemed like a dream.

As the smoke cleared, Sharoud helped Nouri to his feet. It was clear that no bones had been broken, but when the elder dervish asked him if he felt any pain, Nouri did not say a word. Sharoud realized that Nouri's hearing had been damaged, so he started to lead him off to the hospice to be examined. But Nouri knew that in order to be examined he'd have to remove his head cloth. So he raised his hands to his ears and shook his head.

"Please," he said. "Just take me back to the lodge."

Sharoud understood. So he took Nouri's arm and escorted him back up the mountain.

When Sharoud told Sheikh al-Khammas what had happened, the Sufi master wanted to inspect Nouri's ears. Nouri, however, would not allow his head cloth to be touched, and Sheikh al-Khammas—believing the Sufi's body to be a sacred vessel—respected his wishes. Instead, he fetched a sheet of paper and a pen and wrote a message to Nouri:

"God has placed his hands over your ears for a reason. He can remove them whenever he likes."

As the days passed, however, Nouri's hearing didn't return. And while the loss only strengthened his other senses—the roses in the garden smelled sweeter—the sun felt warmer on his back—it was strange to no longer hear the wind rattle his window or the rain pelt the roof or Omar al-Hamid intone the call to prayer. After a lifetime of being pierced by the tiniest vibration, Nouri's world had gone utterly still.

Despite the perfect silence without, it became quickly apparent to Nouri that there was no silence within. For without the roaring and crashing of the day, he was unable to escape the relentless rumble of his thoughts. The concerns and regrets and complaints and ruminations were all there, whether he wished them to be or not. And it was only after weeks of trying to quell them, as he sat on the bench in the garden one morning, that he remembered the refuge of words.

It startled him when he realized how long it had been since he'd put pen to paper. He'd not written a word since he'd fled the brutal embrace of The Right Hand. But now, with the absolute silence without and the constant clamor within, he was again drawn to the tender act of giving shape to his perceptions. As he moved through the lodge, simple phrases would appear. As he toiled in the garden, they would extend themselves into verse. And as the weeks passed, it became more and more clear that he wished to preserve them. So he asked Sheikh al-Khammas for a quill and some paper and began writing them down.

He wrote. And he wrote. And he wrote. And he wrote.

When he was finished with a page, he would place it in the wooden chest beneath his window, where the winter blankets—which he unfolded and laid beneath his bed—had been stored. Then he would reach for the quill and the next sheet of paper and continue writing. It was like traveling back to his cell in Tan-Arzhan or the Court of the Speckled Dove. This time, however, he did not write to celebrate the roses or the sunset or anyone's arms, but to stave off the voices inside his head.

There were times when Nouri wondered if Sharoud, in the deepest part of his being, had known that the explosion would occur, had coaxed him to the workshop in the hope that he would lose his hearing—perhaps even lose his life. What he did not realize was that Sharoud wondered the very same thing. And that even he could not see into his own heart deeply enough to know the truth.

IT TOOK TIME FOR THE BROTHERS to get used to the fact that Nouri now lived in a world of silence. If Abbas al-Kumar asked him to pass the lentils, he would sit there as if nothing had been said. If Omar al-Hamid called his name while he was tending the roses, he would not turn around. Eventually, however, Nouri learned to discern what the others were saying by the movements of their lips, and it was not long before he was able to engage in conversation. So in time his inability to hear simply became another fact of life at the mountain lodge.

Despite the pleasure it gave him to write, Nouri was careful to shield the activity from the eyes of the brothers. He'd learned the danger of being praised for his verse, and he did not wish to lose what he'd struggled so hard to reach by seeming to boast of what he knew. Yet the daily act of transforming the world into words had a curative power. It stilled his mind. It allowed him to bear the silence that surrounded him like a fortress. So he continued on, taking pains to keep his writing hidden from sight.

Sharoud and Abbas al-Kumar and Omar al-Hamid had no idea that Nouri was writing. They noticed the extra time he spent in his cell, but they assumed the sudden silence he'd been thrust into had increased his desire to be alone. Only Sheikh al-Khammas seemed to understand the truth. For one thing, Nouri came to his cell over and over to get paper and ink. But more than that, as Nouri floated from room to room, Sheikh al-Khammas could see the words taking shape behind his eyes. The Sufi master would never have brought the subject up, however, had not fate—that old juggler—arranged for him to stumble upon the verses one day.

It was a quiet morning, even for the mountain lodge. Abbas al-Kumar had gone to town to buy provisions. Omar al-Hamid had wandered high into the mountains. Nouri and Sharoud had ventured off to their respective work at the hospice. So Sheikh al-Khammas was alone, and as he moved through the empty halls, it seemed as if the world had completely disappeared. He ate his breakfast in his cell, taking pleasure from the shapes the rising sun cast through the window. He sat in the garden and listened to the wind stir the argan tree. It was a cold morning, and as the day waxed, the chill in the air did not recede. And that was when Sheikh al-Khammas knew that winter was on its way.

He'd have to make sure that the larder was stocked with dried beef and chickpeas and grains. He'd have to check that the windows were sealed tight and that the brothers kept warm at night. And since the last of these tasks was the only one he could take care of alone, he decided to fetch the winter blankets from the chest beneath the window of Nouri's room.

He would never have thought to invade Nouri's privacy. But when he knelt down and raised the lid of the wooden chest he was so surprised to find the stack of written pages he could not help but pull one out and begin to read. Once he'd read one, he could not help but read another. And another. And another. Until he sank to the cold tiles and read them all.

When he'd finished, he gathered the pages, placed them back in the chest, and lowered the lid. Then he rose, brushed the creases from his robe, and continued on with his day. That evening, however, when Nouri returned, Sheikh al-Khammas went to see him.

"May I enter?" he asked, as he stood at the open door.

"Of course," said Nouri.

The Sufi master stepped into the room. "I must apologize to you."

"For what?"

"I came to your cell today while you were gone. My intention was to fetch the blankets. But I found your verses."

"And you read them?"

"I didn't mean to. But once I began reading, I couldn't stop. You have a gift, Nouri."

"They're a distraction," said Nouri. "A diversion. That's all."

Sheikh al-Khammas shook his head. "They're a sign that you need to empty your cup." He gazed into Nouri's eyes. "I think it's time that you took on a disciple."

Nouri furrowed his brow at the Sufi master's words. "But who would I teach? No one has come to join the order in years."

"He will appear. If he's what you need, I assure you. He will appear."

Nouri knew better than to question his teacher. So he thanked him for his words, and Sheikh al-Khammas left the room.

For a long while after the Sufi master had gone, Nouri stood at the window of his cell watching the light fade from the sky. He knew that what Sheikh al-Khammas had said was true: at a certain point, the only way to progress on the spiritual path was to find a pupil. But Nouri could not imagine anyone arriving at the lodge to receive instruction. Especially from him.

Twenty

The signs were there even before Ryka was born. Only weeks after he'd appeared in his mother's womb, still more amphibian than childlike, the roses on the north side of the house began to wither, while those on the south side began to bloom. At three months, the throbbing in his father's left leg suddenly switched to his right. And just before his mother gave birth, the rust-colored hen stopped laying her eggs in the backyard and began depositing them beside the front gate.

Still, no one connected these things to the frail child who arrived one late-summer morning. Neither did they connect them to the strange bluish cast to his skin, which caused the midwife to cross the village to alert her cousin, who carved headstones, to the prospect of new business. As the day was quite warm, it was clear that the child wasn't cold. And though his mother feared she'd eaten too many of the deep purple figs her husband had filched from their neighbor's tree, she knew the moment she held her new child in her arms that something was wrong with the inner workings of his body.

It was therefore almost a relief—after an hour of thumping and poking and pressing his ear against the child's springy chest—when the doctor who'd come to inspect him explained that the architecture of his infant heart was reversed, that the slick tubes and soft, spongy chambers were transposed, that his blood was shuttled along a different pathway to the lungs, depleting it of its rich, reddening color. All Ryka's mother knew was that her impulses toward the child were not what she had expected. When he cried, rather than scoop him up, she would move farther away. When she held him to her breast, rather than swoon, she would cringe. And since his father had no use for a boy who was fragile and vaguely blue, Ryka's childhood was lonely, his heart marked less by its strange design than by having a mother and father who disliked having him around.

As time passed, the child grew into a delicate youth with a faraway look in his eyes. The other children in the village kept their distance—partly because he couldn't join in their games and partly because they were confused by his strange, distant manner. There was nothing sinister about him, like Sharoud, yet not a single person in the village had ever seen him smile. On top of this was the issue of his spells: at various intervals he would become lightheaded and dizzy and have to squat down low to the ground. The bluish tint to his skin increased, and by the time he rose back to his feet, he'd scarred the surface of the day.

One morning, around the time of his eighth birthday, he scarred more than that. He was heading to the pump to fetch water for the baking. It was a gray day and his mother had decided to make some *khabisa*, whose nutty fragrance always cheered her up. As Ryka walked along, there wasn't a sign of trouble. But a few paces from the well he felt the constriction in his chest and the spinning in his head and, before he could squat down, he toppled to the ground. Had the rake been just a few fingers to the left, it would have gouged out his eye. Instead, one of its tines tore a small patch of flesh from his right cheekbone. When he stumbled back to the house, his face streaming with blood, his mother was so shaken she poured vinegar, instead of rosewater, into the *khabisa*. But she salved and bandaged the wound and when the cloth was removed, a week later, Ryka was graced with a tiny square just beneath his left eye.

Although the spells continued, there was no pattern to their coming. Sometimes he had two or three in the same week. Other times, months would pass without an occurrence. Since he was not made for running or jumping or climbing, he devoted himself to books. And the more he read, the more he felt sure that another life waited for him, away from the heat and the crushing disinterest of his parents.

One afternoon, when he was fourteen, he was sent to market, and as he was standing at the cheese sellers' stall he overheard a pair of men talking about the small band of Sufis who made their home in the clouds. Their description of the simple lodge and the ascetic brothers was enthralling to Ryka. So he decided that when he turned eighteen he would go to join them. He spent the intervening years reading book after book about the spiritual path. Yet he sensed no words could ever convey what real practice was like.

On the morning of his eighteenth birthday, he awoke early and told his parents of his plans. And though time and the sun had tempered the bluish cast of his skin to a muted gray, they were happy to let him go. So he gathered a few things into a satchel and headed off to climb the long, dusty path to the mountain lodge.

It was almost dusk when he finally reached the Sufi dwelling. The door was open, so he stepped inside and wandered down the long corridor until he reached the kitchen, where Sheikh al-Khammas was seated at the table shelling beans. When their eyes met, a look of recognition passed between them. And even before he could say why he was there, Sheikh al-Khammas made a gesture for him to sit.

"It's a long walk," he said. "Even the most devoted of Allah's servants can flag from the exertion."

Ryka stepped into the room and sat down on the bench opposite Sheikh al-Khammas. The Sufi master reached for an empty bowl and filled it with half of the remaining beans. Then they worked together in silence as the light slowly faded from the sky.

There were words, of course, that would need to be exchanged.

"Where have you come from?"

"What do you seek?"

"What will I have to give up?"

But Ryka knew that at last he'd found a place where the rules of life, like his fragile heart, were reversed. And Sheikh al-Khammas knew that Nouri's pupil had finally arrived.

WHILE RYKA WAS GETTING READY to climb the mountain, Nouri was deeply immersed in his writing. Day after day he gave birth to new poems—refining each image, sculpting each phrase, stilling the random chatter in his head, and drawing nearer to God. He waited for nothing and nothing waited for him. The silence engulfed him. Consumed him. Protected him. He ate and he wrote and he prayed and he wrote and he watered the roses and he sat in the garden and he went to the hospice to bandage the wounded and cool the feverish brows of the infirm. And he wrote.

Sharoud, on the other hand, writhed. For despite his long years of penance, he could not free himself from the dark thoughts he harbored toward Nouri. He'd tried to keep them hidden away, like a patch of brindled skin beneath his tunic. He'd refrained from telling the brothers about Nouri's ears, convinced that his efforts to remain silent were proof that he'd mastered his ill feelings. He told himself that the distance he kept from Nouri was a sign of respect. He told himself that he was pleased—even grateful—that the winds of fate had blown him to the lodge. When the explosion at the workshop occurred, however, it brought Sharoud's antipathy to the surface. Nouri's beauty—which had only deepened over the years—made Sharoud feel enraged at the thought of his own sunken cheeks and small, beady eyes. Nouri's grace—which was now counterbalanced by a gentle wisdom—made his own awkward movements seem grotesque. And the beatific state that Nouri seemed to have entered when the clatter of the world had been removed evoked a deep feeling of envy. So what began as disgust, and fanned into outrage, and was covered over by a grudging acceptance, finally burst into full-blown hatred. Which Sharoud knew was utterly intolerable in a servant of Allah.

He could not say where the needle had come from. Perhaps it had fallen from Abbas al-Kumar's lap as he sat in the garden mending his tunic. Perhaps it had dropped from the hem of Omar al-Hamid's robe. He only knew that when he saw it—glinting in the grass like the dagger of a tiny *djinn*—it offered a pathway to redemption. So he slipped it into the folds of his cloak and carried it to his cell.

That night, when the brothers had retired to their separate chambers, Sharoud placed the needle in the flame of the squat taper beside his bed and jabbed it into the sole of his foot. The following night, he inserted it into the palm of his hand. The night after that, he pierced the tender flesh between his hip bone and ribs.

For his spiritual salvation hung in the balance.

And he knew that his time was running out.

WHEN SHEIKH AL-KHAMMAS gathered the brothers in the meeting hall to introduce Ryka, they each had a different response. Since Abbas al-Kumar now found it hard to crouch down to the ground, he hoped the youth might take over the weeding. Since no one had appeared at their door since Nouri's arrival in a basket of laundry, Omar al-Hamid was relieved that the order would continue on after his death.

"He's not very strong—" said Abbas al-Kumar.

"But he's stronger than we are—" said Omar al-Hamid.

"And he's young—"

"Which is refreshing—"

"And which may attract others—"

"If it's the will—"

"Of Allah."

Sharoud felt the youth lacked the vigor and strength that were required of a true Sufi. Yet he could not deny that his arrival brought new life to the mountain lodge. Only Nouri had no thoughts when he gazed upon the new aspirant. For the tender glance and the slender frame and the unusual color of his skin—was it slate?—was it ash?—brought a perfect stillness to his mind. He could only stand there and listen as Sheikh al-Khammas explained that, while Ryka was not ready to be inducted into the order, he was to be treated as a fellow traveler on the path. He would wash the floors. He would weed the garden. He would help Abbas al-Kumar and Sheikh al-Khammas prepare the meals. And he would study with Nouri the basic tenets and principles of Sufism.

To Ryka, it was like stepping into a strange and wonderful new world. He was given the room next to Nouri's, which, though smaller, had the same majestic views of the open sky. And while it was true that he lacked the robustness of a typical boy of eighteen, he made up for it with the strength of his devotion to his tasks. He washed the floors until they gleamed. He removed each weed the very moment that it appeared. And though he curdled his first batch of yogurt and charred a week's worth of *naan*, he was soon indispensable to Abbas al-Kumar.

It wasn't until a fortnight had passed that the youth had his first lesson with Nouri. He was a bit nervous about it. He'd been told that Nouri had lost his hearing and that he conversed with the others by reading lips. But the rest of the brothers were so old, it seemed to Ryka that they might have studied with the Prophet himself. So he knew that if he was going to have a friend in the order, it would be Nouri.

For Nouri's part, he'd tried not to think too much about the task Sheikh al-Khammas had set before him. He assumed that the youth needed time to settle into his new life, and that he'd come knocking at his door when he was ready to begin his studies. He felt utterly unprepared, however, when he turned to find him standing in the doorway.

"I've come for my first lesson," said Ryka.

Nouri studied the young fellow's lips as he formed the words. "Let's go outside," he said. "We can sit on the terrace."

He rose from his desk, crossed the room, and led Ryka down the hallway and out to the small bench that was carved into the side of the mountain. As they sat, he could feel that the boy was no more ready to learn the secrets of the Sufi life than he was ready to teach them. So they'd have to find their way forward together.

"What brings you to us?"

Ryka thought carefully before answering. "Absence."

"Absence?"

"From others. From myself." He brushed a few strands of hair from his forehead. "I'm tired of feeling I don't belong."

"In your village? In your family?"

He paused. Then he shook his head. "In the world."

A hawk flew by and they both turned to follow it as it vanished into the distance. When they turned back to face each other, Nouri noticed the small scar beneath Ryka's left eye.

"Where have you studied?"

"I haven't," said Ryka. "I've read a lot. But I have no formal training."

Nouri nodded. "Then you'll have to begin now."

He told Ryka to return to his chores and then meet him again the same time the following day. Then he went to his room to consider the complex of feelings that stirred inside him. He knew he could explain the rules of the Sufi path. The question was whether he could impart their inner meaning to Ryka. So much of what he'd come to understand had been revealed through pain. What did the words really mean without the struggle that had etched them into his heart? But perhaps it was his role to lay down a foundation for the youth, as Sheikh Bailiri had done for him. And perhaps Ryka had already suffered in ways he was unaware of.

The following morning, Ryka was seated on the bench when Nouri arrived. Nouri was now nearly forty, but when he looked at the youth he could not help but picture himself at that age: lost in the haze of Abdallah's pipe and the whirling madness of the seaside town. The boy who sat before him seemed a good deal wiser. So Nouri shook the thoughts from his head and joined him on the bench.

"Good morning," he said.

"Good morning," said Ryka.

"Did you rest well?"

Ryka shrugged. "Not really."

"It's the altitude. The air is thinner. It takes a while to adjust."

"I don't sleep very well," said Ryka. "But then I never have. I'm used to it by now."

"Perhaps you need a more strenuous task," said Nouri. "When I work very hard during the day, I sleep like a baby at night."

Ryka paused a moment. "I have a problem with my heart."

"Is it serious?"

Ryka shrugged again. Then he turned his head to look out at the mountains, and Nouri fixed his eyes upon him. He had the grace of a panther. He was alert, yet at the same time he seemed fiercely attuned to another world. Before Nouri could study him any further, however, the youth turned back.

"How did you lose your hearing?" said Ryka.

"There was an explosion," said Nouri.

"When?"

Nouri closed his eyes and thought back. "It's been almost a year now."

"And you hear nothing?" said Ryka.

Nouri shook his head. "Not a sound."

Ryka tried to imagine what it would be like to hear nothing. Not the patter of the rain upon the roof. Not the rustling of a leaf.

"Where would you like to begin?" said Nouri.

"That's a difficult question."

"Not really. Wherever we begin, we always wind up at God."

Ryka thought for a moment. "Then explain how to get there. Tell me about the Stages of the Journey."

Nouri was silent. There were so many things that the boy would have to grapple with before he was ready to grasp the Stages of the Journey. But he'd asked him where he wished to begin, so he leaned forward and launched into a description of the lengthy process that led from the Gateway to Awakening through the Door of Self-Denial to the Development of Conduct—and Character—and Principles—and then onward up the perilous slope until one arrived at Unity with God. Ryka sat very still as he listened. And though he stopped Nouri every now and then to ask questions—

"What is the difference between peacefulness and tranquility?"

"How does one move from intoxication to sobriety?"

"How does one submit to annihilation?"

—he mostly listened, his eyes firmly fixed on Nouri's as he spoke.

For Nouri, the experience was both pleasing and troubling. For though Ryka and Vishpar could not have been more different—the one dark where the other was golden—the one frail where the other was fierce and strong—something about the tender youth brought his childhood friend to mind. Nouri hadn't thought of Vishpar in a long while. But as he and Ryka sat on the small stone bench, he could feel that he was falling in love. And whether it was wonderful—or terrible—or both—he knew that there was nothing he could do to avoid it.

Twenty-One

It was a long while before it became clear to the brothers that Sheikh al-Khammas was ill. He'd become so infused with light as the years had passed, they barely noticed that his skin had developed a gray, sickly pallor, that his eyes had become milky and veiled, and that he grew thinner with each passing day. Only when he lost interest in food—for no matter how simple the meal, the Sufi master had always savored each bite—did the brothers begin to suspect that, though his spirit was still strong, the body that housed it was under siege.

"Perhaps it's a chill—" said Abbas al-Kumar.

"The lodge can be quite drafty—" said Omar al-Hamid.

"And the nights can be bitter—"

"And windy—"

"And Sheikh al-Khammas's cell is exposed on two sides!"

The brothers took turns bringing him yogurt and lamb broth and cups of mint tea heaped with honey.

"For the Prophet himself," said Abbas al-Kumar, "claimed that honey can cure any illness."

To Nouri, however, it was clear that Sheikh al-Khammas was suffering from more than just a chill. So one day he asked one of the physicians at the hospice to accompany him back to the mountain lodge. When they entered the Sufi master's cell, the doctor peered into the old man's eyes and examined his tongue and ran his hands over his legs and his chest and his belly and thumped the entire length of his spine. And when he was done, only Sheikh al-Khammas was unsurprised at his diagnosis.

"There are a number of things I could point out," said the doctor. "The liver is weak. The blood is too cool. The kidneys are beginning to fail. But the only real condition he's suffering from is exceeding old age."

The brothers heaved a collective sigh of relief and their lives went on. But one day, Sheikh al-Khammas did not appear for the morning meal and when Nouri went to see him he confessed that he did not have the strength to leave his bed. From then on, all of the meals were prepared by Abbas al-Kumar, *zikr* was conducted by Omar al-Hamid, the maintenance of the lodge was taken over by Sharoud, and the tending of the garden fell to Nouri and Ryka. The hearth fire of the order was now confined to a simple cell. But it was a flame of great strength, and the brothers were convinced that it would burn for years to come.

As a result of Sheikh al-Khammas's confinement, life at the mountain lodge began to change. Without the master's presence at meals, Abbas al-Kumar could not control his eating and in less than a month he swelled to an alarming size. Omar al-Hamid could not refrain from prayer, and often lay prostrate on the cold stone floor until his bones began to ache. Sharoud—whose dark thoughts rose up to fill the space created by the Sufi master's absence—took to pricking himself with the needle throughout the day. And an aching closeness grew up between Nouri and Ryka. From the early morning until late at night, they talked and worked and ate side by side, forging not only the contract of teacher and pupil, but the compact of friend and friend.

There was no reason that the deepening bond between Nouri and Ryka should have bothered Sharoud. But like all things connected with Nouri, his sudden closeness to the new aspirant made Sharoud's ascetic blood boil.

So he waited.

And he watched.

And though at times he wished to stick the needle into the four-eared Sufi or the pewter-colored boy instead of himself, he managed to keep his impulses in check.

"IF THE DISTANCE BETWEEN God and man is even greater than we imagine," said Ryka, "how do we bridge the gap?"

"We must learn how to serve," said Nouri.

"But what can a man possibly do that would matter to God?"

"It's not what he does that matters. It's how he does it." Nouri paused. "Service wears out our sharp edges. And opens the heart."

It was a cool morning in the month of Muharram. Nouri and Ryka were walking in the mountains, and the higher they climbed, the more exalted Ryka's questions became. They'd been working together for nearly six months now. And while their talks had only begun to scratch the surface of the truths Nouri wished to impart, he was impressed with Ryka's ability to move beyond the strictures of his mind.

"And what does the aspirant do when the heart resists?"

"He kneels lower. He bows deeper."

"And if that doesn't work?"

Nouri smiled. "Then Allah will provide the means."

Ryka was silent, and they continued walking. It seemed as if years had passed since he'd first come to the lodge, and at the same time the place seemed as strange as the day he'd arrived. He was inspired by the simple dedication of the brothers and he was awed by Sheikh al-Khammas—who, despite his illness, still cast his benevolent light over the lodge. Yet no one had as strong an effect on him as Nouri. At times—as they sat on the terrace or in the garden beside the pool—he could not bear to meet his gaze. At other times, he could not look away. But he listened quite closely to what he said, and did his best to understand the spiritual map he laid out before him.

"The problem is that you still place God outside yourself," said Nouri. "God is within."

"Then why do we have to work so hard to reach him?"

"We work to become empty. When your thoughts disappear, God will draw near."

Ryka's eyes flashed, and Nouri felt a hand reach inside him and twist his stomach into a knot. For months now, he'd walked with Ryka and sat with Ryka and worked and eaten and prayed with Ryka. And for months he'd tried to resist what he felt when the youth was near. He'd noticed other men over the years—the lanky fellow who sold figs at the market—the youth with the liquid eyes who tended the stables—but he'd always managed to keep the feelings they aroused inside him in check. Ryka, however, evoked a yearning that Nouri had not felt since he'd first arrived at the mountain lodge. He was moved by his tenderness. His beauty. His grace. And he was intrigued by his gravity: in the six months since Ryka had appeared, Nouri had not once seen him smile. He was an enigma to Nouri. And though he did not wish to stare at the youth, the silence he dwelled in forced him to keep his eyes fixed upon him when they spoke.

"The truth is simple," said Nouri. "It's we who are complicated."

Ryka suddenly stopped. Then he took a deep breath. "Do you think we could rest for a while?"

"Of course," said Nouri.

He led Ryka to a cluster of rocks that bordered the path and they sat.

"Are you all right?"

Ryka nodded. "I just needed to catch my breath."

They were silent a while. Ryka focused on the pace of his breathing. And Nouri focused on Ryka.

"You said you had a problem with your heart," said Nouri. "What's wrong with it?"

Ryka turned and gazed into Nouri's eyes. "It's backward."

"Backward?"

Ryka raised his hands to his chest. Then he crossed them over each other. "The parts are reversed. So my blood doesn't follow the usual pathway to the lungs."

"Is it painful?"

"Not really. But it can make me dizzy. And sometimes it makes me turn slightly blue."

As Ryka said this, Nouri saw that the bluish cast to his skin had increased.

"I'm not like other people," said Ryka.

Nouri was silent a moment. "Neither am I."

A strong current passed between them. Then Nouri raised his hand to Ryka's cheek, leaned forward, and kissed him.

"Perhaps we should head back," said Nouri, as he pulled away.

Ryka nodded. Then they rose and started back toward the lodge.

They said no more as they made their way along. But they both knew that things would be different now.

AS THE MONTHS SLIPPED BY, Sheikh al-Khammas grew smaller and thinner and less tethered to the earth, until at last he was like a child's rice-paper toy, brittle and shot through with light. The brothers took turns drawing his drapes in the morning, massaging his feet, sponging water on his brow, and reading him passages from the Qur'an. He no longer had the strength to practice *zikr.* And when speaking, he would often fall asleep between one sentence and the next. But he was still the glittering sun around which the lives of the faithful brothers revolved.

It was therefore troubling when Nouri announced one morning that Sheikh al-Khammas wished the brothers to gather in his cell after the midday meal.

"We should go there now!" cried Abbas al-Kumar.

"If our teacher wants to see us—" said Omar al-Hamid.

"There's no reason to wait—"

"Even a breath—"

"To obey!"

Abbas al-Kumar rubbed his forehead with the palm of his left hand and Omar al-Hamid tugged on his beard. Then they cried out together:

"When the master calls, the servant appears!"

Sharoud, who rarely listened to what the two dervishes said, to their surprise, agreed. "If Sheikh al-Khammas wishes to see us all at the same time, it must be of the utmost importance."

Nouri, however, insisted that if Sheikh al-Khammas wished them to come right away, he would have said so. So he told the brothers to attend to their morning chores and await the appointed hour.

When they finally filed into the Sufi master's cell, the drapes were still closed and a pair of tall tapers stood glowing. In the gauzy light, Sheikh al-Khammas seemed more fragile than ever, and as the brothers spread out around his bed they were unsure that he even knew they were there. As their eyes began to adjust to the darkness, however, he suddenly spoke.

"I smelled the scent of oranges in the night."

The brothers said nothing.

"The loveliest fragrance," he said. "In the darkness, over my bed."

"The orange trees along the path are just beginning to bloom," said Omar al-Hamid.

"Not the flower," said Sheikh al-Khammas. "The fruit." He closed his eyes. "As if someone had sliced one open and held it up to my nose."

"Perhaps," said Sharoud, "it was a dream."

"Not a dream," said Sheikh al-Khammas, as he opened his eyes. "The scent of oranges."

The brothers waited while the Sufi master stared into the darkness. Then he turned to Ryka.

"How are the roses?"

"They're doing well."

"And the daisies? And the oleander?"

Ryka nodded. "Everything is thriving."

There was another silence. Nouri wanted to ask if he could open the curtains. Abbas al-Kumar wanted to ask if he could bring him a blanket. A drink. Sharoud wanted to ask why they'd been called. They waited, however. And after a while, Sheikh al-Khammas spoke again.

"One thinks that the end will never come," he said. "That this eating—this laughing—this breathing"—he paused a moment—"this *existence* will just go on and on." He paused again and the light in his milky eyes grew stronger. "But no matter how small it may be, our order must go on. It is a part of Allah's plan. And in order for it to do so, I must choose a *khalifa* before I die."

"You mustn't speak of dying!" cried Abbas al-Kumar.

"The physician assured us—" said Omar al-Hamid.

"In the clearest terms—"

"That you have years left to live!"

A faint smile traced over the Sufi master's lips. "Physicians are wise," he allowed. "But the All-Knowing Allah is beyond wisdom." His twisted fingers fluttered across the edge of the bedsheet. "As you know, my successor need not be chosen from among you. I myself was brought in from another order to be the *murshid* here."

He paused again, and the brothers could feel their future hovering in the air. "But that was another time. With another purpose. What matters now is that you hold to the path. And that you go deeper. And for that I need not look elsewhere for someone to guide you."

It was only when Sheikh al-Khammas spoke these words that Sharoud knew he'd been chosen to lead the order. He knew that Abbas al-Kumar and Omar al-Hamid had both lived at the lodge for much longer, but the former was not far from being released from his body and the latter, for all his piety, was not a leader. It was obvious that Nouri was not ready for such a role, and there was no point in even thinking about Ryka. What surprised Sharoud was the sudden clarity he felt. His shame fell away. His guilt. His fear. Everything he'd been through had been a test. There was nothing standing in his way.

It was just as clear to Nouri that the office of *khalifa* would fall to Sharoud. His practice was diligent, his knowledge of the Shari'a was absolute, and his devotion to the order was unassailable. Although Nouri could not forget the ill will he'd once borne him, he'd kept his promise not to reveal what was hidden beneath his head cloth. So Nouri vowed that he would do his best to obey Sharoud's will when he took over the order.

"I'm still here," said Sheikh al-Khammas. "But when I die, your new *murshid* will be Nouri."

The room was silent as each of the brothers took in Sheikh

al-Khammas's words. Abbas al-Kumar was surprised; Omar al-Hamid was relieved; Ryka was joyful. And Nouri—who could only wonder if the darkness had caused him to misread the Sufi master's lips—was completely stunned. Yet nothing could match the shattering blast that went off in Sharoud. All of the years he'd struggled to let go of having been cast out of the lodge in Tan-Arzhan, all of the battles he'd waged to melt his anger and resentment, all of the wounds he'd made in his flesh with the tiny needle had come to naught. It was a juncture. A turning point. The wheel of his spiritual ascent suddenly froze. Then—with a roar like the screeching of a thousand crows—it reversed its direction. And his soul began to plummet downward with amazing speed.

Twenty-Two

And then, one day, Nouri's hearing returned.

Abbas al-Kumar had decided to make a carrot jam for Sheikh al-Khammas and since he could not even begin without fresh cubeb, he asked Nouri to head down to the village to fetch some from one of the lay members of the lodge who had an elaborate spice garden. Nouri knew that Abbas al-Kumar could have fetched the cubeb himself. The walk would have done him good. But it was a pleasant day and, if truth be told, he was grateful to get away for a few hours and think.

From the moment Nouri had been chosen to be Sheikh al-Khammas's *khalifa,* his mind had been awhirl. One thought rose up after the next, each contradicting the one that had come before.

How can I be the next leader of the order?

I'm not wise enough.

I'm not selfless enough.

What makes me worthy to follow in Sheikh al-Khammas's footsteps?

There was his writing, of course. Each day, Nouri poured himself into his verse, fashioning a gift that he could lay at Allah's feet. Yet he could not help but feel that each thought—no matter how graceful—no matter how deeply felt—was merely a shadow of the truth.

As he moved toward the village, he tried his best to shake the thoughts from his mind.

Feel the sun on your arms.

Smell the grass.

See the faces of the people who pass by.

But no matter how hard he tried to root himself in the here and now, he could not stop thinking about Ryka. The hollow of his throat. His hands. His eyes. He'd been scrupulous about keeping him out of his verse—in the time since he'd arrived, he'd not written a single line to praise him—yet he knew, in his heart, that the youth was in each word he wrote. It was clear that Nouri loved him. And the Sufi's labor is to love. But what troubled Nouri was that he wanted to touch him, hold him, be with him as he'd been with the men in the dark alleys behind the wharves. And this made him feel that he was not ready to be the next *murshid* of the order.

He did not even realize he'd passed the house where he was meant to fetch the cubeb until he was wrenched from the struggle inside his head by the harsh braying of a donkey, and looked up to find that he was well past the schoolyard and only a short distance from the mosque. At first he thought that his conscience was taunting him about the illicit nature of his thoughts. But when the braying subsided, he heard the gurgling of the fountain, the shouting of the children, the rumbling of the carts rolling by.

It wasn't his imagination.

Without a warning—without a reason—his hearing had come back.

He ran the entire way back to the lodge: across the village, up the mountain, through the front gate. And what delighted him most was neither the cackling of the geese nor the crying of the fruit sellers nor the booming of the call to prayer—but the sweet, sweet thought that he would finally hear Ryka's voice.

REGARDLESS OF THE SOAPS and powders employed—the scalding water—the stinging lye—it's never easy to cleanse a vessel of contagion. A trace can always linger in a crevice or burrow inside a hairline crack. Then, in a flash, it can spread back over the entire surface. It was therefore only a matter of hours after Sheikh al-Khammas announced that Nouri would be his *khalifa* that Sharoud's inner world was completely befouled. For though he'd spent more than three decades trying to cauterize the blackness in his soul, a particle of mean-spiritedness had always remained, and it took only a moment for it to course through his entire system. Nouri Ahmad Mohammad ibn-Mahsoud al-Morad had been a thorn in his side for too long. The only way to save the order—and himself—was to destroy him.

The obvious thing would have been to reveal the four ears that lay hidden beneath his head cloth. But that was what had led to Sharoud's expulsion from the order in Tan-Arzhan, and he was not going to make the same mistake twice. Sheikh Bailiri had been convinced that Nouri's ears were a sign of his spiritual grace. So Sharoud decided that if he was going to taint him in the eyes of Sheikh al-Khammas, he'd have to focus on something that bound Nouri to the earth. And there was no better subject than the closeness between him and Ryka.

In the years between his departure from Tan-Arzhan and his arrival at the mountain lodge, Sharoud had observed numerous intimacies between men. Some were affairs of the mind, involving debates over Qur'anic exegeses and jurisprudence, while others were deep friendships born of shared practice over long periods of time. Every so often, however, he witnessed a connection that seemed to go too far. A pair of brothers at the order in Shariwaz. A clerk and a stable boy at the court in Cairo. Nothing was ever said, of course, and the contact was always subtle. A hand that rested too long on the curve of a back. A furtive glance. But in each case it was clear to Sharoud that something illicit was going on.

He had no proof that anything unchaste had occurred between Nouri and Ryka. The relationship between teacher and pupil was by necessity close, and they were both devoted to the path. But there was no doubt in Sharoud's mind that they felt a physical longing for one another. At times, he could feel the heat rising from them. He could almost smell it in the air. And he felt sure that, sooner or later, they would cross the line. And since he knew that that would be an affront to the All-Seeing Allah, he felt obliged to reveal the nature of their connection to Sheikh al-Khammas.

It was on the morning that Nouri's hearing returned that Sharoud paid a visit to the Sufi master. He'd not been to see him since the day that he'd chosen Nouri to be his *khalifa*, and when he rapped on his door and Sheikh al-Khammas called out to him, Sharoud could tell that he was even weaker than before.

"Come in!" cried the disembodied voice.

Sharoud pushed the door open and when he stepped inside he could feel death in the air. He wanted to flee the room, but he knew there was not much time to convince Sheikh al-Khammas that Nouri was unworthy to take his place when Sheikh al-Khammas passed over to the other side. With the curtains drawn, he could barely make out the tiny figure that lay swaddled in blankets on the bed. As his eyes adjusted to the darkness, however, he saw the stool perched beside him. So he went to it, and sat, and waited for the Sufi master to speak.

"It's strange, isn't it?" murmured Sheikh al-Khammas. "We devote our entire lives to this journey. Yet most people don't even know it exists." He was silent a moment. Then he turned his head and peered at Sharoud through the darkness. "What a privilege it is to see what lies behind the veil."

Sharoud nodded. "A blessing that only Allah can bestow."

Sharoud waited for Sheikh al-Khammas to go on. But the Sufi master remained silent.

"If it's not a good moment," he said, "I can come back later."

Sheikh al-Khammas smiled. "I'm afraid there is no later!"

Sharoud ran his tongue over his lips and took a breath. He knew what he wished to say, but he also knew that he needed to be careful how he said it.

"The work of a Sufi," he began, "is to know God."

Sheikh al-Khammas nodded.

"And to do so," continued Sharoud, "he must cleanse his heart." He paused for a moment. "And banish the dark thoughts from his mind."

Sheikh al-Khammas focused his gaze on the slender dervish. "Be plain. I have no time for riddles."

"Impure thoughts, if left unguarded, will lead to impure actions." Sharoud paused again. Then he leaned in closer and whispered, "Nouri and Ryka."

"What about them?"

"They're always together." Sharoud drew his body up tall on the stool. "I fear that it goes beyond what is proper."

Sheikh al-Khammas shook his head. "A closeness between brothers is an alms."

"But what if that closeness becomes tainted?"

"By what?"

Sharoud hesitated. "Longing," he said. He peered into the Sufi master's eyes. "Lust." He waited, but Sheikh al-Khammas said nothing. "I needn't quote the scriptures to you: *'If two men commit a lascivious act, one must punish them!'*"

Sheikh al-Khammas turned his gaze back to the empty room.

"Where you see darkness, Sharoud, I see light. Where you see impurity, I see only love."

Sharoud wanted to argue that the love between Nouri and Ryka was profane. But he knew that if he said any more he would only anger Sheikh al-Khammas. "Forgive me," he said. "I simply thought I should share my concerns."

"You must be vigilant," said Sheikh al-Khammas. "The enemy tricks us to our very last breath."

Sharoud said no more. But the seed had been planted. And he

felt sure that Sheikh al-Khammas would soon see that what he had told him was true.

BY THE TIME HE REACHED the gates of the mountain lodge, Nouri was drunk with sound. From the snapping of a twig beneath his feet to the lowing of a cow, each noise was like a forgotten song to his reanimated ears. He was so pleased he was barely aware of the fact that his hearing had seemed to lose its hypersensitive edge, that his ears, though still doubled in number, were no longer doubled in sound. He only knew that when he saw Abbas al-Kumar standing in the doorway, he could not refrain from shouting: *"Say something!"*

Abbas al-Kumar placed his hands on his ample hips. "Where's my cubeb?" he shouted back.

Nouri, who suddenly remembered why he'd gone into the village in the first place, laughed. "I completely forgot!" he cried. "But my hearing has come back! Just like that!"

Abbas al-Kumar was not convinced that this was an excuse for having forgotten the cubeb. But he was happy to hear it, just as Omar al-Hamid was when Nouri passed him in the hallway and told him the news.

"The ways of Allah," said the astonished dervish, "are truly unfathomable!"

Nouri agreed, but he was too excited to stand with Omar al-Hamid and discuss God. So he clapped him on the shoulders and hurried off to find Ryka. After searching for him in the garden and the kitchen and the meeting hall, he finally found him sitting on the terrace.

"Say something!" he shouted, as the youth looked up.

Ryka, who thought it was a test of some sort, cleared his throat. *"We return through the words of the Prophet to God. Who is beyond all words."*

Nouri felt a rush of sweetness at the sound of his voice.

"What is it?" said Ryka.

"I can hear you! By the grace of Allah, my hearing has come back!"

When Ryka heard the news, he rose from the bench and embraced his friend. When they found themselves in each other's arms, however, they both felt a charge pass through them.

"How did it happen?" said Ryka, as he withdrew from the embrace.

"I'm not sure," said Nouri. "A donkey brayed, and the silence was shattered."

They stood there a few moments longer, but the tension was too great.

"I must tell Sheikh al-Khammas," said Nouri.

Ryka nodded. Then Nouri hurried off to the Sufi master's cell.

It was only a few hours after Sharoud had paid him a visit that Nouri entered Sheikh al-Khammas's room. He was lying perfectly still in the darkness and when he saw Nouri, his joy bubbled up.

"My child!" he cried.

Nouri, who had not heard his teacher's voice in nearly a year, was moved by the fractured sounds that floated up. He went to the stool—which was still traced with a faint emanation of Sharoud—and sat down. Then Sheikh al-Khammas drew his hands from beneath the covers and held them out.

"Light a taper," he said. "I know it's hard for you to read my lips in the darkness."

Nouri grasped the old man's bony hands and shook his head. "I can hear," he said. "Every word. Every sound. It's come back as unexpectedly as it went."

Sheikh al-Khammas smiled. "It was a labor," he said. "A trial."

"I feel as if I've been inside a cave. Or under the sea."

"Now you know silence. That will help you when the time comes for you to lead the order."

Nouri released the Sufi master's hands. "I don't think I'm ready," he said. "There are many veils that still shield my sight."

Sheikh al-Khammas could not help but think of what Sharoud had just told him. And had the suspicions come to him a year or even a month before, he would have warned Nouri to guard against the hungers of the flesh. But now, as he stood at the doorway to the other side, such words seemed foolish. What else could the flesh possibly do but hunger? Perhaps rather than lose oneself in such yearnings, one might find oneself. "You must not forget that Allah creates the veils as well as the sight. We see through them by confronting them. Not by turning away."

Nouri tried to imagine what would happen if he confronted his desire for Ryka. Would the veil fall away? Or would he find himself twisted up in its folds?

He thanked Sheikh al-Khammas for his advice and took his leave. But for the rest of the day he could not stop thinking of what the Sufi master had said. He walked in the mountains. He sat at the desk in his cell and read the Qur'an. But no matter what he did, he could not wrest Ryka from his mind.

The evening meal brought a host of forgotten sounds to Nouri's ears. The crackling of the fire in the hearth, the burbling of the water as it was poured into the cups, the smacking of the brothers' lips as they ate their food. Throughout the meal, however, Nouri's awareness remained focused on Ryka. They tried to avoid each other's gaze, but this only increased the intensity between them. So when the meal was done and the last call to prayer had been intoned, Nouri gathered his courage and made his way to Ryka's room.

Ryka seemed neither surprised nor alarmed when Nouri opened his door and stepped inside. He could feel his reversed heart beat so fast he thought it would split in two. But he could only remain frozen on the floor—where he'd been sitting cross-legged, reading beside a slender taper—as Nouri crossed the room and knelt down before him.

Nouri's heart was pounding as well, filling his head with blood and making his tender ears burn hot. He searched Ryka's eyes for a sign of protest. But all he could see was love. So he placed his hand on his cheek, leaned forward, and kissed him.

It was gentle at first. A kiss between comrades. A seal of their mutual respect. But the hunger in Nouri was too strong, and it quickly took over. He pressed his mouth hard against the youth's. He grasped his shoulders and pulled him closer. And as the heat flashed through him—clouding his mind and rousing the serpent—he felt Ryka respond.

"Are you sure you want to do this?" he said, as he drew back for a moment.

"Yes," said Ryka.

Nouri wasn't sure himself, but he was too aroused to turn back.

So he rose, reached his hand out, and drew the slender youth to his feet.

"Bring the taper," he said. "I want to see you."

Ryka stooped down and grasped the taper. He felt as if the ground had vanished beneath him. As if the roof had parted to reveal the sky. He was not sure what Nouri intended to do, but he knew that he wanted him to do it. He was flushed with desire. So he followed him across the room to the narrow bed to see what would happen.

When they reached the bed, Nouri removed Ryka's robe and raised his tunic over his head. Then he loosened the tie at his waist and let his trousers fall to the floor. Ryka's prick sprang upward like a cobra, fat and gleaming in the light. Nouri wrapped his fingers around it and Ryka gasped.

"Are you all right?" said Nouri.

Ryka nodded.

"This isn't too much for your heart?"

"It would be too much for my heart," said Ryka, "if we stopped."

Ryka reached out and tugged at Nouri's robe. So Nouri released him for a moment and slipped out of his clothes, until the two men stood naked together. They both noted the differences between them: Ryka was slim where Nouri was solid; Ryka was smooth—except for the flash of curls at his groin—where Nouri was covered with hair. But there was not much difference between the hardness that rose up from beneath their bellies. So Nouri stepped forward, pressing their bodies close, and they kissed again.

Eventually, they lay down upon the small, thin mattress and as they did, it occurred to Nouri that—for all the men he'd been with in his smoke-induced nights—he'd never made love in a bed. He knew that for Ryka there had been no other men. But the light was too dim and he was too inflamed with passion to see that—for the first time in his life—as his body entwined with Nouri's—Ryka smiled.

Twenty-Three

As Sheikh al-Khammas moved closer to the precipice between this world and the next, he requested that Nouri become his sole caretaker. The pattern of Nouri's days, therefore, became fixed: rising at dawn to bow his head and fall prostrate for the first call to prayer, eating the morning meal, carrying a bowl of yogurt to the Sufi master's cell and feeding him, practicing *zikr,* bowing his head and falling prostrate for the second call to prayer, eating the midday meal, carrying a bowl of broth to the Sufi master's cell and feeding him, tending the roses, bowing his head and falling prostrate for the third call to prayer, writing in his cell, bowing his head and falling prostrate for the fourth call to prayer, eating the evening meal, carrying a bowl of lentils to the Sufi master's cell and feeding him, reading in his cell, and finally, as the light bled from the sky, bowing his head and falling prostrate for the last call to prayer. His movements were simple. No excess. No strain. Each day was like the day that had come before. At night, however, when the hallways darkened and the brothers retired to their separate cells, Nouri abandoned himself to the constant surprise of being with Ryka.

It was like nothing that he had ever known. The sweetest tenderness. The fiercest passion. The endless unfolding of their bodies as they gave pleasure to each other. At first, Ryka was hesitant. He seemed to vanish into smoke at Nouri's touch. As time passed, however, he became confident in the feelings that coursed through him and he gave himself over completely. And Nouri only knew that—despite the doubts that rose up as he crept from the youth's cell before dawn—he had never felt closer to God than when he was in Ryka's arms.

Sometimes, when the passion subsided and they lay intertwined in the darkness, Nouri would send up a prayer.

Let me remain here, Allah, and I will never forget you. Not for an instant. Let me remain with him and I will remain with you. Forever and ever.

But the night always passed. And Nouri always had to leave the warmth of Ryka's embrace.

As the days went by, the closeness the two men felt during the night began to spill out into the day. Their heads would tilt close together as they tended the roses. Their fingers would touch as they entered a room. And while these things were too subtle to be perceived by either Abbas al-Kumar or Omar al-Hamid, not a word—not a gesture, no matter how fleeting—went unnoticed by Sharoud.

What surprised Nouri most about his feelings for Ryka was how they changed his writing. His verse became leaner. More muscular. More intense. It also became deeply erotic, for he found that when he raised his pen he could not keep his passion for the youth from pouring out. At times, when he read over what he'd written, he would blush. Yet he could not help feeling that his longing for Ryka was merely an expression of his longing for God.

It wasn't until they'd been lovers for several weeks that Ryka learned what was hidden beneath Nouri's head cloth. He'd not questioned the fact that his head always remained covered, even as they lay in each other's arms. He assumed it was a sign of his respect for Allah and left it at that. One night, however, as they were lying together, Nouri suddenly pulled away.

"What is it?" said Ryka.

Nouri looked deep into the youth's eyes. Then he rolled over onto his back.

"Is something wrong?"

Nouri was silent, his body taut, his breath rising and falling in waves. Then he rose up onto his side and, with an aching slowness, began to unwind his head garment. He remained perfectly still as the strip of pale cloth fell away—like the ashes from a coil of incense—until at last the final layer was removed and his secret was revealed.

For a long while, Ryka neither spoke nor moved. Then he took Nouri's head in his hands and gently kissed each of his ears.

"Allah the Incomparable," Ryka whispered.

Nouri pressed back the tears that flooded his eyes. Then he and Ryka dissolved in each other's arms.

DESPITE THE CONSTANT CARE that Nouri and Ryka took to keep their lovemaking a secret, Sharoud had no doubt that they'd crossed that invisible line. He could hear Nouri slip from his cell and creep down the hallway in the middle of the night. He could smell their scent on each other during the day. Before he could bring the matter back to Sheikh al-Khammas, however, he needed absolute proof. So one night, after Nouri had gone to Ryka's cell, Sharoud tiptoed down the hall, pressed his ear to Ryka's door, and waited for the two men to perform their sacrilege to God.

Sex had been repugnant to Sharoud from the first moment that it had entered his awareness. When he was three, he crept into his parents' bedroom one night while they were making love and from the sight of his father's body over his mother's, and the sound of her cries, he could only conclude that he was taking her life. When he awoke the next morning to find her calmly tending the hearth, he was convinced that black magic had occurred, and he could never look at either one of them the same way again. When adolescence arrived, he was so dismayed by the insistence of his erections that he rubbed turmeric on his penis, which—though it burned like hellfire—made it go limp. He repeated the procedure until the poor thing became docile, in which state it remained throughout his time at the order in Tan-Arzhan. Only when he was alone in the desert did it rear again: one morning, a pack of nomads stopped at the oasis to water their camels and while the men rested, the women disrobed and waded into the water to bathe. When

Sharoud—who'd taken cover behind a cluster of date palms—saw their soft hanging breasts and their voluptuous buttocks, his forgotten organ sprang to attention like a serving boy at the appearance of the Sultan. He was so transported by the sight of them splashing the cool water on their bodies, he could not keep from taking himself in hand. And though he was convinced that the dazzling pleasure he felt was the elixir of the devil, he could not make himself stop. When he reached his climax and found himself covered in a sea of slime, he was so horrified he took a vow that it would never happen again. And from that day on, there was not a flicker from beneath his robes.

Now, as he listened to the sounds that came from Nouri and Ryka, not only was he repulsed; he was enraged. And when he summoned the courage to crack the door and peer through the inky shadows, he knew that such perversity could not be allowed beneath the roof of a spiritual dwelling. So he closed the door and went to the chapel and bowed his gaunt body in prayer. Then, when morning came, he paid another visit to Sheikh al-Khammas.

When he reached the cell, he rapped loudly on the door. But no answer came. So he pushed it open and went to the narrow bed where the Sufi master lay. The room was so dark it was hard to discern where the bed linens ended and Sheikh al-Khammas began. But his eyes were wide open, and they gave Sharoud the signal to speak.

"Forgive me for disturbing you," he said.

"If one is truly inclined toward Allah, one has already been forgiven," said Sheikh al-Khammas.

"And what if I told you I'd seen something that goes beyond forgiveness?"

"Then I'd counsel you to cleanse your eyes."

Sharoud hesitated. He knew that he had to be careful. But he felt sure that if Sheikh al-Khammas had seen the foulness he'd seen, he'd condemn it with all his heart. "I know he's dear to you," he said. "Like a son. But what he and the boy are doing cannot be condoned."

Sheikh al-Khammas remained silent for a while. Then he parted his withered lips and spoke. "I cannot leave this world while there is discord among you. You must stop this, Sharoud. Or you must go."

Sharoud was incensed. But he knew that there was no more to say. "I won't speak of it again. I assure you."

He bowed his head. Then he rose from the stool and left the room.

As he made his way back to his cell, Sharoud vowed that he would not speak of Nouri and Ryka again to Sheikh al-Khammas. But there were other ways to destroy them. And with Allah on his side, he knew that he couldn't fail.

THIS TIME ABBAS AL-KUMAR wanted fenugreek.

"Nothing stimulates the liver better than fenugreek," he announced one day over the morning meal. "I'll put some in Sheikh al-Khammas's *khoofteh berenji*. He'll live forever!"

He knew that there was sure to be some at the bazaar, so once again he asked Nouri to travel down the mountain to fetch it.

"Try Aftab Hamiwallah's stall," he said. "Or if you want the best price, Rashid al-Hamid's."

Nouri was reluctant to leave Sheikh al-Khammas's side. But if it meant prolonging the Sufi master's life, he would have traveled to Cairo to pluck a hair from the head of the vizier. "I'll set out after *zikr.*"

Abbas al-Kumar nodded and the matter was settled. As they rose from the table, however, Ryka asked Nouri to let him go in his place.

"I haven't left the mountain in months," he said. "And it would be a gift to be able to help Sheikh al-Khammas."

Nouri was afraid that the trip would be too hard for his friend's fragile heart. But Ryka was now nearly twenty, and he understood his wish to serve. "We'll go together."

"No," said Ryka. "You should stay here." He reached out and placed a hand on Nouri's shoulder. "I haven't had a spell in weeks. I can do this alone."

Nouri was not convinced. But he did not wish to undermine the youth's confidence, so he agreed. "Just promise me you'll take your time. And that you'll stop and rest if you need to."

"I promise."

So Abbas al-Kumar gave Ryka the money to buy the fenugreek and he set off.

As he started down the mountain, he felt as weightless as a gooseberry husk. The air was fragrant and the sight of the fields in the distance filled him with joy. As he approached the village, he spied the colored awnings and heard the plaintive cries of the bazaar. And before he knew it, he was swept up in the sea of goods. There were tooled leather saddles and beakers of blown glass; there were carpets and caftans; there were reed pipes and ink-pots; there was jackfruit and passion fruit and carob fruit and kepel fruit and quince. Ryka wanted to stop at each stall and examine its wares. But he knew that Abbas al-Kumar was in need of the fenugreek for Sheikh al-Khammas. So he continued on until he found an inconspicuous stall that sold the leafy herb.

He was just placing his purchase in his sack when he heard a voice.

"I suggest that you get some rose of Jericho as well."

He turned and, to his surprise, he found Sharoud standing behind him.

"Fenugreek is good," he continued. "But rose of Jericho will help to purify his blood."

"I'm afraid I've spent all the money Abbas al-Kumar gave me on the fenugreek," said Ryka.

Sharoud peered into his eyes and then smiled.

"Allow me."

He reached into the pocket of his robe, drew out a coin, and purchased some of the bitter herb. Then he handed it to Ryka.

"We wish to keep our master alive, don't we?"

"Of course."

Ryka lowered the rose of Jericho into his sack.

"There's a merchant that makes a nice apple tea," said Sharoud. "Will you join me for a glass?"

"It's kind of you to offer," said Ryka. "But I ought to get back."

"As you wish. Just remember that it's an arduous climb."

At Sharoud's words, Ryka thought of how strenuous the journey up the mountain would be, and of the promise he'd made to Nouri that he would take time to rest. "On the other hand," he said, "it would be good to take some refreshment before I start back."

Sharoud smiled again. "It will do you good."

Sharoud led Ryka past the silk sellers and the cheese sellers and the men discussing the Hadith to a small tent where a man with an extravagant mustache sat beside a steaming kettle perched over an open fire.

"Some apple tea," said Sharoud. His eyes scanned the pastries that lined a table beside the fire. "And a pair of *baslogh*."

The man combed his fingers through his lavish mustache. Then he went to one of the sacks that were propped up along the wall, scooped out some pieces of dried fruit, and placed them in a teapot. He carried the teapot to where the kettle sat, filled it with hot water, placed it and a pair of etched glasses on a wooden tray, and laid a pair of warm pastries beside them. Then he handed the tray to Sharoud and returned to the fire.

"Come," said Sharoud. He led Ryka to a table and a pair of chairs that were perched outside the entrance, lowered the tray to the table, and they sat.

Ryka waited for the tea to steep and for the dervish beside him to speak. In all the time he'd lived at the mountain lodge, he'd barely spoken with Sharoud. He made Ryka nervous, with his beady eyes and his imperious manner. Regardless of how enticing the *baslogh* looked, he wished that he'd headed straight back to the lodge.

"You seem to be adapting to the order," said Sharoud. "It's not a path to which many can adhere."

"I thank Allah for giving me the courage to search for Him."

Sharoud poured the tea into one of the glasses. "And may He give you the strength to find Him." He handed one of the glasses to Ryka. "The pastries are rather sweet. But even a Sufi must give over to the senses now and then. Don't you agree?"

Ryka—who entirely missed the insinuation in Sharoud's comment—reached for one of the pastries and took a bite. It was quite delicious. For a few moments, the two men were silent. Eating the *baslogh*. Sipping the tea. Then Sharoud lowered his glass to the table and spoke.

"You and Nouri have become quite close."

Ryka nodded. "He shows me the way to God."

"Perhaps." Sharoud paused. "Or perhaps he obstructs it."

"I don't understand."

"You're young. It's natural that you would place your faith in someone who's older." Sharoud took a sip of his tea. Then he gazed into Ryka's eyes. "But what you're doing is unnatural. And deeply offensive to God."

Ryka said nothing, but Sharoud knew that his words had pierced him.

"You need look no further than the Qur'an for confirmation. *'Will you commit abomination before the Lord? Will you lust after men instead of women?'* "

Ryka felt the ground give way beneath his chair, the pastry turn to granite in his stomach.

"Take heed," said Sharoud. "Allah sees into the darkest corners. There is nowhere to hide."

He took one last sip of his tea. Then he headed off into the crowd, leaving Ryka alone.

For a long while Ryka just sat there, unaware of the tea growing cold or the bodies moving past him or the man sitting distracted by the fire. It had never crossed his mind that what went on between himself and Nouri in the deep hours of the night might be wrong. It was so full of joy—so consistent in its power to move him beyond the boundaries of his existence—he could only think of it as a blessing. Now it was as if a veil had been lifted and what had seemed good was suddenly evil. And though he could not name the feeling that coursed through him as shame, he knew that his connection to Nouri would never be the same.

Twenty-Four

The fenugreek did nothing. Neither did the rose of Jericho, the parsley, the turmeric, the coriander, the gray verbena, the basil, the marjoram, or any of the other herbs Abbas al-Kumar added to Sheikh al-Khammas's food to reinvigorate his blood. Day after day he lay in the darkness—his eyes open—his body inert—until it seemed as if he'd go on in that state, perched between life and death, until the end of time. He ate the simple food Nouri brought him. He murmured the Shahaadah. He glowed as if he'd swallowed the sun. One day, however, he stopped speaking and then a few days later he stopped eating. And that was when Nouri knew that the end was near.

From then on, Nouri remained at his teacher's side: eating the meals Abbas al-Kumar carried in, responding to the call to prayer with a fervent whisper, sleeping when he could no longer resist. He found it hard to believe that a heart so great could actually stop beating. That a man so profound could ever draw his last breath. But Nouri kept his hand on the Sufi master's chest, determined to feel that final moment when his spirit broke free.

Later—when he tried to reconstruct the exact order in which things had occurred—he could not remember whether the cat had shrieked before or after the shutters had crashed open or whether the mirror had shattered before or after the taper had gone out. He only knew that when he heard the sound he drew his hand from Sheikh al-Khammas's heart, and when he placed it back, the shrunken body was still.

Death had finally come.

And Sheikh al-Khammas was gone.

WHEN NOURI ANNOUNCED that Sheikh al-Khammas had died, the brothers were grief-stricken. The Sufi master had been their compass, and they could not picture life in the mountain lodge without him. They knew, however, that there were strict rules regarding the mourning of the dead, and sacred rites they had to perform. So they reminded themselves that their beloved *murshid* was now with God, and then set to work.

The first thing that needed to be done was to carry the body to the meeting hall for cleansing. And since Ryka was too frail and Abbas al-Kumar and Omar al-Hamid were too old, the task fell to Nouri and Sharoud. As they raised the lifeless body from the bed, they did not exchange a glance or utter a single word. They simply carried it from the cell, down the stairs, and into the hall where the others were waiting. They laid the body on a table that Omar al-Hamid had placed at the center of the room. Then Abbas al-Kumar removed the clothes, drew a rag from a bucket of perfumed water, and began washing it from head to toe.

When the cleansing had been performed three times, Omar al-Hamid began the shrouding. The Sufi master's turban was used and—just like the washing—the shrouding was done three times. Then the brothers chanted the Salaat-ul Janaazah, and the body was carried to the garden, where a simple grave had been dug beside the shimmering pool where the Sufi master had loved to sit.

They placed the shrouded corpse in the grave and covered it over with soil. Then Nouri knelt down and lowered his forehead to the ground. He remained there for a very long while, bidding farewell to his beloved friend. And when he rose to his feet, it was clear that the mantle had been passed.

Over the following days, a hush fell over the lodge. For despite the fact that Sheikh al-Khammas had been bedridden for months—barely moving—barely speaking—his death was like the arrival of winter on a bright summer day. The brothers went on as before: taking their meals, chanting their prayers, practicing *zikr*. But the future of the order was unclear, and no one knew this better than Nouri.

To complicate matters, Ryka became ill. For from the moment Sharoud dropped the doubts into his apple tea, his fragile heart began to falter. Before he even left the bazaar, he suffered one of his spells, which caused him to knock over a stand of melons. He took the climb up the mountain so slowly the sky was dark when he arrived. And though Nouri pressed him to explain what had happened, he would not say a word. That night, when Nouri came to his cell, Ryka said that he was too tired to be intimate. And the following morning—when Nouri began his vigil at Sheikh al-Khammas's side—Ryka vowed that they would never make love again.

It was clear to him now. It was wrong. And what was even more clear was that the fault lay with him. He must have been sent to Nouri as a test of strength. To see if his friend could move beyond the yearnings of the flesh. So he decided that he would use his unorthodox heart to remove the temptation.

At first the illness was feigned. He'd been through it so many times it was easy to fake the dizziness, the shortness of breath, the frenzied fluttering in his chest. As the days passed, however, the false manifestations began to give way to the real ones. His guilt over his impassioned nights sapped his blood. And the loss of those nights caused a sorrow that he could hardly bear. With each day he grew weaker, until it was clear that something had to be done.

Nouri instructed Abbas al-Kumar to prepare Ryka ginger-and-honey tonics and strong cups of hawthorn tea. When these had no effect, he called in the doctors. But after endless examination and much shaking of heads, they explained what Nouri already knew: Ryka's heart was not like other hearts, and its fate was uncertain. So once he'd finished his vigil beside Sheikh al-Khammas, Nouri devoted himself to tending to Ryka.

When Sheikh al-Khammas died and Nouri took over the order, Sharoud did his best to remain silent. When the doctors appeared at the gates of the mountain lodge to see Ryka, he escorted them to his cell. But when Nouri began spending his days at Ryka's side, Sharoud could no longer hold his tongue. So one morning, as Nouri was taking a bowl of *maast-o khiar* to the youth, he intercepted him on the stairs.

"I need to speak with you."

"Can it wait?"

Sharoud frowned. "I'm afraid not."

Nouri had not slept well in weeks, and the last thing he wanted was to struggle with Brother Shadow. But he knew better than to stir up Sharoud's wrath, so he acquiesced.

"Meet me in the garden," he said, "after the next call to prayer."

Sharoud nodded, and Nouri continued on. Then—after an hour had passed and they'd performed the *salah*—they met on the stone bench beneath the argan tree, just a few paces from Sheikh al-Khammas's grave.

"You wished to speak with me," said Nouri.

Sharoud nodded. "I believe it's important."

"Well, I'd be grateful if you'd keep it brief."

Sharoud turned to face Nouri directly. "It's not my place to give you advice. But it's an important moment for the order. You cannot be blind to it."

"The loss of Sheikh al-Khammas is a terrible blow. It will take us time to adjust."

"Sheikh al-Khammas was a great man. And he led this order with great wisdom for many years." Sharoud paused. "Perhaps, in his greatness, he kept it alive." He paused again, careful to choose his words. "Or perhaps—Allah preserve him—he kept it from moving forward."

Nouri felt the heat rise to his cheeks, but he fought the impulse to respond.

"I do not question your assumption of the mantle," continued Sharoud. "For whatever reason, Sheikh al-Khammas chose you to take over as our *murshid*. But I do question whether you realize what's at stake. Either the order flourishes"—his eyes grew even darker—"or it collapses."

"And what would you have me do?" said Nouri.

"I'd have you focus your energy on ensuring that it's the former and not the latter. Grounding our order in a new set of disciplines. Searching for ways to increase our ranks." His mouth curled. "Not sitting all day in a dark cell beside a sickly boy."

"That boy is our brother."

"Perhaps. But he seems to evoke the lowest part of you."

"No, Sharoud. The highest part."

"You cannot—"

"No!" cried Nouri. "I won't hear you! I won't let you speak about what you don't understand!"

Sharoud's eyes glittered. He wanted to shout that what Nouri had done with Ryka was an abomination. But he knew that he'd said enough. So he rose from the bench and left the garden.

For a long while, Nouri just sat there—letting the blood drain from his throat, urging his heart to stop pounding, willing the thoughts from his mind. He knew that, in part, what Sharoud had just said was true: the order was at a crossroads and it was up to him to shepherd it forward. But he was unable to do that until he was shown the way. So he sat there until his spirit had regained its balance. Then he rose from the bench and returned to Ryka's side.

DESPITE THE EXOTIC ELIXIRS that Abbas al-Kumar concocted, despite the bed rest, despite Nouri's loving attention, Ryka's condition did not improve. He tried to return to his daily chores, but he soon found that he grew weak while tending the roses, he felt dizzy while practicing *zikr,* and the grayish-blue cast to his skin became its permanent hue. What troubled Nouri the most, however, was the wall that Ryka had erected between them. He no longer shared what he was thinking or feeling. He would not allow Nouri to hold him. Something had damaged his trust and Nouri felt sure that if he could learn what that was—and put it right—Ryka's health would return.

One morning, Nouri suggested to Ryka that they go walking together. He knew of a path that was quite gentle and he was convinced that the fresh air could only do him good.

"We'll take it slowly," he said. "I promise. We'll stop and rest whenever you need to."

Ryka—who longed to spend time with Nouri even as he tried to avoid him—could not refuse. So he accompanied him to the kitchen for a bowl of *shaami* and they set out.

Neither said a word as they moved through the gates and out along the curving path. The sun warmed their faces and the ground felt solid beneath their feet. As they made their way along, Nouri was reminded of that morning when he and Vishpar had been sent to the Darni Sunim to fetch the fountain. So much had occurred between that moment and this one. Yet he was just as affected now as he'd been then by the nearness of his friend.

At first, Ryka seemed to revive from the exertion. His pace increased, and the warmth returned to his cheeks. Eventually, however, he could feel his strength begin to drain away.

"I need to rest," he said.

Nouri placed his hand, ever so gently, on his back. "Take as long as you like."

They looked around, but there was nowhere to sit. So Nouri removed his robe and laid it out on the ground. Then he took Ryka's arm, helped him sit, and lowered himself beside him. Again they were silent, Nouri waiting for a sign from Ryka, Ryka waiting for the fury in his chest to subside. Then Ryka brushed the hair from his brow, raised his eyes to Nouri's, and spoke.

"You've said that everything happens as it must. That each action—each breath—is the will of Allah."

"It cannot be otherwise."

"Then how can we know if our actions are supporting our aim? And not blocking the way?"

Nouri saw the conflict in Ryka's eyes. "It's not what we do that matters. It's whether we can maintain our connection with God while we do it."

"But surely certain things are wrong—"

"Of course."

"And yet they're still the will of Allah?"

Nouri leaned closer. "We each have a path to follow." He paused. "Not all of them lead to awareness."

Ryka tried to make sense of what Nouri was saying. "So even if we think we're moving closer to God, we may be wrong."

"It's possible."

"Our actions—our thoughts—may still draw us away."

Nouri said nothing. It was clear that someone had made

Ryka doubt the closeness between them. And that someone could only be Sharoud. But Nouri decided that, for the moment, he would say no more.

When Ryka was ready, Nouri helped him to his feet. Then he took his arm and escorted him back to the lodge. Over the following weeks, however, his condition only worsened. There were times when his breath was so short he was unable to eat. There were days when his head was so light he had to remain in bed. The weaker he grew, the harder it was for Nouri to broach the subject of the distance between them. Yet he remained convinced that if he could remove the doubt that Sharoud had inserted in his heart, Ryka's heart would regain its strength.

One morning, when Nouri went out to the terrace, he found Ryka seated on the bench. "May I join you?"

Ryka nodded, and Nouri seated himself beside him.

"It's good to see you out of bed," he said. "I hope it means that you're feeling better."

Ryka was silent. Then he shook his head. "Not really."

Nouri gazed at the youth and felt his stomach clench: the heightened awareness he felt when Ryka was near was only increased by the fact that it had been weeks since they'd touched.

"Abbas al-Kumar found a book that explains the medicinal uses of wildflowers. He thinks it can help."

"Abbas al-Kumar means well. But some things are not fixable."

"Perhaps. But I'm not giving up."

Nouri's words seemed to pierce something in Ryka. And though he knew that the youth would prefer him to say no more, he decided to press on.

"The love that we feel is a blessing."

"It isn't the love that concerns me. It's how we express it."

"And how is that wrong?"

Ryka blotted his brow. "The Sufi must embrace sobriety."

"Yes," said Nouri. "And intoxication. What we do can't be wrong if it brings remembrance."

"And what if it brings forgetfulness?" said Ryka. "What if it places a wall around the soul?"

"I don't believe you."

Ryka raised his eyes to Nouri's. "I think it's a test."

"Then you can pass it."

"Not for me." Ryka paused. "I think it's a test for you."

Nouri was silent. Then he shook his head. "The only test is whether we can bear the fire. And keep God in our hearts."

Ryka wanted to believe this. And the truth was that he'd never felt closer to God than when he was in Nouri's arms. But the poison Sharoud had sprinkled into his heart seemed to have damaged its fragile workings. And he could not take the chance that he was the devil on Nouri's path and not the dove.

"Who's done this?" said Nouri. "Who's made you doubt?"

"No one."

"I don't believe you."

Nouri raised his hand to Ryka's cheek just as a tear trickled down.

"Don't—"

Nouri looked into the youth's eyes, but they were firmly barred. So he leaned in to kiss him. Ryka tried to pull away, but Nouri whispered in his ear: "Whatever Sharoud has told you, it's a lie. Trust your heart."

Sometimes, when things are the most confused, a light penetrates the darkness and grace is restored. This is what Nouri thought had occurred when Ryka threw his slender arms around him and held him tight. But he would never be sure. For Ryka's tender heart could not sustain such a vigorous battle. And when his grip relaxed, he lay dead in Nouri's embrace.

Twenty-Five

At first Nouri thought that Ryka's damaged heart had been swapped for his: the pain was so great he could barely breathe. He cradled the dead body in his arms and carried it back to the lodge, but by the time he reached the gates he was on fire. He paced the hallways. He wept. But there was no escaping the torment.

When the time came for the cleansing of the body and its placement in the ground, Nouri could not take part. But once the shrouded vessel had been interred—just beside the remains of Sheikh al-Khammas—he could not tear himself away. He seated himself on the grass between the two graves and there he remained. Abbas al-Kumar brought him food and Omar al-Hamid knelt before him from time to time and intoned the *salah*. The rest of the time he sat alone—eyes closed, arms folded tightly across his body—and burned.

The days passed. The nights passed. And Nouri's grief continued on. Whether the sun blazed or the rain pelted down, he sat on the grass and mourned. One morning, however, he heard a voice. And when he opened his eyes, he found Sharoud standing before him.

"You were chosen to be our leader," said Sharoud. "Well, it's time to lead."

Nouri looked into Sharoud's eyes and felt a hatred so deep he did not recognize himself. He wanted to leap up and throttle the life from his body. But he closed his eyes and bore down against it, and Sharoud went away.

Another day passed. And another. And another. And then, one night, he remembered the curative power of words. He went to his room, lit a taper, found some paper and a pen, and sat down at his desk. He reached for the pen and his thoughts and feelings began to flow. He wrote about Ryka's eyes. Ryka's smile. About life. About love. About loss. But the words, no matter how graceful, seemed false.

He threw down the pen and raised his head to the rafters.

"You take everything I care about!"

He reached for one of the pages on which he'd written the pointless words.

"Then take it all!"

He placed the edge of the page in the flame of the taper and watched as it began to darken and curl. Bit by bit it became particles of crackling ash that flew up into the darkness. He prayed that it would combust into a blaze that would ignite the room and consume his grief. But it burned quite slowly, until he held a singed scrap between his fingers, and the flame died out.

He sat there a moment. Alive. Awake. He went to the trunk and scooped up the written pages that lay inside. He removed one of the blankets from his bed, spread it out upon the floor, piled the pages on top, and tied the corners up into a heavy bundle. Then he lit an oil lamp, hoisted the bundle over his shoulder, and headed out into the night.

He moved like a wraith through the gates and out over the path that led to where he and Ryka had gone walking. The night was cold and the stars glittered like signposts overhead. When he reached the place where they'd stopped and talked, he lowered the lamp and the bundle to the ground. Then he knelt down, untied the corners of the blanket, and exposed the pages to the night. For a moment, he was still: a soldier in the Prophet's army before a battle, Abraham with Isaac before the knife was raised. Then he slid open the cover of the oil lamp, touched one of the pages to its flame, and set fire to the entire stack.

He remained there until the flames died out, and the first streaks of light traced the horizon. Then he blew out the lamp, rose to his feet, and headed off down the mountain.

HE WANDERED FOR DAYS, moving out past the farms and the villages into the river valley that skirted the northern edge of the desert. The land billowed before him like a wave he implored to carry him away from the lodge, from the world, from himself. At times he would pass a small band of pilgrims or a cluster of nomads, but for the most part he was alone. The fire inside him still raged, but the constant movement seemed to keep it at bay.

He walked for days, resting only when his body could go no farther, scooping water from the river only when his head became so light he was afraid he'd collapse. One day, however, he could walk no more. So he found a small cave near the river where he could take refuge. It was oddly shaped, with a trio of walls that rose to a dome overhead and a jagged entrance that let in the morning sun. But it gave shelter from the wind and Nouri knew that he could be alone there with God.

It did not take long for him to establish a daily routine. He awoke as the sun streamed in and went out to wash in the river. Then he gathered some dates and nuts and returned to the cave. At first his mind was blank, but soon the thoughts began to come. So he reached for prayer. The repetition of the ninety-nine names of Allah. The recitation of verses from the Qur'an. Eventually, however, he settled on the six words *There is no god but God*. Day after day, they trickled out in a gentle stream, over and over and over. And as they did, the memories rose up.

He and Habbib planting crocuses in the garden.

He and Vishpar lying beside the fountain, beneath the stars.

The fear that gripped him as the marauder thrust the blindfold over his eyes.

The pain that seized him as The Right Hand defiled him.

The startling whiteness of the snow outside Enrico's barn.

The numbing pleasure of Abdallah's pipe.

The blissful encounters with the men in the dark alleys.

The thump of the laundry rod as it hit his head.

The boom of the explosion as he hit the ground.

The sweetness of Ryka's embrace.

As each memory flashed and died away, Nouri grew emptier inside. Until even the words of prayer disappeared and there was only silence. He hovered in the tiny cave like prayer itself, humbled to find that the closeness to God he'd reached through his love for Ryka was surpassed by what he had received through its loss.

Nouri lost track of time. The days, the weeks, the months slipped by. But eventually, the pain began to diminish and one morning he awoke to find that the fire inside him had gone out. So he left the cave and started the long trek back to the lodge—finally ready to lead the order.

IN ALL THE TIME THAT ABBAS AL-KUMAR had been a member of the order, he'd never hung the laundry up to dry outside the entrance to the lodge. He usually strung a rope between the oaks that bordered the southern wall, which more than sufficed to drape the tunics and bedsheets and robes of the tiny gathering of brothers. When visitors came, he'd hang a few pieces over a ledge or place a line between the kitchen and one of the columns of the north portico. Now, however, there was so much to dry he had no choice but to string a rope from the front door to the grillwork of the gate and hang the items there.

"It looks like a market stall," said Omar al-Hamid. "Or the inner courtyard of a harem."

Abbas al-Kumar paid no attention to the comments. It was a lovely day and he could not help humming a little tune as he drew the clothes from the basket and hoisted them over the line. He was thinking about the fresh herring he'd found that morning at the market; if he hung out the laundry in time to roll out the crusts, he would bake a herring pie for the midday meal. As he squeezed the excess water from the tunics and smoothed out the creases from the sheets, he imagined the fishy fragrance rising from the hearth. His song was interrupted midnote, however, when he saw the stranger making his way up the mountain path.

He was as slender as the stamen of a hibiscus flower, his head tightly wrapped, his beard untrimmed, his body clothed in a tattered shift. Abbas al-Kumar couldn't tell whether he was an aspirant or a mendicant, but he knew that after the long, arduous climb he would be hungry. So he went to the kitchen, fetched a piece of *naan* and a cup of water, and returned to the gate.

"It's a long trip!" he called out.

The man said nothing. He simply continued walking until he reached the place where Abbas al-Kumar stood.

"It's always good to refresh oneself after the climb," said Abbas al-Kumar, as he approached.

He offered him the cup and he drank. Then he held out the *naan* and the fellow tore off a piece, placed it in his mouth, and began to chew.

"You always sustain us, Brother Abbas."

The man raised his eyes to Abbas al-Kumar's and only then did the corpulent Sufi realize that it was Nouri.

"You've come back!"

Nouri nodded. "I've come back."

"We thought that you'd been eaten by a mountain lion! Or that you'd fallen from a cliff!"

"I should have come to see you before I left. But I didn't know that I was leaving. I just started walking. And I couldn't stop."

"The heart is a bafflement," said Abbas al-Kumar. "It can torment us even more than the stomach!"

Nouri wanted to explain that his heart had surrendered. But he could not find the words. "It's been a battle," he said. "But I'm back. And I have an order to lead."

Before Abbas al-Kumar could respond, he heard a voice.

"Forgive me for interrupting, but I need your help."

The two men turned to find a frizzy-haired youth standing before them.

"Brother Omar asked me to come find you."

"What's wrong?" said Abbas al-Kumar.

"One of the grates in the bathing chamber is clogged."

"And what does Brother Omar think I can do about it?"

"He wants to borrow one of your cooking utensils to dislodge it."

"One of my cooking utensils!" Abbas al-Kumar turned a bright crimson. "Tell him I'll be right there! And don't let him touch a thing!"

The youth bowed, and vanished into the lodge.

"It seems that we have a new initiate," said Nouri.

"Oh, there's more than just one!" said Abbas al-Kumar. "I'm afraid things have changed a great deal while you've been gone!"

Before Nouri could learn what he meant, Abbas al-Kumar hurried off. So he followed him into the lodge to find out for himself.

As he stepped over the threshold, he felt as if he was entering a place he'd never been. The floors were covered with rich woven rugs, the windows were draped with colored silks, and a strong smell of sandalwood filled the air. A series of lamps was strung from the ceiling and the walls were piled high with books. What startled Nouri the most, however, were the dozens of men moving to and fro. They were all ages. All shapes. All sizes. And they all seemed to be at home in the mountain lodge.

When Nouri reached the doors of the garden, he stepped outside. There was a youth trimming the hedges, another pruning the roses, a third edging the footpath that led to the pool. Nouri's attention, however, was instantly drawn to the pair of graves. So he crossed the well-cared-for lawn and knelt down before them.

He closed his eyes and felt not pain, but communion. Gratitude. Love. Then—like the base note of an old, insistent song—he heard the familiar voice: "I knew you'd return. But I didn't think it would take this long."

Nouri was silent. Then he rose to his feet and greeted his friend and foe. *"Assalamu alaikum,* Sharoud."

Sharoud bowed his head. *"Alaikum assalam."*

The moment crackled. Then Sharoud spoke again.

"We have things to discuss. Follow me."

He turned and headed into the lodge, and Nouri followed. They moved down the corridor to one of the small prayer rooms that flanked the meeting hall. When they entered, Nouri found that it had been transformed into a private chamber even more lavishly appointed than what he'd already seen. Glittering objects adorned every surface and—despite the enormous Qur'an that lay open on a silver stand—the room was devoid of grace.

"Please be seated," said Sharoud, as he gestured to one of the velvet cushions that were scattered across the floor.

Nouri sat. Then Sharoud closed the door and sat beside him.

"You vanished," he said. "Without a word."

"I grew tired of words."

"That's commendable." Sharoud paused. "Especially for you."

Nouri felt something stir inside him. But he did not respond.

"The fact remains that you were chosen to be our *murshid*. And you abandoned us." Sharoud paused a moment. Then he smiled. "But Allah always achieves what He desires. So it seems clear—from a more detached point of view—that you were removed so that we might prosper."

Nouri knew that Sharoud's words were meant to wound him. But they had no effect.

"We have twenty-three new members," continued Sharoud. "Fourteen have come from other orders and nine are new initiates. We have a dozen new lay members. We're growing. Thriving."

"And you are the new *murshid*?"

"There are no rules about what to do when the head of an order disappears. Someone needed to grasp the reins."

Nouri raised his eyes to the polished lamp that hung like an ill star over their heads. He hated the thought of so many brothers pledging their love and devotion to a master like Sharoud. Yet he knew even he could not stand in their way if their paths were true. It was clear to Nouri that he could not exert an authority he'd walked away from or use a voice he'd given up. He would not subject the order to a struggle for power. And he would not waste a single moment arguing with Sharoud.

"May Allah be with you," he said.

Then he rose to his feet and left the room.

As he moved down the corridor, he saw how intently the new

members of the order approached their tasks. He wanted to tell them that their bodies were too clenched—their words too emphatic—that what they yearned for was not in some distant future but right before their eyes. But he knew how much they would have to go through before they would understand. And how much had to fall away.

When he reached the entrance, he paused for a moment. The sun felt warm, and the world seemed perfectly still. As he crossed the threshold, he realized that once again he was setting out on a journey. This time, however, he knew his destination. So he passed through the gates for the last time and started off down the mountain.

PART SIX

Twenty-Six

As the wagon approached the city of Tan-Arzhan, it was as if time folded back into a pleat, causing the present moment, in which Nouri sat on the wooden seat plank, weary from the lengthy journey, to lie flat beside the moment, more than thirty years before, when he'd last laid eyes upon the town. The cows and the chickens and the yards were like the ones he'd known then. Yet everything seemed smaller, as if the rain and the sun had shrunk them, made the trees and the stones more compact, boiled the essence of the place down to a more concentrated version of itself. Despite the fetid smell of the goat hides that lay stinking in the back of the wagon, Nouri was grateful for the ride. For while the ten-month trek had been interrupted by fleeting passage on the back of a camel or the deck of a boat, for the most part the journey across the blazing sand and over the rutted roads had been made on foot. Nouri's bones ached, and his feet were in shreds. But he was almost there. So he closed his eyes and tried to rest before the wagon pulled in and he had to travel the final stretch of the journey.

When the shout came, and the wagon lurched to a stop, Nouri saw that—for a few blissful moments—he must have nodded off. As he thanked the driver and stepped down to the ground, he tried to shake off the night and the lingering traces of sleep. But as he walked through the streets—past the town square—past the schoolhouse—past the Darni Sunim—he felt as if he were moving through a dream.

When he reached the Sufi lodge on the outskirts of town, it seemed to be deserted. The gate was rusted open and the walls were covered over with twisted vines. As he stepped into the forecourt, the memories rushed in. Sitting on the bench for a lesson with Sheikh Bailiri. Polishing the stones with Jamal al-Jani. What struck him the most as he stood there, however, was the quiet of the place. Even the laughing ghosts of his old friends could not disturb the silence.

He climbed the weathered steps and reached for the handle of the door. It opened. So he stepped inside and moved down the vacant hall past the empty rooms. It was as if the order had been consumed by the hungry flames he'd ignited that night on the mountain. Not a trace of the work or the prayer or the devotion remained.

When he reached his former cell, he paused in the doorway. The bed, the table, and the washbasin were just as they'd been so many years before. But he could not bring himself to step inside. He could only stand there and wonder at the strangeness of time.

When he heard the pensive note rise up, it seemed another trick of memory. But as the note stretched into melody and progressed into song, he knew that the sounds were actually occurring in the space. He followed them, and when he reached the courtyard he found a slender man, about a decade older than himself, seated cross-legged on the ground. He was playing a wooden *ney*, and the sounds seemed to issue from every part of him, from his dirty toes to the cloud of fuzz that surrounded his head. And even before he looked up and the old, toothless grin spread across his face, it was clear to Nouri that it was Ali Majid, the odd serving boy from his youth.

"I thought they ate you," said Ali Majid. "Or skinned your hide and stretched it out to make a *tombak*."

Nouri moved closer, the memory of the gangly youth peering out of the deep seams that lined the face of the fellow before him. "You're still here."

Ali Majid lowered his *ney* to the faded tiles. "And where else would I be?"

Nouri crouched down. "And the brothers?"

"All gone."

"And you've stayed here? All of this time? All alone?"

Ali Majid—as he had done so many times—poked his finger in his own ear. "Who said I was alone?"

He gazed at Nouri a moment. Then he grabbed his flute, rose to his feet, and started away. Nouri felt his heart begin to pound, but there was no time to either think or hope. All he could do was follow the wiry fellow across the courtyard, down the corridor, and out through the low stone archway that led to the small enclosure between the chapel and the southern wall of the lodge, where a tiny figure sat pulling up weeds.

When Nouri saw him, he felt a dam break inside him and a lifetime of longing wash over him.

"He always said you'd come back," said Ali Majid. "I never argued. But I never believed him."

Nouri crouched down and gazed into the old man's eyes. His skin hung loose and he was missing more teeth than Ali Majid, yet there wasn't a doubt in Nouri's mind that the withered fellow who sat before him was the loving caretaker and sweet companion of his childhood, Habbib. What surprised him was that he was wearing a head cloth—for his beloved friend had never shown the least sign of any desire to become a Sufi.

"I'm sorry I took so long," said Nouri. "So many things happened."

Habbib raised his fingers to Nouri's cheek, which only then did Nouri realize was wet with tears. Then the old fellow smiled, and Nouri took him into his arms.

When Nouri drew back from the embrace, he turned to thank Ali Majid for looking after him. But Ali Majid had scampered away, so Nouri turned back to Habbib. He gestured to Nouri to lower his head and, when he did, he reached out his hands and began to unwind Nouri's head cloth. Bit by bit, the fabric unfurled until the four ears were exposed. Habbib raised his fingers and gently stroked them. A smile spread across his face. And Nouri knew that he no longer needed to hide them away.

Nouri rose and reached out his hand to Habbib. But Habbib

wouldn't take it. Instead, he patted the place where Nouri had just been. So he crouched down again.

"What is it?"

Habbib said nothing. But then, with a determined slowness, he began to remove his head cloth. He kept his eyes fixed on Nouri's as he gently pulled the tattered layers away. And the calmness behind them was the only thing that kept Nouri from crying out once his head was bare.

His ears were gone. Like a sea-washed stone, his head was a lumpen sphere, the two holes on either side surrounded by mottled scar tissue grown hard over time. Nouri could feel his heart constrict, but before he could speak Habbib pressed a bony finger against his lips. Then he reached for his hands and placed them over the savaged flesh.

The two friends remained that way for a long while. Then Nouri lowered his hands, rose to his feet, and helped Habbib rise to his.

There was so much to ask.

And so much to tell.

But Nouri had ears for them both.

And they had plenty of time.

Twenty-Seven

The following morning, when Nouri awoke, he went out to the courtyard and asked Ali Majid to explain how Habbib had lost his ears. As he suspected, it had happened on that day when the lodge had been attacked by the marauders. According to Ali Majid, Hajid al-Hallal had been slain just moments after Nouri had been carried away. With the others already felled, only Sheikh Bailiri—whose grace seemed to deflect the villains' weapons—and Jamal al-Jani—who was off pissing in the woods—and Ali Majid and Habbib had survived the attack. The latter had remained frozen in place as the men stormed the lodge, seizing the prayer stands and the lamps. As the men were leaving, however, Habbib had cried out Nouri's name. And like a huntsman slicing a pair of bright apples from a tree, one of the barbarians turned back and lopped off his ears.

According to Ali Majid, Jamal al-Jani was so troubled by what he found when he returned to the lodge that he retired to his cell and remained there for the rest of his days. Sheikh Bailiri, in contrast, went to the chapel, where he bowed down in a prolonged state of prayer. When men arrived offering to rebuild the order, Sheikh Bailiri instructed Ali Majid to send them away. As a result, the daily maintenance of the lodge fell to the flute player and the six-fingered fellow with the broom. And when the two Sufis died, they simply carried on as before.

"I make the meals," said Ali Majid. "Habbib tends the garden and keeps the place clean. If you've nowhere to go to, you're welcome to stay."

It was clear to Nouri that he'd been drawn back to the lodge in Tan-Arzhan in order to care for Habbib. For though his friend was still able to sweep the floors and tend the garden, he moved so slowly it took him the whole day. So besides the obvious joy that his presence would bring, Nouri could help to reduce Habbib's workload.

Despite the fact that his ears were gone, Habbib could still hear. The sound was muffled, but if Nouri leaned in when he spoke and Habbib cupped his hands around the damaged holes, he could perceive every word. Each night, therefore, before bed, they would retire to Habbib's cell and, by the light of a taper, Nouri would retell the stories that Habbib had so lovingly told to him when he was a child. Like a thread being wound back onto its spindle, each image would rise up as if Nouri had just received it the night before. And Habbib would sit and listen as if he were hearing it all for the very first time.

Time passed and the two friends watered and weeded and swept. Nouri and Ali Majid took turns preparing meals, and Ali Majid sat in the courtyard for hours making music with his *ney*. One day, however, while Nouri was replacing a tile in the floor of the chapel mosque, Ali Majid came to see him.

"I'm leaving," he said.

Nouri looked up.

"There's still time for me to learn a new song," said Ali Majid. "Even have an adventure."

It was only then that Nouri saw that Ali Majid had remained at the lodge all these years to care for Habbib. So he bid the loose-limbed fellow farewell and—after a simple good-bye to Habbib and one last impossibly haunting melody on the *ney*—Ali Majid headed off.

The days grew colder. Then warmer. Then colder again. Nouri and Habbib continued on. Nouri knew that he could not give his friend back his ears or the years that had slipped by, but he could give him his love. And that was all that Habbib seemed to need.

The days grew longer. And shorter. Then longer again. And gradually, like a spring winding down, Habbib began to falter and had to take to his bed. His skin became ashen. His eyes became veiled. Then slowly the illness crept in, sucking the breath from his lungs and wracking his little body with pain. Nouri sat beside him mopping his brow, spooning the broth into his trembling mouth, holding his withered hand.

When the end finally came, there were no words. Habbib gazed at Nouri, and Nouri—his mind empty—his heart full—gazed back. A world passed between them. Then the worn-out lungs took their last breath, and Habbib was gone.

The silence in the room after Habbib died was even greater than the silence that had greeted Nouri after the explosion. But for all the seductive peace that it offered, Nouri knew he could not remain at the lodge. So he gathered up Habbib's lifeless body, carried it out to the garden, and buried it beneath the fig tree that his friend had loved. Then he whispered a brief prayer, retied his head cloth, and headed out through the gates.

Twenty-Eight

When Nouri left the lodge, he made his way along the curving path that led to the heart of the city. He had no idea what lay ahead. The future seemed as unreal as the past. After the quiet of his time with Habbib, however, he felt enlivened by the throb and clatter of the streets. So he walked past the public bath—past the countinghouse—past the grand bazaar—and drank in the vivid life that surged all around him. At night, he found a patch of grass in the town square where he could sleep. Then he awoke the next day and continued roaming the streets. Past the schoolyard, where the children laughed and played games. Past the stables, where the horses grazed. Each day the city seemed new, as if it had been razed to the ground and carefully reconstructed while he slept.

One morning, as he was walking through the northeast quadrant, a door flew open and a man dashed out. As he tore past Nouri, another man—dressed in expensive robes and clutching a broom—appeared in the doorway. When the second man saw Nouri, he handed him the broom, ran into the street, and shouted after the first man:

"And don't show your pox-ridden face in my house ever again!"

By the time he'd finished shouting, the fellow had disappeared. So he turned and—still shaking with rage—started back to the house. When he saw Nouri holding his broom, he folded his arms over his chest.

"Can you sweep?"

Nouri—who could only think of Habbib—nodded.

"Can you write?"

Nouri nodded again, and the man took a step closer.

"Can you tell stories?"

Nouri nodded a third time. So the man ushered him into the house and he began his new existence.

For the most part, his job consisted of caring for the man's children. Aban, the boy, who was as frisky as a newborn goat, was eight. Sanam, the girl, who was as plump as a freshly picked fig, was six and a half. Nouri would awaken them and feed them and escort them to school. Then he would return to the house, fetch the broom, and sweep the inner courtyard and the rooms. When school was done, he would fetch the children and then retire to his room while they ate their supper with their parents. Then he would tuck them into bed and tell them one of the stories he'd learned from Habbib.

No one—either in or outside the household—knew that

Nouri was a Sufi. But Nouri knew. Each morning, before he awoke the children, he would sit in his room and affirm his connection to God. Each afternoon, when he'd finished sweeping, he would sit in the garden. And listen. And look. What he was forging inside of himself had no texture, no sound, no scent. But it was real, and it was growing stronger each day.

From time to time, Nouri thought about his ears. They'd marked him as different from his very first breath, but after a lifetime of keeping them concealed, he could only wonder that they'd seemed so important. He still didn't know if they were a quirk of nature or a sign of his spiritual calling. But he knew that without them his life wouldn't have been his life. And since he could not wish away his life—not one moment of it—he could not wish away his ears.

The children grew from eight and six to twelve and ten to sixteen and fourteen. Nouri cared for them and swept the house and communed with God. At times—despite the fact that he was now more than fifty—the old questions would reappear:

Who am I?

Why am I here?

Which of the Nouris is really me?

He knew by now that he was not the Nouri who studied or the Nouri who suffered or the Nouri who prayed. Those were the chalice. The vessel. The shell. The only Nouri that came close to who he really was was the Nouri who loved. That was who would remain when all the other Nouris were gone.

One day, while he was sitting in the garden, he heard a voice:

"The children are old enough to care for themselves now. It's time to go."

When he turned, he saw his old friend Soledad standing at the entrance to the garden, her hair tied back in a slender braid, her dark eyes shining. He wanted to go to her and enfold her in his arms. But he knew that she was not really there. The following morning, however, he placed a few things in a satchel, left the house, and headed out to the ruined room in the clearing on the outskirts of town where he'd lain, beneath the stars, beside Vishpar, a lifetime before.

When he reached the clearing, he paused for a moment and gazed at the forgotten structure. The crumbling walls were overgrown with weeds, the stone floor had been worn away to reveal patches of dark earth, and the small piece of roof that had framed the night sky that had spat stars over him and his friend seemed to have blown away. He did not know what awaited him in the little room. A flash of lightning? A final struggle? But he knew that, whatever it was, he had to face it alone.

He crossed the clearing and climbed over the wall. He found a place where the floor was still intact and settled himself in. Then he opened the satchel and—one by one—lowered the items he'd brought with him to the stones.

A bowl to catch rainwater.

A blanket.

A knife.

His tattered copy of the Qur'an.

And a sack that held a small stack of paper, a pot of ink, and a pen.

For though he knew by now that words could never enter the invisible world, they could carry him to the threshold. And despite what he'd been through, he still felt the need to praise.

Twenty-Nine

Nima could never resist a dare, and no one knew that better than Azad. Whatever challenge Azad, who was twelve, posed to Nima, who was only ten, Azad knew that the boy would embrace it with gusto. Climbing to the top of the Darni Sunim. Stealing eggs from Hasam al-Farid's hens. Jumping into the River Tolna in the middle of winter. Nima would do anything to win Azad's favor. For although Azad was small and possessed of a lateral lisp, he had the combative confidence of a bulldog. With his approval, the other boys moved more freely through the streets, and slept more soundly at night.

It was therefore without hesitation that Nima agreed to head out to the abandoned room by the river and bring something back to prove that he'd faced the spectral figure that dwelled there.

Some said he was the ghost of the man who had built the tiny structure. Others said he was a *djinn*. Still others said he was a wandering saint who'd grown tired of wandering. They only knew that he'd been there as long as anyone could remember. And that if someone called out to him, he'd just sit there—eyes open—hands resting gently in his lap—as if nothing had been said.

Nima didn't know which of these theories was true. But he knew that if the fellow was a *djinn*, he was not likely to respond kindly to a visit from a thieving boy. So while he had every intention of meeting Azad's dare, he did not approach it without trepidation.

The night before he was scheduled to set out, he lay flat on his back, taut with excitement, until the first glimmer of light traced the sky. Then he bolted up, pulled on a pair of trousers, and headed out into the morning mist. As he made his way along, he tried to press back the thoughts that crowded in of what might happen when he got there. Perhaps the fellow was mad and as Nima drew near he would grab him and slit his throat. Perhaps he really was a *djinn* and would transform him into a toad. It occurred to Nima that he did not have to go at all. He could easily find a cup or a jug and tell Azad that he'd taken it from right beneath the fellow's eyes. Azad would never know he'd been too frightened to see the challenge through.

But Nima would know. So he wiped the remaining sleep from his eyes and continued on toward the clearing.

Nima was going to be a great man when he grew up. He was not sure if he would become a caliph or a magistrate or a judge. Or perhaps even a sorcerer. But he knew there were important things for a man to know, and he was determined to find them out.

By the time he reached the edge of the clearing, the mist had dissolved. So he slowly made his way toward the roofless room, where he found an old man wearing an odd-looking head cloth seated cross-legged on a blanket. To his left sat a bowl and the remains of a small fire. To his right stood a pot of ink, a quill pen, and a sheet of paper folded over into a square. The old man's eyes were open wide, yet he did not seem to notice Nima as he approached. So the boy scrambled over the wall to see what he might carry away.

It was only when he was standing right beside it that he saw the snake. It was a dull brown covered with pale zigzag stripes that seemed to flash through its supple body as it slithered across the stones. And he knew—from the countless lectures he'd been given by Azad—that it was not only a viper, but the deadliest kind.

Nima was well past the clearing and deep into the woods before it even occurred to him that he might have called out to the old man before dashing away. Yet he sensed that—even if the fellow had a hundred ears—he would not have heard him. So he continued running until he reached the safety of his home.

Nima spent the rest of the day hiding from Azad. And that night, just as the night before, he barely slept. He kept seeing the snake sink its fangs into the old man. He kept seeing the old man writhe in pain. But he also kept seeing Azad's face when he went to him empty-handed. So when dawn came, he summoned his courage and headed back to the room.

As he approached the clearing, he pictured the old man lying lifeless on the stones, his skin a ghastly greenish black. When he reached the room and climbed over the wall, however, he found that it was empty. Only the handful of objects strewn about gave any sign that the man had ever been there.

As Nima scanned the room trying to decide what to take back to Azad, his eyes fell upon the inkpot. The pen was also nice: a perfect goose feather, dappled with gray. When he turned to the bowl, however—to his surprise—he saw the viper curled up inside. And since he did not know whether it was sleeping or dead, he thought it best not to go near it.

He turned back toward the clearing. There was no one watching him, yet he felt he was being watched. Then—just as he was about to give up—he saw the small square of paper lying at his feet.

Perhaps the old man had written a message upon it.

A secret.

A spell.

Perhaps when Nima read the words they would change his life.

He knelt down and reached for the piece of paper. A shiver ran through him. Then he slipped the folded page into the waistband of his trousers and hurried off to find his friend.

Thirty

The light filtered in through the trees, casting scalloped patterns on the grass, as Azad stared at the sheet of paper he'd just unfolded.

"You don't even have the guts," he snarled, "to take a dare!"

He shook his head a few times. Then he balled up the paper, threw it onto the ground, and walked away.

Nima's heart thundered loudly in his chest. He could not imagine what the old man had written that could have angered Azad so. So he went to retrieve the crumpled page to find out.

He crouched down and raised it from the dirt, and as he pulled back its edges his mind flashed with images. Fierce constellations in a cobalt sky. Splashes of wine on a tufted divan. A boat crossing a slender sea. A ribbon of smoke curling up from a dying fire.

When he smoothed out the paper to read it, however, he found, to his surprise, that it said:

Nothing.

Nothing.

Nothing.

Nothing.

He folded up the page and slipped it back into his trousers. Then—filled with an excitement he could not really explain—he ran off through the clearing toward home.

ACKNOWLEDGMENTS

One can never acknowledge all the exchanges and encounters that find their way into the rich loam from which a novel grows. I'm grateful for all who shared their experience and understanding of the spiritual path.

Among the many books that aided me, I'm especially thankful for *A Sufi Rule for Novices,* translated and edited by Menahem Milson; *The Adventures of Ibn Battuta* by Ross E. Dunn; *A Dervish Textbook,* from the 'Awarfu-i-Ma'arif of Sheikh Shahabuddin Suhrawardi, translated by Lieutenant Colonel H. Wilberforce Clarke; *Essential Sufism,* edited by James Fadiman and Robert Frager; *Daily Life in the Medieval Islamic World* by James E. Lindsey; *Divine Governance of the Human Kingdom* by Ibn 'Arabi, translated by al-Jerrahi al-Halveti; *The Sufis* by Idries Shah; *Islam* by Karen Armstrong; *Sufis of Andalusia* by lbn 'Arabi; and *Islamic Art and Spirituality* by Seyyed Hossein Nasr. Most of all, a deep bow to the great Sufi poets, whose beautiful light still dazzles.

I cannot imagine a more wonderful editor than Will Schwalbe. His passion for the book, from the first reading through the various stages of publication, and his warm friendship have been a blessing. Likewise, I could not have had a better team than the one at Picador: my publisher, Stephen Morrison, who is smart and kind and elegant; Emily Mahon and Henry Sene Yee, whose cover design is magical; Kolt Beringer, Emily Walters, and Kim Lewis, who went over the manuscript with a fine-tooth comb; Shannon Donnelly, James Meader, and Darin Keesler, who put their hearts into the marketing; Cassie Mandel and Isabella Alimonti for their media wizardry; and Bryn Clark and Kara Rota, whose intelligence and grace helped make the process a joy.

Every writer should be so lucky to have an agent like Gail Hochman; her huge heart and lightning mind are fantastic allies. Thanks also to Marianne Merola, Jody Klein, Lina Granada, Jody Kahn, and all the other folks at Brandt and Hochman.

For inspiration, courage, and love, I thank my son, Joshua. For a lifetime of unconditional love, I thank my mother. For her warm support, I thank my sister. For lessons in how to bring humor to life's struggles, I thank my father and my stepfather, both of whom are deeply missed.

To the many friends who have sustained me over the years, who have shared their stories and listened to mine, who have comforted me, taught me, and helped me to keep on, I'm forever indebted. A special thanks to Jean Taylor, Thomas Fenn, Jo Anna

Mortensen, Mari Reeves, Elizabeth Blake, Jeanne Chapman, Brigid Moran, Daniel Labensohn, and Gwendolyn Marks for being the first to read, and for offering their loving encouragement.

There are no words to thank my teacher, Robert Burton, for he has taught me how to go beyond words. His love and unwavering insistence on what is true have changed my life.

FOOD GLOSSARY

aash-e aloo: a rich soup made with walnuts, spinach, peas, beans, and lentils

baghali polo: rice mixed with lamb, dill, and fava beans

baslogh: a pastry made of wheat flour and roasted walnuts

bureg: pastry triangles filled with cheese

ceviche: raw fish cured in citrus juice

dolmeh seeb zamini: potatoes filled with ground meat, rice, and herbs

ghee: clarified butter

kashk: a fermented dairy product made from yogurt

kefir: a fermented milk drink

khabisa: a sweet made of walnuts, honey, and starch

khoofteh berenji: large balls of rice, ground meat, onions, walnuts, and herbs *khoresht annar-aveej*: a stew made of chicken, walnuts, pomegranate juice, and garlic

khoresht baadenjaan: a stew made with meat, eggplant, onions, and lime juice

maast-o khiar: yogurt mixed with cucumbers and mint

mirza ghasemi: roasted eggplant in a tomato and garlic sauce, with egg

naan-e barbari: a furrowed, oval-shaped flatbread

naan-e sangak: a large flatbread sprinkled with sesame seeds

naan-e taftoon: a round, leavened bread sprinkled with poppy seeds

panir: a cheese made by curdling heated milk with lemon juice

ranginak: a sweet made of dried wheat flour, dates, walnuts, pistachios, cinnamon, and cardamom

shaami: ground meat mixed with eggs, bread crumbs, milk, and tomatoes

sharbat-e limoo: a drink made with fresh lime juice, honey, and water

tagine: a stew cooked in an earthenware dish

yakh dar behesht: a sweet made with rice flour, rosewater, pistachios, and milk

ABOUT THE AUTHOR

Michael Golding's first novel, *Simple Prayers,* was published in 1994 and has been translated into nine foreign languages. *Benjamin's Gift,* his second novel, was published in 1999. He is also a screenwriter, whose works include the adaptation of Alessandro Baricco's *Silk.* He lives in the foothills of the Sierra Nevadas in Northern California.